ALWAYS A PRINCESS

Clyve Rose

www.BOROUGHSPUBLISHINGGROUP.com

ISBN 978-1-951055-83-7

For Beautiful Bella, who always belongs to herself.

And for Jenn, Julie, Sara, & Stuart:
The ones who catch you before you hit the ground never lose their
wings.
Thank You. xxx

4

ACKNOWLEDGMENTS

Big thank yous to my editor, Susan, and to Liesl Leighton, Andrea Thatcher, and Boroughs Publishing Group.

ALWAYS A PRINCESS

Romany Rhyme *(trans. c. 1625)*

Ride a cock-horse
To Banbury Cross;
Where the Romany lady
Rides a fine horse.

With rings on her fingers
And bells on her toes
She shall have my love
Withe'er she goes

Prologue

February 1814
Mayfair

White's whist room was hazy with too much tobacco smoke and tension. Wil frowned, shuffled the deck, and replaced it. The stakes were higher tonight than the other three gentlemen knew.

"Time to declare the stakes," murmured Lord Maynooth, glancing at the men on either side of him. "We stake our pot." He glanced briefly at Wil.

Wil nodded, adding his gold pocket watch to the small store of cravat pins, signet rings, and other objects of value. That was it. All he had apart from his horse, and Nero was as necessary to his new commission as having the money to purchase it. He had to win this hand or it was all over. He watched the Earl of Horsham place the papers down for another mount.

The players lifted their cards in silence. Horsham slopped his drink down his front. All three earls were a little foxed this night, but Wil would not drop his guard with so much on the line. Steadying his nerve, he lifted his cards, turning them—

A discreet knock sounded at the door.

"Come," called Maynooth, not without irritation.

The hall butler sidled into the room, signalling to Wil particularly. Wil's face warmed as he rose, aware of his partner's glare as he laid his cards on the table face down and strode over to the servant. "I beg your pardon, Lord Maynooth."

"Is it life or death, man?" Wil asked the butler, trying to hide his vexation. He was so close to his win he could feel it. No delay was welcome. The butler bowed, offering up a silver salver, on which lay a single letter, addressed to Captain Warwick Clifton, Esq., care of White's on St James's Square. Not bothering to scowl at the use of his hated Christian name, Wil nodded his thanks and took it, recognising the additional direction scrawled on the flap. The note came from his brother Roger, who'd agreed to up their stakes. His pulse quickened.

Stuffing the rest of the letter in his empty watch pocket, Wil returned to his rubber. He glanced at his companions. "Lord Clifton stakes his Lune River mill."

This sudden increase in the size of the pot mollified all three peers at once. They'd been playing all evening, and Wil knew each earl to a man by now. Without lifting his head, he eyed them in turn. Each man's appearance of stoicism was a failure and Wil recognised which trick to take first.

"One, no trump," he muttered, watching Maynooth's nod.

His partner placed his card. Their opponents laid down theirs. This was the final hand. Gathering in his tricks, he closed the game quickly. All three hands were won, with Maynooth no less delighted than Roger would be with their joint result. Roger had his hunters, and Wil would make a cavalry major now. He tasted his port and rose to bow.

"Good night, gentlemen. It has been an excellent rubber."

"Well played, Captain," Lord Maynooth replied. Halving the monies, his partner handed the notes across. "Yours, I believe, Captain. May it assist you in being made."

Wil inclined his head. "It's Wil when we win the pot, my lord."

"Very well, Wil," Maynooth replied. "You ought to call me Charles. Come, stay for a drink."

Wil shook his head at the proffered glass. "Another time, my lord. I leave town tomorrow and have much to arrange."

He changed his mind when he remembered his letter. Standing by the fireplace, Wil pulled out the rest of the pages and read it through.

"Damn his eyes." Wil's shout made all three earls jump as he smashed his glass into the fire.

"What the—," Lord Maynooth paused. "News from Lord Clifton, I take it. Is your brother quite well?"

Wil blinked and unclenched his jaw. Ripping his letter into tiny pieces, he swore again, throwing every scrap into the fire. Grabbing the poker, he stabbed viciously at the flames before looking up.

"Lord Clifton is quite well. A pressing matter of business has gone awry." He banged a fist against his open palm. *Damn the duke and his meddling.*

With a last glare into the fire, Wil turned and stalked to the door.

Maynooth was still staring at the smashed whisky glass by the grate. "Where the deuce are you going?"

"To the devil."

Chapter One

Few sensible folk were abroad this night. Syeira envied the carefree slumber of small woodland creatures tonight. All seemed tucked away in their warm dens and burrows. The moorland wind whipped cruelly about her face and hands, and she thought longingly of the great central cooking fire at her Romany camp and the warmth she'd find there. Warmth that was nowhere in evidence in her journey across the Lancashire moors where snow remained in small pockets on the heights. Blowing warm breath onto her cramped hands, Syeira flexed her fingers before re-threading them through Grygry's mane.

"Have you found it yet?" she said in Romany, her whisper ringing loudly in the pre-dawn silence. She glanced around. Nothing stirred.

"If I had, do not you think I might say so?" Her eldest brother, Valkin, uttered several Romany curse words as his speech died to an undertone. Syeira cleared her throat to remind him that she, the princess, did not like his language. Valkin gave no indication of hearing her, nor did he beg pardon, but the curses ceased.

"I know the fence is poor along this path. There is most certainly a way in," he said.

"If you say it is here, Valkin, it is here."

Syeira strained her eyes in the dark, watching the country all around as her brothers walked slowly along the northern boundary fence of the greatest estate in Lancashire. It was essential they find an access point that would admit their horse. She rode the animal up and down the fence line at a trot, keeping an eye on the horizon as she did so.

Though it was night, she had as assured a sense of direction as the horse. No one suggested leaving their mount on the open moor. Grygry was as much a part of the royal Romany House of Brishen as any of them, and valuable breeding stock besides.

"Something we two have in common," Syeira spoke under her breath, leaning forward to stroke the proud soft ears in front of her. The animal snorted, stamping a hoof in the freezing air. Syeira encouraged him to walk on, keeping him moving and his powerful equine frame warm. There was no telling when this Romany family would need to move quickly, especially so near the estate of a notable English peer. A rapid gallop might be needed at any moment and the animal must be kept ready.

Her younger brother, Janfri, moved silently beside Valkin, testing each paling with his boots. The boundary fence held true so far, but the Romany House of Brishen knew this estate, given they stopped in this part of Lancashire each winter. It was well known that sections of the fence were in sad need of repair.

With no roads on this side of the estate, it was the safest way to enter the grounds unobserved. Though the wind dropped off, Syeira felt colder than ever. She tugged her shawl more tightly about her. It was the warmest one she'd yet made, but she sometimes wished for the heavily furred cloaks fine English ladies wore.

"Is it so important that we enter under cover of dark, Valkin? We have an appointment at the estate, after all."

"We cannot risk being seen."

"We cannot risk *you*, my *prala*, my brother," she replied, so quietly he might not hear it.

His sigh spoke otherwise. "You worry too much my sister, my *pen*."

"Perhaps you do not worry enough." Even as Syeira said the words, she knew they were unfair.

"We have no choice, Syeira."

Valkin was right. No Romany risked their family lightly. All of them, even Janfri, risked this midnight journey for the good of House Brishen. If there had been another way out of trouble for her Romany House, her brother would have found it. She took a breath, trying not to think about the people she'd already lost. For her brother's sake, for the sake of the Royal Romany House of Brishen, she must not give in to her fear.

Syeira glanced up at the stars glimmering overhead. Inhaling deeply, she drew in the scent of furze and pine needles. Distant wood smoke tingled in the back of her throat. The call of a night bird reached her ears. A splash sounded somewhere close by. Perhaps a flying fish or a moorland owl chasing a meal. There must be a lake near the estate. No doubt crafted for the pleasure of the Englishmen who resided here, rather than one naturally formed from the earth. Anger curled through her. That anyone should border an open woodland to declare "these are my lands and no other shall walk in them," then tamper with it in such an unnatural fashion. It was not the Romany way, and the cause of much trouble between her people and the English.

A deeper black space in the fencing opened before her. Her anger falling away, Syeira pulled Grygry to a halt and leapt down. Using a fistful of mane to keep a firm but gentle hold on her mount, she inspected the hole and the jagged edges of wood that bound it. It was large enough to lead Grygry through. Exactly as Valkin had described it.

"Valkin," she called as loudly as she dared.

"Ah." The prince hurried towards her, Janfri at his heels. "Well done, my sister, my *pen*. I shall go first, in case—"

Syeira didn't stop to wait for him, leading Grygry through the boundary fence, one hand beneath the horse's chin.

"Syeira," the prince called in alarm. "I said I'd go through first. You do not know what dangers await."

Syeira clicked her tongue in irritation. "I can take care of any dangers as well as you, Valkin. Besides, we're the only ones mad enough to be out at this time of night." Nonetheless, she stopped as soon as she'd cleared the fence and turned to wait for her brothers.

"Good boy, Grygry." She stroked the sleek nose of the horse, huddling against his flank for warmth. "Well, we have arrived in safety it seems. Shall we wait out here in the open?"

"Hmmm, I think not." Her brother took her arm, moving forwards. Janfri led their horse close behind them. "We may seek shelter in that copse. The field is not far from here and the trees offer some protection from this wind. It will be warmer among the trunks in any case."

Already Syeira felt the welcome of the woodland. There was little foliage to afford them any cover, but the trees had trunks and early green growth. It was at least somewhere to stay better hidden. It would not do to be charged for trespass under the English law. A stupid law to be sure, as most English laws were. There was no such equivalent charge among her Romany. All Romany agreements allowed room for re-negotiation and compensation. *Not quite all,* she amended, anger and grief flashing through her at the thought of the promise that bound her.

They reached the trees after a brief walk, their horse glad of fresher grass and new leafing buds. Her brother was right. It was a little warmer here than out in the open, at least until the sun rose. She thought longingly of the sun's warm rays. Better to think warm thoughts than focus on her numb hands. She made a mental note to trade some herbal remedies for gloves as soon as she could.

Gazing upward, Syeira wondered if any Romany had studied the stars. She took another deep breath and released it slowly, feeling the night air move into her body and out again. Somewhere, stubborn stalks of lavender still scented the air. A smudge of grey tinged the eastern sky. It wanted a few hours to the dawn.

"And now, Valkin?" she asked, doing her best to find his face in the shadows.

Her brother took her cold hand in his, placing his other arm around Janfri's thin shoulders. Drawing them all in closer to Grygry's warmth, Valkin spoke in a low voice, full of wariness and tension.

"Now, we wait."

Chapter Two

Wil kept his eyes shut tight against the needle-sharp pain at his temple. Someone was moving about his room. The susurration of pouring water, the rustle of cloth-on-cloth, and an occasional rattling pierced right through the fiendish agony behind his eyelids. The perpetrator of these multiple assaults on his delicate sensibilities deserved a whipping at the very least. Peering ever-so-slightly out of one eye, he surveyed his blurry surrounds.

This wasn't his room.

Far too much peach and gold brocade glimmered on the bedclothes in this chamber, and a good deal too many ruffled ribbons masqueraded as drapery. The fussiness was positively dizzying. A false floral scent cloyed his nostrils. He held his breath, feeling distinctly ill. Lying quite motionless, he closed his eyes against what little light there was, attempting to recall what he could of the previous evening.

A lamp was lit. Bright light speared directly through his eyelids, eliciting a grunt. Clearly this person was determined to disturb him. A discreet cough told him that the person who deserved a thrashing was Hudson, his valet. He suppressed a groan. If Hudson was already present, then arrangements were well underway.

His man cleared his throat, loudly this time.

Grimacing, Wil tried to sit up. A mistake. His head throbbed like a volley of musket-fire shot loose inside his skull.

"Good morning, Hudson," Wil croaked, feeling every agonising word.

Hudson inclined his head towards the lovely form sprawled over on the other side of the expansive bed. Wil glanced over his shoulder. Lady Gresham was deeply and irretrievably asleep. Bits and pieces of memory from the Valentine's Day rout at Gresham House came back to him. It must have been a blinder, judging by the state of himself and his hostess this morning.

It would have been terribly poor form to disappoint Lady Gresham last night. She'd been remarkably persistent. He was not sorry he'd allowed himself to be persuaded to attend her party or her bed. He'd enjoyed pleasing her. Besides which, this liaison would end with the dawn. He was, after all, merely the second son of the Duke of Carston. With the duke hampering his advancement at every turn, Wil could not reckon on an increase in income any time soon.

How dare the duke prevent him purchasing a new commission? The anger in his gut had not lessened any since he'd read Roger's letter. Wil wondered how long the rumours about his wild behaviour would take to reach His Grace. He hoped the duke might choke on the scandal. No doubt His Grace sought to keep his spare son docile and dependent by bribing him into the kind of marriage Wil especially despised. From what he'd seen, marriage within the ton appeared a sort of misery shared. He shuddered. Glancing out the window, he saw the sun was not yet up.

"Hudson," he began again, keeping his voice low. "Why—?"

"There is a dawn appointment, captain." His valet handed him a cup of cool water, gesturing toward the fresh linen already laid out in the dressing room. "At the hall."

A dawn appointment at Clifton Hall? But that was several hours' hard riding. And on Pancake Day? Wil gulped his water, rising gingerly to his feet. He sat down again immediately, head swimming. It would not do to black out, even in front of his valet.

"What idiot arranged this?"

Hudson's expression did not alter. "You did, captain."

Wil groaned, aloud this time. "I was afraid of that. I am meeting whom?"

"The Earl of Haversham," Hudson replied. "Your offense against Lady Haversham last week in town, captain." The slightest shade of disapproval coloured his tone.

Wil did nothing more than lift his brows, his man having long earned his trust.

Wil had never backed away from a physical challenge in his life. He sighed. Haversham was a fool. Calling him out was incontrovertible proof of this. The earl had insisted they duel, despite the bodily risk. He'd also insisted the duel take place at Clifton Hall—private land owned by the duke.

"You are aware that duels are illegal, even on private land?" Hudson seemed to read his thoughts. "If the law is alerted, it will be Clifton Hall's responsibility."

"I am aware of that, Hudson. I thank you."

The fact hadn't been lost on Wil when the earl issued his challenge. It marked his opponent as a coward. "A man so afraid of scandal that he gives up a home ground advantage is no threat." Besides, Wil was an excellent pistol man, and the earl could not hit a farmhouse wall with a blunderbuss. This morning's appointment was a pointless exercise. Haversham was certain to be hurt.

"Is this the best way to return home?" His valet continued, ever determined to make his point. "It's some time since you were furloughed, captain. His Grace expects you to pay your respects at the hall. He will be livid this is the way you choose to do it."

Wil waved his hand, used to being the target of his father's ire. "His Grace likely will. As for demanding I pay my respects, I understand the duke to be en route to London. Haversham may be satisfied at no inconvenience to His Grace." He forbore to add that he would not bestow attention on his father that was so little deserved. "As for the duel itself, we are safer on private land than on his common. You can't save a fool from his folly, Hudson."

Wil swallowed slowly past the nausea washing through him. Dear God, what *had* they been drinking? He shrugged off his tension, accepting the valet's hand to haul him to his feet. He took a moment to steady himself, blinking in time with the thudding in his brain.

"Is there hot water at this hour?"

Hudson gestured toward the dressing chamber. "I thought it best to prepare in the other room, captain, and—ahem—to avoid disturbing Her Ladyship."

Once again, his valet's face conveyed no expression, but Hudson had occupied the room directly beneath theirs last night and he'd been Wil's valet for some years now. He conjectured that his man had heard most of last night's activities. Her Ladyship was nothing if not enthusiastic. His ears might still be ringing. His headache was so severe he couldn't be sure. "Remind me, Hudson, what vintage was I drinking last night?"

"I believe it was the house brandy, captain."

"That explains it," Wil muttered. "Remind me not to drink at Gresham House again."

"Noted, Sir." The valet handed Wil his wound pocket watch. "We must be leaving if we're to make Clifton Hall by dawn."

"Thank you, Hudson. I shall be down directly. Have you breakfasted?"

Hudson, who had most likely been up for several hours already, nodded.

"Excellent." Wil pulled on his boots. "There will be no occasion for disturbing the family." He glanced meaningfully at the woman in the bed behind him.

Hudson took the hint, averting his attention entirely from Her Ladyship. "Something to eat may be a good idea for yourself, captain."

Wil shook his head, wincing at the sensation of being clubbed. A Gresham House soiree would not tempt him again. "Lord, no. Not after that god-awful brandy and never before a duel, Hudson. I aim best on an empty stomach."

"And a clear head," his man responded as he left to see to their horses.

Wil dismissed this parting shot with a wave of his hand. That was true too, of course, but the earl was no formidable opponent, and one out of two would have to do today.

Wil damped a monogrammed cloth in the bowl, and wiped the hot water over his face and shoulders. Splashing some into his eyes for good measure, he shook his head again.

The ride home would take several hours and the winter road was hard. The snow had ceased but the Lune remained frozen and the way icy. They would be riding into a rising sun as well, and visibility would be poor. Hudson was right to get their journey underway, no matter how vile his master's head might be. Wil must arrive at Clifton Hall well in time to secure his honour. After all, this was nearly the only thing of value he had left.

A murmur from the bedclothes sent Wil straight out the door. He groaned quietly, putting his hand to his head as he awaited Hudson in the dark relief of the downstairs hall.

The valet still deserved a thrashing.

Chapter Three

Syeira shivered in the shadow of the trees, holding Janfri's hand tightly in both her own.

"Janfri should not be here," she spoke up. "He is too young to see this."

"He is thirteen," the prince countered. "A Romany man. With Papa's health so poor, I require Janfri present in case I can no longer lead House Brishen." He placed his hand on her shoulder.

Again, Syeira tasted her fear, glancing down at her younger brother. Janfri was next in line for *sher-engro,* Head of the House of Brishen.

"The fewer witnesses to an illegal duel the better," she reminded Valkin.

"I cannot disagree with you there," her brother sighed. "You do not have to remain, my sister, my *pen.*"

"I can take care of myself," she replied, bridling as her brother shook his head at her. "You do not trust me to do this?" Syeira's voice rose in warning.

"Of course I trust you." He shrugged impatiently, cutting off further debate. "It is the Englishmen I do not trust. Their behaviour, even with English girls, is not always honourable. I will not leave you unchaperoned with Captain Clifton. You are the pride of Brishen after all." He smiled as he said this, calling on Janfri to agree. This the young boy did, nodding firmly at his sister.

"Your honour is a matter of importance for all of Brishen," Valkin added quietly. "Janfri is here for us both. He is a man of Brishen now."

Syeira shook her head at Valkin's stubborn adherence to such an outdated tradition. It was true that Romany children grow up quickly and most married young. Janfri would probably find himself betrothed before his sixteenth birthday. Janfri was the second son of the centuries-old royal Romany House of Brishen, and she had no doubt *his* marriage bed would prove satisfactory. *Unlike my own.* She tossed her head in regret. There was no point dwelling on what cannot be changed.

Syeira studied Valkin closely. "You are truly uncomfortable," she observed, catching his dark, worried gaze with her own.

A knot settled heavily in her stomach and stayed there. Until this moment, it had not occurred to her that Valkin might be afraid. That he might be at risk of losing this silly contest. Her brother succeeded in everything he did. He was rarely bested by the English in any trade. Indeed, success in his parlay with the English was one of his greatest strengths.

Now he was as tense as she'd ever known him. Syeira swallowed her sour-tasting acrimony. The prince was the one facing the pistol this morning, after all. He likely did not need her to voice what they both knew to be true in their hearts. None of this felt right. None of it was fair, and still, Brishen must see it done. With their mother dead and their father ill, care of the royal Romany House rested with its prince and princess.

"Do you know much about this Englishman you are to face?"

The prince lifted his shoulder in a half-shrug. "Captain Warwick Clifton is the second son of the Duke of Carston. I am acquainted only with his brother. Lord Roger Clifton is heir to this entire estate."

Syeira gazed around her. All these woods and lands belonged only to one man? One man who had but two sons? She shook her head.

The estate was truly an abundant bounty, even in winter. Rich mosses hung from giant trees and she breathed the cold-weather herbs on the air. There were some midwinter blooms still about. Snowdrops and pale heather graced the little copse in which her family stood hidden among ancient elms and towering oaks.

Oh, what she could do with these woodland plants. Syeira expelled an impatient breath, eyeing a lichen-draped bough dripping with growths.

"The English always have more than they need," she said softly.

"You are right, my sister."

Looking up at Valkin, her chest swelled with pride. He was handsome and strong and would make a fine *sher-engro* when their father passed on. He was nineteen, a year older than her, and he took his duty to Brishen seriously.

Syeira frowned as her brother's quick smile faded and he looked back across the field, jaw stiff with tension. Duels like this one were against the law. There was always the chance that the earl had tricked their Romany family into the crime of trespass. Haversham wouldn't be the first Englishman attempting to stir up trouble between the law and Brishen. Clearly, Valkin had similar concerns.

"Stand back. Stay under the trees. Our house has history here at Clifton Hall but it would be as well not to trust these English too far." Valkin did not make requests. He was a Romany prince and knew what it was to give orders and be obeyed.

"If the constabulary arrive, take Janfri and ride back swiftly. Say nothing to anyone about this. I will not have you in trouble with the law."

Syeira made an irritated noise again. "I still do not see why you have to stand up as the earl's second. You never so much as touched his sister."

"This is true." Valkin made a terribly un-prince-like face and shuddered.

His sister raised a brow, trying not to grin.

"But Papa gave Haversham his word. This way the earl forgives our poaching debt, which is considerable. You know the year we've had, Syeira. We cannot pay this any other way." He didn't say, "Father is ill and may not last much longer," but Syeira heard it in his careful tone.

As the most skilled healer of House Brishen since her mother's passing, Syeira ministered to their father daily. She knew his time was not far. If Papa died while they were here playing proxy for a foolish earl… Syeira's temper flared as she cursed the Englishman for forcing them all away from their father at such a time.

"It is not our way to pay at all. He could have had fortunes told, or handwoven silks in exchange, or curing herbs. Even one of your new-bred horses. Do you truly think a few game hens are worth your life, brother?"

Her response drew a smile. "It's more than a few hens, Syeira. We're talking over two dozen deer, countless grouse, braces of partridge by the dozen and geese too. And some hundreds of rabbits." His voice lightened.

Syeira guessed he was thinking back to the outrage Brishen had caused by camping at the far end of an estate no one appeared to examine thoroughly. They'd managed rather well from Michaelmas to Christmas, until the sot of a gamekeeper eventually sobered up. Now, their house was being threatened with prosecution if they did not make good the debt.

"Don't forget the salmon," Janfri chimed in.

Valkin chuckled.

"Or the trout," Janfri said again. "We took his gamefish too."

This time Syeira laughed with them, her slender shoulders shaking as she allowed herself a brief respite from the tension. The moment was all too fleeting. Surveying her surroundings like a wary fox, she sobered again, feeling the joy fade from her face.

The change did not escape her brother. "I swear, when I am head of our house, I will find a way to help you to happiness." Valkin reached for her shoulder, holding her steady.

Syeira took a breath, trying to smile again. "I thank you, my *prala*, my brother." She heard Valkin make that vow out loud at least once a day but was no closer to seeing it fulfilled. Her father, and only her father, could make her situation right, and he was in no fit state to do so.

This was not something Brishen discussed. It would not serve their people to have it known that the Romany king, and *sher-engro* of the oldest Romany house in England, was fast losing his reason. The prince, especially, had warned his siblings never to speak of Papa's illness to the English, and Valkin had more knowledge of them than any other Romany.

Janfri tried one more time to lighten the mood as the chill winter sun began its glow over the horizon. "Then there was also—" his voice was drowned out by hoofbeats as two riders galloped into view.

"Hush, they're here." Syeira shivered again in the icy air. "He is a coward not to stand up for himself then," she whispered to Valkin.

Her brother looked as if he didn't disagree, but he'd never say so. It was not his way. The Romany king's oath was given to the peevish Earl of Haversham who believed her brother's life of less worth his own, even though Valkin was a man ten times better than the earl. The earl's behaviour was little different to that of other Englishmen. Many peers of the realm treated Romany men poorly, and their women worse. It did not help the peace the English king fought so many wars to keep.

Shaking out her hair, the princess Brishen stationed herself against the trunk of a great oak, erect and ready for whatever might befall her family this morning. These English and their pride: Miss Haversham ought to have stopped the duel if she could. What sort of sister would risk her brother so? Syeira would never permit such a foolhardy display on her own behalf. She'd borne too much loss already.

Syeira sighed and reined in her temper. It would only get her into trouble. Besides—she looked down at Janfri—she ought to set an example. Drawing back beneath the shelter of the trees, Syeira wrapped her woollen shawl more closely about her. As Valkin advanced to meet the man who'd apparently insulted the honourable Miss Haversham, Syeira examined his opponent as best she could at such a distance.

If Clifton had said something ungentlemanly about the earl's sister, Syeira was willing to bet it was no slander. It was common knowledge among the Romany that fine ladies of the English aristocracy were not as unstained as everyone pretended. Her handsome, virile brother knew this at least as well as some of the *gadje* English ladies knew *him*.

Now that the mist was lifting, Syeira saw Clifton clearly. He approached with his valet as his second. His man bore a flamboyantly crested case of duelling pistols. She was surprised at the captain's height, which was over six feet, she guessed. He had the subtle strength of a military man and moved with an easy grace. She allowed her gaze to follow long, strong rider's legs up to a hard-looking chest and broad shoulders, leading to a muscled neck and handsome face with a clear-cut, angular jaw. The rays of the rising sun picked out the golden strands of his hair.

Captain Warwick Clifton was a fine-looking man. She shivered again, and this time it was not from winter's chill. Syeira knew a fair amount about *camello*, or lovemaking. Romany girls received their instruction from the women of their house when they came of age at thirteen. It wasn't her Mama's fault that Syeira would never come to practise these lessons.

Feeling his gaze move over the woodland, she shrank back with a gasp. She had the oddest feeling he guessed they were there. A warm tingle passed through her belly. She pressed further into the shadow of the trees. Had he seen her? Had she wanted him to?

The captain wore nothing but his linen, breeches, and boots. His red coat was slung casually over his arm with the rest of his attire. Clifton appeared to be arguing heatedly with her brother as his voice carried in the crisp air. Deep and powerful, the sound was currently overlaid with harsh, angry tones.

"...damned coward, where the *hell* is he? Granted that sister of his isn't worth the trouble, but why in thunder the cad had to drag you into it, I can't say. I've no wish to injure you, Prince Brishen, but the *Code Duello* is absolute. If I had to leave a warm, favoured bed to duel on time, then that blasted Haversham can bloody well—" and there followed further vigorous expletives.

Syeira placed her hands over Janfri's ears, who repeatedly and determinedly tried to push them away. She smiled. A passionate man, then. Immoderate too. She liked his fire. She shook her head. What was she thinking of? None of this mattered when he was about to duel her brother.

Clifton was shouting something, signalling with his hands for Valkin to remain stationary while he set up a shot. Her brother shook his head. The prince's pride would have none of a dumb shooting as he turned his back to the captain, taking his place on the duelling field.

Janfri's hand squeezed hers. Syeira held her breath, heart in her throat, praying she would not need the herbal poultices she had prepared. She tensed as the duellists stood back to back. The two men paced out, her brother standing proud. Clifton moved as though his head hurt. The terrible thought came to her that Valkin might kill the captain, and immediately, she pushed it away.

She could not bear it and couldn't think why.

Clifton's second dropped the white kerchief. Syeira froze, not daring to breathe. Both men turned and fired.

Chapter Four

Two shots rent the air at nearly the same moment, smoke curling into the watery morning light. The Romany prince shouted as he crumpled to the ground, scarlet blooming through his shirt.

Wil ran forward, sliding to his knees beside the downed man. God, what the hell had he done? The prince's eyes were glazed with pain and the shock of hot lead tearing flesh. The faintly metallic scent of blood rose from his torso. A wild, feminine cry stabbed the air from behind. Wil looked around open-mouthed at the woman racing towards him, a bundled rag-bag swinging from one arm.

"What have you done? *What have you done?*" The accusation flew from her lips as she arrived beside him, swinging her bag, knocking Wil bodily away from the prostrate prince. Falling to her knees beside Brishen, she began slashing at his shirt with a knife from her bag. Wil stared as she administered a kind of greenish poultice to Brishen's mangled, bloodied skin.

"Who the devil—"

"Valkin?" Her panicked whisper cut Wil to the quick.

"It's all right. It…it should not be much of a wound." Wil's shaking voice sounded far from reassuring.

"You will stay out of my way," the Romany woman ordered, without looking at him.

Sprawled in the mud on the other side of the unconscious man, Wil could do little else but watch her fingers at work. She had long, slender hands, hands a man might like to feel on his skin. He blinked in a futile effort to clear his head as he regained his feet. For God's sake, he'd only left a woman's bed a few hours ago, and this was hardly the time. He looked down at the Romany prince he'd bested and sighed heavily. This definitely wasn't the time.

Wil glanced at Hudson. The valet shook his head, obviously as mystified as his master. Wil was terribly afraid he'd shot a man in front of his wife. He had truly tried not to do any damage. He put his hand to his head again. It hurt like the very devil.

He heard Hudson behind him. "I do not think we ought to remain here too long, captain. These people may have alerted the law."

Wil dismissed this. "I know of no Romany who willingly engages a constable. Especially on private land."

It made the presence of the woman even more puzzling. *What kind of man brings his wife to a duel over another woman?* He tried desperately to think. It was damned difficult, and not merely because he'd not yet breakfasted since riding for several hours after their pre-dawn departure. Drawing closer now, he saw the Romany nurse was quite young. She was a girl rather than a woman.

Wil cleared his throat. "I beg your pardon. May I be of assistance?"

The girl did not respond. She hardly seemed to notice him at all. Her focus on the wounded prince was absolute. How could she possibly know how to treat him?

"The herbs will soothe the pain," she glanced up, speaking quickly. "It is vital he regain consciousness as soon as possible." Trickling water over the prince's lips, she tipped a little over his face as well. Next, the girl laid her dark head over the Romany prince's heart, listening intently.

"Staccato, but steady," she said aloud. "I must slow his blood loss."

Wil heard her breathe the prince's name again.

"Thank God you are strong." She kissed Brishen's cheek.

Wil felt a pang of envy. The care she took, and the skill. He wondered how old she was.

"The Romany prince said nothing about witnesses, captain." Hudson muttered in his ear again, his voice scarcely audible. "These gypsies may be attempting some kind of trick."

"Shh." Wil raised his palm, feeling the previous night's impairment to his faculties tenfold. "I do not think so," he replied. "Those are real tears on her cheeks."

Real tears and the girl's shoulders shook, but no further cries beyond her first terrified shout. If the girl had attended the duel to leverage some kind of blackmail attempt, she'd have addressed herself more specifically to Wil. He would also have expected a much greater (and less genuine) ululation. His tensions eased further as he saw that she seemed no more interested in demanding recompense than the fallen prince she tended.

Moistening one slender fingertip, the girl dipped it in a vial of olive-dusted powder.

"Belladonna," she explained. "The smallest dose will dull his pain. It will dull his senses as well, but this cannot be helped."

Slowly, the prince's dark eyelids rose, mouth moving convulsively at what Wil supposed was the strange taste on his tongue.

"No, you will please be silent," the girl ordered when the prince's mouth opened as if to speak. Her hands moved with sureness, tightening bandages and securing poultices. She paused in her flow of movement long enough to deliver Wil a furious glare and say something aloud in her language, before returning her attention to the Romany prince.

Wil did not know the meaning of the word, but he could not mistake her tone. He blinked, actually stepping back from the furious force of her gaze, even as he admired the way her eyes flashed. She had some spirit in her. If a man must take a wife, it ought to be a woman like that.

Where the hell had that come from? He mentally shook himself. Marriage was hardly part of his plans. The Romany girl's appearance had startled him. *I'm not used to being surprised, that's all.* He watched the girl's face. She looked, and sounded, furious. Furious and frightened. At him, presumably, and of him as well. Well, at least that made sense. Still, what was she doing here?

"We'd best find out what she's about." He moved closer again, waiting until the girl's remedies were secured with clean linen cloths before he spoke.

"The prince cannot travel in this condition." It was not a question. "Quite apart from the pistol wound, what reason can be found for your presence on the Duke's estate that will not bring the law down upon us all?"

Dark violet eyes regarded him with barely suppressed fury. "You will call out the law?" The girl half-stood, crouching as she kept one stubborn hand on the prince's chest. The awkwardness of her pose did nothing to defuse her anger. "The county constables give the Romany short shrift. I am sure you know this already, Captain Clifton." Flicking a glance towards the prince, she took a breath, before returning her direct gaze to Wil. "If you call in the constabulary, there is no hope for him." She choked on her words.

"I will not hesitate to call out the law if the reputation of Clifton Hall is at stake," he replied, choosing his words with care.

"I am not here to attack Clifton Hall, captain," the girl broke in. "I have come to assist the Romany prince. Alone, if I must." She knelt again, taking pains to tighten the binding on the dressings. Turning away from Wil entirely, she laid her head over the Romany prince's heart once more. Sitting upright directly, she shook her head, appearing far from satisfied.

Watching her lift one shaking hand to her mouth decided him. Wil knelt to ensure he met her eyes. "Then will you please consider that your prince is in no condition to be moved any great distance?" He had caused quite enough trouble for one day, and it was barely breakfast time.

The Romany girl did not disagree. "I cannot explain this," she whispered. "My father...and all my other family. None of Brishen will bear seeing the Romany prince in this condition. There is already—" she looked away.

Wil wondered what it would take for her to accept his assistance. She could not bear the prince's prone body any great distance on her own.

"Are you camped nearby?"

The girl shook her head. "We dare not. We hear of sickness in the White Chapel village. It is so, yes?"

Wil's brows shot up. "I am not certain," he responded. "I have this moment arrived on furlough."

"You think I lie?" Her blazing eyes raked him from head to toe, suppressing none of her anger this time.

"I did not say so." Wil winced, his headache increasing in intensity alongside his irritation. The girl's pretty mouth opened in retort, but he cut her off, determined to put this kind of suspicion to bed.

Biting back a curse, he continued. "I see no reason to doubt the word of a Romany." Gratified to see her start of surprise and that fiery gaze fall to her feet at last, Wil adjusted his tone. After all, she'd witnessed him shoot the Romany prince. An unprotected Romany girl had good reason to distrust Englishmen.

"May we address the current matter now?" His query wanted politeness and he knew it. Desperately weary and worried, he glanced again at the Romany prince before turning his gaze back to the girl. She bit her lips, rubbing awkwardly at her cheeks, unaware she smeared blood through her tears. She hesitated, her eyes on the too-rapid rise and fall of the prince's chest.

Wil had been guarded too well from the horrors of French battlefields, but his war service had not been for nothing. While the girl's remedies had been applied cleanly and well, the prince needed a professional. "Haydock should see him," Wil ordered. "Take him to the hall. It's nearest."

"Sir—" Hudson began.

Wil levelled a quelling glance at his servant. "To the hall, Hudson."

Hudson tightened his lips and said nothing, though Wil could guess his man's mind. No one at Clifton Hall would like this, but it was not their decision. It was not strictly Wil's either, but as neither the Duke nor his heir was in residence, the next male in line had to do what he believed to be right and bear the consequences. Such behaviour had been the *modus operandi* at Clifton Hall for centuries.

The girl acquiesced, wrapping her shawl around the Romany prince as she blinked away tears. She still looked frightened. Wil ran a distracted hand through his hair, wishing he could put her at ease. "I am so terribly sorry," he said quietly.

"Are you indeed?" An edge of panic tainted her voice despite the fury in her eyes. "Are you sorry enough to give up such games as these, captain?" She exhaled sharply, standing as tall as she was able and hardly reaching Wil's shoulder. "This is not truly about honour. This is *dinnelipénes*," she finished, her glare spearing him with ire.

Wil received every bitter word knowing he deserved it. There was nothing he could offer in response but his aid.

"Here. You must let me help." With Hudson's assistance, Wil hefted the prince onto his horse, slipping the man's foot into a stirrup before attempting to mount behind him. His eye caught movement at the edge of the wood. A boy on a Romany-bred horse trotted out from under cover of the trees. Wil tried not to look as nonplussed as he felt. It was high time the duke's fences were repaired to address this issue of trespassers.

Syeira called to the boy in Romany before turning back to face Wil with an awkward curtsey. "This is Janfri, our younger brother. He must bear Valkin's body. He is next in line. You may address me as Princess Brishen."

Wil stared at Janfri. *Next in line.* He understood how that felt, and who was he to flout tradition? He too, was a backup. The perpetual second, should anything happen to Roger. He nodded.

"It'd be easier if—Janfri is it?—If Janfri rode Nero and went back with Hudson here." At the princess's nod, Wil assisted the young boy onto his own horse.

"It's all right, Hudson." He eyed Hudson's set mouth. In the eyes of most Englishmen, Romany houseguests were certainly *not* 'all right'. That's as may be, but Wil was responsible for this situation and determined to do what he could in remedy. After all, he hadn't been cut off yet. He adjusted the boy's seat to accommodate his brother's much larger frame. Under Hudson's guidance, they trotted awkwardly away.

Our younger brother, had she said? So, they were family. Wil raised his brows at this. Something stirred within him that he could not quite credit. Envy? He couldn't see either of his siblings coming to be by his side for a duel. He didn't think anyone in his family cared so much about anyone else that they'd do that. Well, perhaps Lydia. She did enjoy having him for an older brother. Roger would attend if he thought Wil might be killed, but that wasn't the case here. The princess didn't think that, did she? One look at the girl's stricken face pulled him up short. *Oh, God.*

"You do know it was a first-blood duel, do you not?" Wil was suddenly desperate to ensure this was clear. "Surely that damn...I beg pardon...earl mentioned it?"

"I do not know," the princess replied. "He may have told Valkin, who forgot to tell me." The princess shook her head, uttering a word Wil was certain was Romany for the one he was thinking.

He snorted. "Quite." An overwhelming need to make sure this girl understood washed through him. He couldn't bear to have her think poorly of him, although why this might bother him, he could not say. Plenty of people thought poorly of him and he never gave them a second thought. "I truly did not mean to hurt him. I was aiming for a grazing, but he moved at the last second...," He couldn't meet her gaze, watching the disappearing horses instead before returning his attention to the Romany princess.

Her hip-length black hair stirred about her in the early morning breeze, framing shapely curves. He'd rarely been so struck by the mere sight of a pretty woman. Beautiful too, rather than merely pretty. She wore no bonnet, no lace or ribbons, and yet he couldn't tear his eyes from her.

Her well-made dress was silver-blue patterned silk in the Romany style, sensuous fabric clinging to gently swelling hips and firmly rounded breasts pressing tightly in the cold morning. He stepped forward, placing his officer's coat over the girl's shivering shoulders and helping her fit her arms into the sleeves. This close to her, his senses reeled. He detected the smell of fragrant herbs and something irresistibly sweet like cinnamon and wild roses. He didn't think he'd ever inhaled a scent more delicious.

His gaze ran up from the dress, over her golden skin, to her dark gemstone eyes and then down to her rich, plum-coloured mouth.

His body hardened as his gaze fixed on her mouth.

Damn. What was the matter with him today?

Slowly, Wil lifted his hand to her face, wiping away the smeared blood on her cheek. She started, then relaxed when she saw the stain on his fingers.

The curve of her face reminded him of sunlight on lake water and those eyes of hers—deep indigo set with full, tear-fringed lashes as her wary gaze tracked him, held him. He stood so close to her now, much too close. Barely conscious of what he was doing, Wil breathed her scent deeply into him, feeling it fill every part of him, surround him, bewitch him. He wanted to curve his arms around her, pulling her closer still until those lips of hers opened beneath his own. Drawing back, Wil attempted to breathe normally and still his shaking hands.

He was unaccountably pleased there remained only one horse. The idea of holding this wild girl in his arms as they galloped back to the hall heated his blood. That's if he could mount a horse at all. The thought gave him pause. His body twitched.

He smiled. "Well, my dear, shall we ride back together?" he murmured into dark silken hair, in no fit state to withstand that powerful pull on his senses again.

The princess looked away, a deeply conscious blush blooming in her cheeks. Wil watched her breasts rise and fall on a deepening breath. She looked up and held his gaze.

"I am sorry," she blurted out, dancing backward. "I cannot ride with you." Grabbing her horse's mane with both hands, she swung herself onto the animal's bare back, astride, mind you. Wil could barely believe it, and for some reason the sight of it stoked his heat painfully. She galloped off after her brothers, silken black hair streaming behind her.

Leaving her would-be seducer to make his own way back without his coat, his horse or even his dignity.

Wil grinned at himself, glancing down at his mud-splattered breeches. He felt decidedly rough. The walk would do him good. He couldn't remember any woman having this effect on him before. And simply from looking at her. He'd never even...

He let out a frustrated groan as he marched the three miles back to Clifton Hall, trying hard to keep at bay the images of all the things he'd like to do to Brishen's sister if he ever got the chance.

Chapter Five

"I hope you know where you're going, boy." Syeira reminded herself that this was Valkin's horse, bred for intelligence as well as speed. The prince's progress would be slower than her own. Syeira prayed the ride from the duelling field did not jar his wound too much. She'd secured her poultices as best she could, but the effects would last no longer than the belladonna. Her mother's instructions echoed through her memory: *In wound healing as in love, my daughter, timing matters.*

Timing. Urging Grygry to even greater speed, Syeira ducked her head, willing him onward as though the beast's pounding hoofbeats could drum the fear from her mind. The animal moved easily through overgrown fields and tumbledown walls, seeming to find his way by instinct. Syeira watched for Janfri, but they met no one.

The sights of the duelling field were seared into her memory so that even behind her eyelids, she saw Valkin falling, heard his pained shout amid her own cries. She remembered her mother, another fallen Romany man, and her ailing Papa. Shaking her head, she sat up a little straighter. This was no time for wretchedness, but the sick feeling worsened as Grygry's steady rhythm brought them closer to the hall. She would not let the English see her fear. They loved to exploit such weakness.

Allowing the motion of the horse's canter to soothe her, Syeira exhaled. She always felt better on the move. The great house was in sight, though there was no sign of the others. She must have ridden a different route to the hall. The knot in her belly tightened.

She did not slow Grygry until they reached the gravel drive, and then merely out of some irrational fear that putting the stones out of place might impair the assistance the captain had promised on the duelling field, assistance Valkin needed so badly. Not that Syeira would rely on it. She would take no Englishman's word on faith alone, no matter how handsome.

Syeira blushed, forcing that thought away. She must focus on her duty. She and Janfri stood for Brishen now. Her younger brother had not dealt with the English directly, and Syeira had never yet met them without the Romany prince. She needed to be strong. The unexpected arrival of Romany royalty did not necessarily secure a welcome. Quite the reverse in fact.

Swinging herself into a dismount, Syeira pulled the horse towards a shadowy corner out of sight of the main entrance. Shivering in its shade, she gazed upward at the ancient stone building. It did not surprise her that Clifton Hall was old. The estate dated back to the twelfth century. But she was not expecting the poorly kept portico marked with mould and spotted with decades of lichen growth. Might there be a connection between this neglect and the dishevelled soldier she'd met on the duelling field?

There was such care in the Romany notion of home. The pride with which so many of her people built and maintained their temporary dwellings with such thought and joy. The warmth of belonging to the Romany was always within her. Syeira drew strength from this and was grateful.

No wonder the captain did not choose to live at Clifton Hall. The sheer size of the over-built stones oppressed her. There was unhappiness here, built right in to the weighted walls around her. A shiver of revulsion raced down her spine.

She hoped Valkin healed quickly and they were able to join the rest of Brishen soon. Gazing at the hard, immovable stone of Clifton Hall made the Brishen camp seem somehow further away. Syeira did not like to be still. She did not like these cold stone walls, and she especially did not like to be beholden to an English household such as this.

The grand main door creaked open and she shrank further into the shadow of the stonework.

"I am certain I heard hoof beats, Mr Oates," a young voice quavered, uncertainty in every utterance.

"You are mistaken, young Yates." An older man's voice this time, endeavouring to conceal his impatience with the youth. "It is nothing to feel ashamed of, boy. I am sure your father has no need to wait on any one resident at the hall while His Grace and Lord Clifton are from home."

Syeira distinctly heard a profound sniff as the presumably senior member of the household delivered his reproof. It had been some time since she had attended on an English household, but she guessed the cadaverous Mr Oates to be a head butler, and the younger man an under butler. She nearly regretted her refusal to ride in with the captain. Improper though it certainly was, at least the staff here knew him. She could not recollect the proper manner to introduce herself into an English household without an Englishman to recommend her.

"Next time, be certain of what you hear before summoning the footmen." Another sniff, as though the man had missed his snuff this day. "They have their duties, Yates, same as you, and we none of us can spare time for your fancies."

Syeira led Grygry forward. "The boy is not mistaken, sir."

The head butler swivelled his head so fast Syeira feared his stiffened neck bones might crack.

"Good morning," began Mr Oates, his lips thinning. Another audible sniff seemed to imply the air at Clifton Hall somehow fouled. "Gypsies can find scraps at the back entrance. Perhaps the kitchens—"

"I am here at the behest of Captain Clifton."

"Are you indeed?" Oates's tone was widely disbelieving.

Syeira had nothing with which to prove her claim. Shrugging her shoulders loose of the scarlet coat, she flushed but held the butler's gaze.

"This belongs to your master, does it not, Mr Oates?"

The man started at the use of his name.

"Would you be so good as to indicate the way to your stillroom?" She smiled inwardly at the useful old Romany knowing, sure to wrong-foot the other party in any exchange. Out of the corner of her eye, she saw a broad grin move over the face of young Yates, gone as quickly as it came.

"A red coat is no indication, Miss." The knot in her belly grew heavier as a coterie of footmen exited the hall, forming a line as though for battle. Further hoof beats interrupted them all. Syeira jumped herself astride Grygry once more, riding forward to assist Janfri and the valet. Looking down at the servants, she indicated the approaching riders.

"Speak with the valet. He knows our business here."

It would not be wise to mention the duel. Besides, she had more pressing matters to attend to. She met Hudson and Janfri at the top of the gravel drive. Adjusting her seat, Syeira sat up as tall as she was able, addressing herself to Hudson.

"How will you manage the dismount?"

The valet, who was attempting to balance the prince's prone frame between his mount and Janfri's, did not answer. He did, however, stare unabashedly at the sight of a woman seated astride her mount. Syeira bit back her irritation. She needed this man's help. Not even with Janfri's assistance could she hope to bear the prince indoors alone.

Matching Grygry's stride to the thoroughbred's, Syeira assisted in the support of her eldest brother as they approached the doors to the hall. Instructing Janfri to hold the prince as steady as he could, she kept one hand on Valkin's leg. Swinging herself down one-handed, she stood looking up at Hudson.

"You will please assist, sir." She glanced at Valkin's chest, his breathing shallowing as she watched. Panic stirred.

"Sir," she repeated. "Hold his upper torso and head as still as you can." She swallowed and took a breath. "I shall manage his lower body, with Janfri's assistance."

Hudson dismounted, leaving Janfri with the full weight of the prince. Syeira swore in Romany, bracing Valkin's frame against her own and that of the horse. She silently thanked whomever had trained this English horse for the steadiness with which the beast held himself. Had he moved, or even shifted weight, Valkin's unconscious form would have crashed to the ground. The animal did not alter his stance at all, merely snorting as he remained still. Syeira found it almost amusing that the most cooperative Englishman was a horse.

"Take the prince," she gasped, all of her upper body strength focused on keeping Valkin from slipping.

Stepping around to the side, the valet added his support to her own. Slowly, they shifted Valkin's weight between them until Hudson had the prince in a gentleman's hold.

"I have him, princess," he muttered.

"Just so." Syeira stepped away, calling Janfri to take her place at Valkin's side. "Now, *gently*," she released an inheld breath. "I believe at least one rib to be broken. The smoother the prince's transport, the better."

The mention of prince and princess had the gazes of all the servants moving curiously from Mr Oates to Syeira and back again.

"Good morning, Mr Hudson," the head butler said.

Syeira noticed that Oates addressed himself solely to Hudson, ignoring the Romany family and the injured prince entirely. The princess held her focus and curbed her temper. The important thing was to secure the supplies needed to heal her brother.

"Mrs Edwards has not notified us of your arrival," Mr Oates continued, still addressing Hudson.

"She did not know of it, Mr Oates," the valet replied. "There has been a—an accident near the moor fence line. These are, ahem, guests of Captain Clifton."

"Guests, did you say?" Oates glared at them all, eyebrow raised, lip curled.

"Enough of this," Syeira broke in. "Janfri and I together can bring prince Brishen inside." She stood at the prince's head, arms out for the weight of her brother's torso, but the valet did not move.

"Captain Clifton's orders were to convey the injured Romany prince inside and render aid." The man stared unflinchingly at the head butler.

"Very well," Oates responded. "Since this is Captain Clifton's doing, convey the guest to his room." He nodded to the six young men. Stepping forward in formation, the small team of footmen did exactly that.

"Which is the room?" Syeira turned to the head butler, ignoring the faint flush to his face. His embarrassment was justified. His want of courtesy was not.

"Second floor, third door on your left," Hudson replied.

Syeira nodded. "Thank you." Straightening her shoulders for one more attempt, she repeated her query regarding the stillroom. "It is essential that I access your stores." Inwardly, she quailed. There were things she needed, and this was the fastest way. She thought of Valkin, lying unconscious somewhere in this great house. She would not fail her family.

Oates's glare could have cracked glass. "Was this part of the captain's orders as well, Miss?"

"His orders," Syeira replied, "were to render aid." She swallowed, speaking words forced from her mouth. "I require your assistance to do this."

"The stillroom is off the kitchen," Hudson replied again. "Down the left stairs as you enter here."

Syeira hardly nodded. Was everything at Clifton Hall grounds for some kind of standoff? The sooner they left this place the better. Turning to Janfri, Syeira spoke in Romany, listing the items she required him to gather. Her brother glanced uneasily at the Englishmen. Syeira exhaled, reining in her annoyance.

"This is for Valkin," she urged him in Romany. "We can waste no more time, Janfri."

He nodded as she completed her list. "A twist of salt, as coarse as possible. Brandy or fortified wine. The heavier the better. Linen cloths if you can find them." Then, without caring that her tone sounded harsh, she spoke her last requirement aloud in English. "Do not forget a full scuttle of coal. We require a large fire."

She wished the whole household to hear of this expense. If they resented it, well, they could whisper about the evils of the Romany princess all they wished. Her sole desire was to heal Valkin.

"I must see to the prince." She swept the head butler and the valet with a glance she hoped was regal enough and ascended to the oak door. At the top of the ancient stone steps, she turned, addressing the head butler one more time.

"You may address me as Princess Brishen." Her whole body shook as she turned away, taking the stairs far too fast in her haste to both attend her brother and escape the horrified look on the face of this English servant who refused to see her at all.

Chapter Six

About a mile from the gates of Clifton Hall stood the steward's cottage, a stone building about as ancient as the hall itself. A smallish park and a produce garden made up the landaulette, on which the steward of so great an estate was permitted to keep his own poultry and farm enough for his family. Wil waited at the old wooden gate, which he noted stood in a far better state of repair than Clifton Hall's boundary fences. Apart from an old bloodhound, the farmyard appeared deserted. The animal rose slowly, limping arthritically over to lick lazily at Wil's outstretched hand.

"Not much of a guard dog, are you, old fellow?" He rubbed the ageing muzzle, feeling a sudden kinship with the worn out beast. His headache worsened and he feared if the steward did not make an appearance soon, he'd find the heir's spare lying face down in the muddy puddle that marked the distance between the gatepost and the homestead door.

The dog lay down and rolled for him, brown eyes and a lolling tongue encouraging this new visitor to play. Wil shook his head, grimacing with pain.

"Not today, fellow." He must dispose of his business quickly. He wondered if he could borrow a horse, or even a mule. And what reason could Captain Clifton give the duke's steward for requiring a mule to carry him the last part-mile home? *Tell him I was hurt in the war?* Wil grinned faintly as he leaned against the stone lintel, knocking loudly on the door. The grounds seemed unusually quiet. He was sure the steward had a family. Wasn't there a wife and several children? What *was* the man's name? He knocked again.

After what seemed an interminable wait, the door was answered by a flustered young girl, who smartened up immediately when she recognised him.

"Beggin' yer pardon, captain, but Mrs Yates is that sick wiv the young 'uns." She curtsied, showing him into a prettily fitted-up parlour.

A rustle announced the arrival of Mrs Yates. The woman came in as distressed and flustered as Wil had yet seen any of her sex.

"Good morning," he bowed.

"Good morning, Captain Clifton." Mrs Yates curtsied in her turn, a flush colouring her cheeks. "Forgive me for not receiving you properly. Your arrival this morning has taken me quite unawares."

Wil shook his head. "I beg your pardon for any undue alarm, Mrs Yates. I've this moment arrived home." *Home.* The word tasted foreign as it left his lips, like the lie he knew it to be. Belatedly, he considered how he must present in this moment. Dishevelled, certainly. Unshaven, definitely. Disreputable? He shrugged away such compunctions. The sooner he ascertained the state of things, the sooner he could find rest at the hall.

His hostess still wore a look of deep concern, though she bid him be seated and rang for tea. Wil sat at the edge of an overly plump velvet loveseat, feeling ridiculous. He cleared his throat. "I shan't intrude upon you long. I wished to speak with Mr Yates regarding the rumour of illness I heard on my way here." He looked around. "Is the steward not at home?"

"He is in Lancaster." Mrs Yates reddened again. "The duke's new linen works takes him from home a great deal." Her voice wobbled. "It is quite a burden to have him so far off, when his children are so ill." At this she failed to suppress a sob, looking to Wil for a kerchief he could not offer. Such niceties remained in his coat, likely already returned to the Hall. He located a lace piece in his waistcoat.

"Th-thank you, Captain Clifton." The distraught woman wiped her eyes and straightened, meeting his gaze. "I shall do my best to assist you."

Wil flinched at the redness he saw there, feeling the need to depart this place but knowing he must stay and offer what aid he could. "Then it is true, Mrs Yates," he pressed. "The incidence of fever in the White Chapel village?"

"Not merely in the village, captain." She waited as tea was brought in, pouring a cup for the captain and then herself.

"Is it one lump, captain?" She looked up, her tongs hovering above the sugar bowl.

"None at all, I thank you, Mrs Yates." Wil accepted his tea, taking a cautious sip. Hot and strong, his aching head could hardly stand it. He hurriedly replaced the cup and saucer on the table.

"Oh yes, it's His Grace who is fond of sweet things." His hostess nodded, then seemed to gather herself to answer his question. "The illness has spread to Preston and Chorley villages as well."

"What is being done?"

Mrs Yates stared. "I am sure Mr Yates is doing all that's required, captain." The woman's eyes glistened ominously. "Why, with my own poor bairns coming down with the fever this very day, Mr Yates can do no less. If he is not sent away every other week..." Her voice trailed off as she buried her face in the scrap of lace, sobbing outright now.

"I do not doubt it, ma'am," Wil replied. "Is there anything else amiss among the estates I should know?"

The lady looked up with a half-smile, and it was not kind. "*You* should know?"

Wil bit back an impatient curse, his manners waning with his energy. "Lord Clifton has not received the estate reports for the past three quarters to my certain knowledge." His clipped tone sounded harsh even to his own ears. "Be so good as to have Mr Yates deliver these to the hall at his earliest opportunity. Have Haydock summoned likewise."

"Doctor Haydock is greatly stretched just now." Mrs Yates took refuge in the solemnity she ought not to have displaced. She glanced significantly towards the upstairs rooms where her ill children lay.

"The illness is severe then?"

"Severe enough, captain."

Another upward glance had Wil on his feet, nodding. "Understood. I shall expect Doctor Haydock's attendance only at a time it may be safely bestowed." He bowed as he spoke. "Thank you for the tea, Mrs Yates. Now, if there is no other—"

"Oh, but there is." The woman's cheeks displayed a blush so crimson she appeared feverish herself. "If you'll take the pup away with you, captain, I'd be much obliged."

"The *pup*?" Wil repeated, wondering if his hearing was failing him too this day. "I beg your pardon, Mrs Yates. I do not understand."

The steward's wife was already on her feet. "Follow me." Her flaming cheeks and downcast eyes preceded him out the side door, onto a kind of small square bordered by outbuildings. She led him over to one and pointed.

"In there."

Wil stuck his head over the top part of the stable door. Inside, a tiny ball of white and ginger fluff snored contentedly on a pile of hay.

"Take him," his hostess said. "Please, captain."

"I'd be happy to if you deem it necessary, Mrs Yates," Wil replied. "But I still do not understand."

The woman blew her nose loudly on his lace and looked at him. "The duke insisted I have him," she explained. "He—he would not allow me to refuse." Her eyes stared earnestly into his.

Yates sent too often from home on the duke's orders. His pretty wife alone at home with the children—and His Grace less than a mile away, 'pressing his gifts'. Wil bit his lips, swallowing epithets he could not utter aloud.

"He p-pressed the little chap on me and I... I did not know what I should do." Mrs Yates's voice was low and earnest. "I wish to be perfectly clear with you, captain. As clear as I am with His Grace when he comes here and—and offers me—gifts and *things I do not require*." She stood there, stammering it all out. "I *do not wish it*. I do *not*." Regaining her composure, she spoke again in her usual sedate tone. "I cannot have it in the house. Mr Yates would not like it."

Wil found himself quite unable to meet the damp eyes of his hostess.

"I will be most exceedingly obliged if you'd take him back to the hall, captain." The woman's blushing confusion excited pity rather than anger.

Wil rubbed his face and nodded, remembering too late that any head movement at all was a bad idea. "I comprehend you perfectly," he sighed. He had some recollection Yates had a son. "How old is your eldest, Mrs Yates?"

"Why, he is thirteen, captain. He removed to the great house at Michaelmas, in service to your family as under butler."

Wil faced Mrs Yates. "It is no distance from your cottage to the hall at all. I see no reason why the boy cannot remain billeted in your home, ma'am. At least while your husband is asked to be away. Will this," he paused meaningfully, "*assist* at all?"

Even his voice sounded used up. He remained but a mile away from rest and refreshment and still it seemed at least ten. He was desperate to be gone, to see Lydia, and how the prince did. To calm that firebrand of a Romany princess and see if she needed him, which he took leave to doubt. She didn't seem to need a great deal, but others did. The relief on Mrs Yates's face deferred his impatience to be on his way.

"It will assist, sir. It will assist greatly, I thank you." His hostess gazed at him so long that Wil began to feel far too consequential. He'd done nothing but attempt to safeguard her from his father. That such an action was necessary he was too weary to resent.

He thought back to the letters he'd received only last week. When it came to the duke, it appeared no woman was safe. An image of the late duchess passed through his memory. He shook his head, repressing a groan. This was turning into one of the longest mornings he could recall, but that, he reflected, was Clifton Hall in summary.

Mrs Yates was speaking. "You will send William home to me when his father is absent?"

"The direction will be given the moment I return to the hall. He shall return to you this eve." Wil bowed and, leaning down, scooped the spaniel pup into his arms. "This little chap need trouble you no longer." He smiled as the little creature's attempt to lick Wil's face was foiled by stubble.

"He is a dear little dog." She smiled through more free-flowing tears. "But I cannot accept such gifts."

"I commend your discretion, ma'am." Wil bowed again. "Allow me also to beg your pardon."

He felt an urgent need to apologise somehow and offer some sort of reparation but could think of no way to phrase this with any delicacy. He remembered the scathing look in the eyes of the Romany princess. The Clifton charm had certainly deserted him this morning. He quickened his pace. Refreshment and repose would have to wait. There was still much to do.

***

Belatedly, Wil remembered it was Pancake Day. At least a dozen children from the estate clamoured around the servants' doors at Clifton Hall. Though small, there were enough of the little terrors to overset Cook as they stood in a ragtag, ill-formed column, grinning irresistibly up at her.

"Please, a pancake," chorused winsomely shrill voices as the army of small boys and girls jostled each other. Their goal was to get as close to Cook as possible as she dispensed the sweet treats for this day. A kitchen maid blew uselessly on a whistle in an effort to restore some order, but it had little effect. Wil grinned at the expression on the maid's face. No doubt the whistle had been the housekeeper's idea. The maid was not much older than some of the children and seemed far more interested in the treats than asserting any kind of authority over the recipients. Children were not soldiers, and Pancake Day was supposed to be a little unruly.

Cook did her best to look cross, but it seemed to Wil that she was in truth trying not to grin back at the children. He watched as one of the sternest staff members at Clifton Hall gave up, bursting into laughter as she gifted gingerbread and toffees into twelve pairs of excited, pint-sized hands. Next came what remained of the orchard fruits and the almond harvest.

Observing the children, Wil frowned. Weren't there usually *several dozen* of the little imps? This illness was likely serious then. He'd find out more soon enough. *First things first*. Spying an open door off a side entrance, he slipped through, deftly avoiding the dozen-strong pack of springer spaniels usually resident in the lower rooms. He had no intention of broadcasting the events of this morning to any member of the duke's staff. No good could come from any mention of the illegal duel. In fact, he saw no reason to offer any explanation at all. At least not until he'd ascertained precisely what assistance the House of Brishen required from Clifton Hall.

He mounted the stairs to find his bedroom commandeered by the princess Brishen. Mr Oates hovered in the hall, clearly at a loss.

"She won't let me in, captain. Stole stores from the stillroom, she did. Pushed right past the staff. Mrs Edwards is livid."

Mrs Edwards ran Clifton Hall like her own personal fiefdom. There wasn't a member of the household staff who thought of her with equanimity.

"Too much for you to handle, Oates?" Wil bit back a choking desire to laugh at his father's butler. The man was as puffed up as Wil had ever seen him. He was practically emotional. How could he let this little family get under his skin so? How could the head butler let a mere girl tell him what to do? Handing the puppy off to his valet, Wil approached the door of his bedroom.

Prince Brishen lay on the bed, hangings gaping wide. His eyes were closed and his face pale. His sister was placing a coarse cloth over his mouth and nose. She kept one palm on his chest, measuring his breath. Herbs simmered in hot water over the fireplace. Janfri sat nearby, stoking a massive fire and using all the coal he could find. It was the house brandy the girl had requisitioned, presumably for the pain. The air smelled sweetly of flowers, berries and an overpowering type of mint. Wil recalled the scent and thought he understood. Pennyroyal, poppy seeds and brandy. The prince's siblings were administering some sort of pain relief remedy. He stepped over the threshold.

Chapter Seven

"Get out," Syeira snapped, without turning her head from her brother's pale face.

"I beg your pardon, Princess Brishen. This is *my* house," Captain Clifton shot back.

"This is *your* doing," she responded without looking up. "So I will not apologise for accessing the stores I require." She hated the still-visible tremors along her arms: hated that an Englishman had to see them, and that she felt them at all.

"No more should you," her host affirmed.

"I must treat the wound." Syeira hoped she sounded less scared than she felt. This was no time for giving way to nerves. Eyeing her companions, she steadied her voice. "You served on the Peninsula, captain?" Seeing him nod, she continued. "You will please now assist me."

Captain Clifton paled perceptibly, holding an unsteady hand to his head. No doubt about it, the man was in pain.

"Oughtn't we to wait for Doctor Haydock? I have no wish to test my limited experience of field surgery on the prince, and you're still in shock yourself." He stared meaningfully at her arms. "If there is even the slightest error, Clifton Hall will be responsible for a lot more than an illegal pistoling." He rested one hand on his gut, looking as if he was struggling to keep his breakfast down. "I say we wait."

"This is not wise, captain. Fetching the physician may take hours, with ill children to attend in your villages." Her mother's words again: *Timing matters.* Yes, yes it does. "The shot must be removed, or the risk of infection becomes very great. It is not the wound that is deadly. It is the sepsis." She gazed into cool green eyes, willing him to agree. To simply nod his head and progress her work here.

The captain flinched from the look she levelled at him. Clifton clearly knew his culpability. No doubt the son of a duke was not used to having so much demanded of him. Still, if he thought he could shoot her brother with little to do in the aftermath he did not know Princess Brishen. This Englishman had no claim to stand upon his dignity. Syeira shook her head, determined to clear the visions of scarlet staining Romany linen, gun smoke wreathing beneath a rising sun.

A closer examination of the wound told Syeira the shot itself was less dangerous than she originally thought, which spoke either to the captain's skill or Valkin's luck. She did not much care which and breathed a prayer of gratitude that most of her eldest brother's bones and organs seemed to have been spared.

"Most, but not all," she murmured to herself. She was right to be concerned about his broken ribs. The bruising was unmistakeable and Syeira's heart sank. She did not wish to remain in this place of walls and under-butlers any longer than she must, but bone healing could be slow. She must take even greater care when seeking the ball. Whether there would be any lasting damage or not now depended entirely on her. Her hands did not shake with shock, but with fear.

Desperate now, she dropped all pretence at hauteur. "There is no one else, sir. I will be only one more moment."

Syeira closed her eyes, placing her palms together. Beside her, Janfri did the same. Brother and sister inhaled and exhaled as one. They repeated this twice more. Syeira's hands stilled and her shoulders dropped by inches.

The calmness of breath steadied Syeira's nerves when there was nothing else to which she could cleave. This practise was her mother's legacy, along with the herblore her eldest daughter had mastered, and the princess Brishen had never been more grateful for her mother's careful instruction than in this moment. She breathed deeply, feeling the stoicism hold her ready. She glanced carefully at Captain Clifton, weighing her presumption.

"Captain?" She held her breath. "Are you ready?"

Clifton stepped away from the fireplace. "Haydock may be some time yet." He locked his gaze to hers, and nodded.

Certain of her knowledge and proud of her skill, Syeira looked down at her brother. A wound was merely another form of illness, and with illness she knew precisely what she must do. Silencing all inward doubt, she turned to her work.

Removing the poppy-scented cloth from her brother's mouth, Syeira nodded in satisfaction. The belladonna, poppy and brandy solution had done its work. Valkin was now as unresponsive as could be expected.

With his hands wrapped in clean linens, Janfri handed his sister a set of callipers from the boiling pot over the fire. There was no longer much bleeding. Her clotting poultice appeared effective, and her bandages were tight enough. She hefted her brother's arm as gently as she could, motioning for Clifton to take the weight of his limb.

"I am not sure," he whispered, holding the prince's arm out so as to offer the best possible access to the injury.

"If you please, captain?" Syeira breathed out the request slowly, patiently probing the raw flesh at the edges of the wound.

Further protests seemed to die on his lips. Syeira held her breath. Her host appeared to be doing the same as she cautiously explored the depth of the damage. Digging gingerly into the open wound, she worked with a sea sponge to absorb additional blood flow. She located the shot and steadily drew it out, placing the lead ball on yet another linen cloth. Janfri relieved Clifton of the weight of Valkin's arm. Syeira permitted herself a small smile of relief.

Measuring two drops of iodine solution into her mortar, she added the salt Janfri had liberated from the stillroom. Next, Syeira handed the whole thing across to Captain Clifton.

"If you would be so good as to mix the remedy against sepsis, Captain Clifton."

Her host ground the pestle in silence, staring at the bloodily smeared lead ball. Perhaps he was contemplating other means by which grown men might settle their disagreements. Syeira silently prayed for Brishen to consider such as well.

She retrieved the bowl once the mixture looked to be thickening. Painting generous dollops of her paste over the open wound, she used the callipers to pack more of the salt around the now-pale flesh. Using the last of her linen cloths, she rebound the wound and released the bandage constricting her brother's upper torso.

"Now he will sleep," she whispered, looking at Janfri. Her younger brother had hardly spoken, but he'd done all that was asked of him. He must have been as frightened as she. Smiling reassuringly, she held out her arms. With a stifled sob, the child held onto his sister for the merest second before stepping back and lifting his chin. He resumed his seat by their brother's bedside without another sound.

Syeira cleaned her healing tools with methodical efficiency, tossing the bloodied cloths into the fire. She stilled her flurry of activity only once the attendant fear was over. The danger was past. She felt it, her instincts and skill telling her that Valkin would be all right—thanks in no small part to the minimisation of the initial attack. For which, she supposed, she owed Captain Clifton her gratitude. Valkin would expect her to feel grateful and in a queer way she did. Brishen's debt to Haversham was paid, and her brother would recover. Still, an unaccountable risk had been taken by two men of sense and honour, to appease another who seemed possessed of neither quality.

This thought surprised her; she hardly knew Captain Clifton. His attentions to Brishen showed nothing more than a man acting responsibly. His assistance was welcome—but what might he demand in return? Terms of trade, or *kin aley*, were decisions she and Valkin usually made together on behalf of Brishen. Syeira suddenly missed the prince's counsel more than she ever had. So much now depended on her alone.

No Romany woman could afford to be at a disadvantage in an Englishman's house, but what trade could she offer this man? Would the captain ask for her virtue? A shiver swept through her. A warmth that had nothing to do with the fire Janfri stoked in Valkin's sick room, or the aftermath of the duel. Gratitude notwithstanding, she must always remember her status—among the Romany and the English. She could no more take such risks with herself than Valkin could have refused Haversham's duel. Still... *what if he wanted her?*

What on *earth* was she thinking? How often had she disdained the English girls who swooned in too-tight stays? Syeira supposed her disorientation was due to the relief of her brother's wellbeing, or perhaps she'd simply been indoors too long.

If this man wished to seduce her, he was sadly mistaken. It seemed important to make clear to Captain Clifton that those few moments alone on the duelling field were all there would ever be. She'd known he stood too close, yet she'd been mesmerised by the scent of leather and cordite rising from his coat, and the musky aroma of his skin. From the way his linen shirt lay against his chest, she could tell his torso was powerful and firm. His chin, roughened with pale gold stubble, framed a sensual, powerful mouth that looked as if it knew secrets about her body even she wasn't aware of, like how she wanted to be touched, and exactly how to quicken the slow-burning tingle within.

An odd warmth rose in her breasts, and that gentle tingle was fast becoming a throb. *Too fast.* Especially for her. What had Valkin called her? The Romany princess was the pride of Brishen, her position among her people unique. Syeira could not afford this sort of foolishness, especially over an Englishman. She had far more pressing concerns to deal with in this moment than the thunder of her pulse beneath her skin, and the dangerous warmth flowing from Captain Clifton's gaze into her own. That curiously heated sensation seemed to linger in her body even now and she did not trust it. She was not sure why it mattered. Perhaps it was the way her cheeks warmed when he stood close to her. Or the way he'd attempted to apologise for winning the duel. Or it could be the way he looked at her. It was certainly strange to be stared at so intently. Syeira wanted this man to feel the pointlessness of pursuit. Still, he was doing his best to assist her family. The least he deserved was courtesy.

Taking a deep breath and hoping her pulse rate slowed enough to cool her burning cheeks, Syeira prepared to address this Englishman who inspired such wild thoughts. Speaking the Romany rules aloud would serve as a timely reminder for herself as well.

Chapter Eight

"You may sit," she told him, inclining her head slightly.

"Thank you," Wil muttered dryly, hardly daring to move.

"I thank you, Captain Clifton." The princess kept her eyes on her hands. "I believe you did your best not to injure my brother." She lifted her head and stared at him, a flash of something flickering in those purple eyes.

Gratitude? *Well, that's something.*

"Er—yes. I thank *you.*" He cleared his throat. "Will you nurse your brother until he is well?" Wil asked, hovering nervously now in his own doorway. *His* doorway. Was he afraid to be too near the girl?

The room was full of steam and herbs. The heat generated by the enormous blaze in the fireplace made the air shimmer. He felt hot all over but desperately wanted to move closer to the heat. What *was* the matter with him today?

"She cannot stay alone in a man's house." The young boy spoke, clearly taking up the mantle of leader until the prince awoke.

Princess Brishen explained she needed to be chaperoned. "Properly," she emphasised.

Wil's eyebrows shot up. "Properly?" He was afforded another opportunity to watch those golden cheeks darken as she blushed deep rose and looked down, lustrous lashes fluttering against her glowing face. She was undoubtedly beautiful. Striking, and unconsciously sensual like the patterned silk she wore and the dark opal mystery of her eyes. At least now he knew she wasn't married. Married women did not blush about courting. At least, not in his experience.

"That is, not like your English ladies," she hastened to add. "When the Romany say chaperoned, we *mean* chaperoned. Romany women do not travel *anywhere* without a chaperon. Any girl who does so brings great dishonour to her House. The men of the disgraced House are seen as poor caretakers of their families and will find it difficult to offer for brides in the future."

Wil did nothing to correct the princess's critique of his fellow English. She merely spoke the truth as it was known throughout the country, after all. He shrugged, inclining his head in accord. "Travelling alone is unsafe for any woman." He suddenly realised that his lovers had borne this risk on many occasions to meet with him. The personal risk they carried had not occurred to him before. He was careful to ensure they were seen safely home by Hudson, if not by Wil. He flushed now to wonder if they'd felt his carelessness as keenly as he did in this moment. None of them had seen fit to mention it. *They might, if you'd ever asked*, a voice inside him piped up. His conscience might be long out of practise but it was, apparently, still there.

"One of the men of my house must have me in sight at all times," his guest continued, her gaze meeting his. "It is a dishonour to my family to disobey."

It seemed to Wil that the princess issued a warning. Was his behaviour now so wild that his affairs had even reached the ears of the Romany? His face heated further as he acknowledged this was more than possible.

"Your honour is quite safe at Clifton Hall, Princess Brishen." He lowered his eyes, stopping himself from shifting uneasily. His room was impossibly hot, although the others did not seem discomfited.

He studied the princess again through half-closed lashes. Her wariness of him was obvious. Wil shoved a frustrated hand through his hair, feeling thoroughly out of his depth. He didn't want her afraid of him. He wanted—well, he wanted what he'd clearly been warned *not* to want. Forcibly turning his thoughts from his troubling desires, he gestured toward the prince.

"Is he very bad?"

The princess breathed out, seemingly relieved at the change of subject. "The worst of the danger is past. He needs rest and time for his ribs to heal. One is certainly broken. Another may be grazed or cracked. You can see the bruising here." She traced a line along the prince's left side.

Wil saw mottled markings on the paler flesh above the wound itself. His stomach turned over. At the same time he felt stabbed with a kind of dawning wonder. His arguments regarding Haydock had been ignorant. The princess had been right, and he'd been wrong. However did she manage to treat such a wound without squeamishness? He knew of no other woman who could have done it, and only a very few men.

"The prince will need to stay entirely still for some weeks. This is not easy for a Romany. Especially for my brother." The girl seemed to be searching her bag for something. "I must keep his wound completely dry and clean. I will stay if Janfri may stay also. This is permitted."

"Of course you must." Dragging his focus away from her lips he noticed the princess was offering him something. A small green leaf lay on her palm. "For me?"

She nodded. "For your headache, Captain Clifton. You chew it."

"Thank you," he said, taking it and placing it on his tongue. In a very few minutes he began to feel remarkably better. A girl who cured a man's hangover? Now *there* was a rare breed. He ran his hand over his stubbled jaw, studying her again.

Her fingernails gleamed slightly in the firelight as she twisted a cloth around the lead shot. Wil watched slender hands efficiently packing dried herbs and bits of cloth into a black leather pouch. Her tongue played hesitantly with her lower lip when she concentrated. She rubbed her moistened mouth together, pressing it closed. He'd never seen anything so unconsciously sensual. Wil caught his breath, swearing silently at himself.

Chapter Nine

Valkin's eyes opened. He paled perceptibly, throat convulsing. Syeira hurried to his side with her mortar, smiling with relief. Her brother was awake—it was the best possible sign that he would recover. She scarcely had time to offer up a silent prayer of thankfulness before the Romany prince turned his head, managing to be violently sick into her proffered receptacle. She heard Janfri's exhalation of breath behind her and squeezed the prince's shoulder tightly. Her brother shifted away with an impatient movement of his head. Syeira did not care. He was awake. She could have kissed him.

"It is the belladonna, Valkin. I gave you the smallest dose for your pain. It is a powerful emetic." Wiping his mouth, she attempted to steady his injured torso with trembling hands of her own, but her brother resisted this too.

"Your pride is greater than your sense," she whispered in Romany, voice catching.

It hurt to see her beloved brother like this. Pressing her lips tightly together, Syeira straightened her back, clamping down on the shivering shards of fear low in her belly. Until her brother was healed, she must be strong enough for them both.

Valkin hardly seemed to hear her as he stared around the room, surprise in every feature. Syeira explained the situation in rapid Romany, not forgetting Haversham and the unclear terms of the duel. Captain Clifton bowed briefly on hearing his own name before she fell silent.

"*Bostaris.*" Valkin scowled, referring to Haversham.

"Indeed," Captain Clifton agreed as Valkin smiled faintly at him. "Welcome back, Prince Brishen. We must see about breakfast for your family. And please, send word to your House. They have my leave to camp by the trout lake until you are well enough to travel." He bowed again.

Valkin spoke a few halting words to Janfri. The boy left at a run to carry his brother's message back to their House. The prince looked ruefully down at his bandaged torso, accepting the cup of greenish tea Syeira handed him. Syeira saw the relief in his face as the pain receded. She had done her work well then, but recovery from a broken rib could not be immediate.

"Thank you, Captain Clifton, for your trouble. We will repay you as soon as we can." Valkin's voice was weak.

"Nonsense. The fault is mine and so must the remedy be."

"We will still find a way to show you our gratitude," Valkin said firmly. "The duel is immaterial, except that it concludes our trade with Haversham. Brishen always pay our debts, and your generous assistance places us in yours, captain."

Syeira gazed at Captain Clifton, nodding in agreement with her brother.

"Wil, please," he insisted, shrugging off any further discussion of their trade.

The captain's charm was hardly understated. He had excellent manners for an Englishman. Syeira hoped he might say similar of the Romany royals. It was difficult to be sure of the correct etiquette in such circumstances as this. What *was* the polite mode of address for a duellist who'd pistoled one's brother? Syeira bit back a smile. No doubt there would be a pamphlet in a library somewhere for young English ladies to follow.

A sound at the door caught her attention. A pretty child looked in, her tear-streaked face smudged with faint traces of charcoal.

"There you are, Wil." The little girl all but flew at their host uttering a shriek of delight. "I'm so glad you've come back. Eddy's in a frightful snit because some Gyp—*Oh*." She stopped when she saw the injured man on her brother's bed, fair childish cheeks flaming scarlet. "I'm frightfully sorry."

Her brother cleared his throat. "Prince and Princess Brishen, may I present my sister, Miss Lydia Clifton?" He announced. "She is *supposed* to be learning to sketch and how to behave like a young lady. I do apologise." But he was smiling.

"You needn't apologise for *me*," the little girl retorted. Turning to Syeira and Valkin, she bobbed a short curtsey. "I beg pardon unreservedly if I've been rude. I'm upset. I've this moment learned Father is not at home for Easter."

Syeira could not feel insulted. "I understand how it is to miss your father, especially when you are young. How old are you, Miss Clifton?"

"Twelve." The little girl looked at Wil. "What happened here? Why is there a prince lying in your bed?"

Captain Clifton seemed to find a change of subject expedient. "What do you mean the duke's not coming up? What's to hold him in London, I'd like to know?"

"He wrote my governess." Lydia sniffed. "Miss Lee says that there's something *political* he has to take care of." His sister hunched into her body, looking thoroughly sorry for herself.

"Never mind, Lydie. I'm here now."

"Do you mean to stay to Easter?" The plaintive voice was so pitiful Syeira wondered how Clifton could resist.

"I am due back in London. I had not—"

Miss Clifton began to cry in earnest, and for lack of any other person to run to, flung herself against Syeira's skirts, sobbing for all she was worth.

"Lydia." Their host's embarrassed alarm was so terribly English that Syeira cringed inwardly for *both* Cliftons. "I beg your pardon, princess," he began.

"Oh, it is all right." Syeira knelt down until her eyes were level with the little girl's. Folding the soft little hands in her warmer dark ones she looked earnestly into overflowing eyes that were greener even than her brother's.

"I am sorry for your upset, Miss Clifton." She pulled the child against her in a soothing embrace. The shuddering sobs subsided to sniffles. In a moment these too ceased. A few moments passed before the child leaned back, shamefaced.

"I b-beg your p-p-pardon," she offered.

"There is no need." Syeira smiled brightly until the child's lips began turning up at the corners. The girl leaned in close.

"Are you truly a *p-princess*?"

Bending forward so that her lips were beside the little girl's ear, Syeira cupped her mouth so only the two of them might share the secret. "Truly, I am."

A shy and wobbly smile greeted this statement. The arms wrapped too tightly around Syeira's skirts eased their hold. The child's presence felt strangely comforting. Similar scenes occurred many times among their younger siblings. Syeira looked to the prince and saw the answering warmth in Valkin's eyes. She missed Brishen a little more now, but the oppressiveness of the hall's stone walls seemed to lessen.

Syeira straightened, one hand resting on the child's shoulder. Turning curious eyes toward their host, she arched a brow as she surveyed Captain Clifton.

"You are required in London, captain?"

Wil cleared his throat, shifting where he stood. "I am to see about my commission, and I have—ah—other business to attend to."

Other business? Syeira wondered if he referred to a lover. Or *lovers,* if rumour served. She mentally chided herself. What Captain Clifton did was none of her business after all. Could he truly spare so little time for his sister?

"In that case, we cannot remain here." They must risk the journey back to the Brishen camp. It was not a good idea to move Valkin with a broken rib, but this could not be helped. Syeira recalled the expressions of the valet and the head butler. If left to themselves, the duke's household would not aid the Romany prince's healing. They'd received their assistance from Clifton Hall, and while it might be less than Brishen had hoped, at least it absolved her House from offering any kind of recompense.

Syeira saw a kind of alarm on Clifton's face at the mere suggestion of an early departure.

"You must stay until the prince is healed," her host insisted. "I shall remain here if you need."

"I thank you, captain." It seemed the captain was as astute as she'd first thought him.

"Wil, please. Everyone here knows me as Wil." He turned to Lydia. "Roger will be returned from Iberia soon and I shall be here—" he stopped, remembering his unfinished business with the duke. "If I am able," he repeated. "We'll make it merry for all of us."

He spoke soothingly in that soft voice of his again, put his arm around his sister and led her gently from the room. Whispered conversation continued for some minutes at the door, Lydia's small sobs audible to the guests. An older woman stepped forward to take charge of the child. Syeira guessed this to be the redoubtable Mrs Edwards, housekeeper at Clifton Hall. The woman hardly curtsied, but she took the little girl's hand in her own.

"Find Hudson, Eddy," their host suggested quietly. "He has something for Miss Clifton."

The housekeeper managed to communicate her sentiments regarding this morning's activities with one outraged glare and a muttered, "You've not heard the last of this, Master Wil."

Syeira—and her injured brother—caught every syllable. Syeira glared right back at the departing Mrs Edwards, though as she stood behind the housekeeper the older woman could not notice the princess's fiery expression.

Chapter Ten

Wil frowned at Eddy as she stalked away with his sister in tow. Her displeasure was clear in the rigidity of her posture and the harrumphing noises she made every fourth step. Prince and Princess Brishen were his guests, and their residence at the hall would be of some duration. He'd best meet with Eddy and attempt to get her on side. Where she led, the rest of his father's staff would follow. He doubted the staff held his father in any greater esteem than he did, but Eddy was another matter. The last thing he needed was someone informing His Grace that Clifton Hall was playing host to an entire camp of Romany. That'd fetch the duke home all right—and quickly—but it wasn't the sort of visit Wil was keen to front.

He studied the princess as she watched over Prince Brishen and thought of the small boy who'd helped carry his brother to the house and sat with him until ordered to leave. Wil didn't think anyone could part this Romany family from each other. He wondered at the affection that did not shrink at duty. That always did what was expected, not as a chore, but out of a kind of love and a true sense of belonging to one's family.

An image of Lady Gresham skittered across his memory, fading too quickly. He felt an odd sort of shame. An emptiness in his soul widened. He'd never had that close sense of family, not even while his mother lived. He knew few families of 'quality' who did. There was little quality in a family connection that could not be relied upon. His own parents had lived separate lives, his father in London and his mother here at the hall. The duke expected his children to do the same.

His thoughts returned to his sister. Lydia's tears were about more than this single disappointment. A muscle jumped in Wil's jaw. Parliament did not sit over Easter, and the duke's reputation was little better than his own. No doubt a woman held his father in London, and His Grace had chosen the company of a whore over his own family. Wil felt the pain of it, unclenching his fist with an effort. He stared back at the Romany royal family. Smiling stiffly at the Princess Brishen, he remembered his duties as host.

"Now, breakfast..."

***

"I don't know what this world's coming to, I declare I do *not*." Mrs Edwards sputtered as she answered his after-breakfast summons in the library. Wil set his jaw and prepared for resistance. There were a few things he needed to get straight.

"His Grace will not approve this," Mrs Edwards began, preparatory to opening fire on her own.

Wil acknowledged the truth of this with a sigh. He also found the ire of his father's staff mildly satisfying. Sometimes he suspected himself of being a rather small-minded man.

"Prince Brishen was injured on our land, Eddy. By my shot. It was an accident. A shooting accident. I am simply attempting to put it right."

He bit his lip. Eddy had known him all his life; she'd come to the hall when the duchess took up residence. Indeed, it was his mother who first engaged this woman as her lady's maid. Wil had never been able to lie to Eddy with any success. It was akin to lying to his Mama, who had been more than usually perceptive when it came to her children, especially her sons.

"I'm not a fool, sir," Eddy replied, exhibiting a show of spirit no other member of the duke's household would dare display. Not even to his 'spare' son. She eyed him closely. "Why, pray tell, are there gypsies on the estate to begin with?"

"I ask you to remember, Eddy, that Mama thought highly of the House of Brishen. They prefer to be referred to as *Romany*, and they are royalty among their own people."

"They're not 'among their own people' now," the housekeeper countered. "It's Mrs Edwards if you please, Master Warwick, and I hope I know my duty."

"As do I," Wil replied, leaning forward to make his point. "In any case, from what I've seen, almost anybody can enter the estate. A situation I intend to rectify as soon as possible. As to our guests, they are here at my express invitation until the prince is healed.

Anything they require is to be given them although I do not imagine they will require a great deal."

"Very well, captain." Her tone was as stiff as her back.

He rubbed a hand over his chin and took a breath. Making an enemy of his father's housekeeper was no way to begin his homecoming. "I understand this is difficult for you, but I must do my duty. Speaking of which, is there anything else you wish to tell me of?"

The housekeeper's lips remained tight but her tone gentled a fraction as she said, "What you say about the boundary fences is true enough. There are one or two other matters as well. There is illness in White Chapel. The schoolchildren. Haydock may need our assistance."

"I have left word with the steward about the children. Clifton Hall will of course aid the affected families of White Chapel." He took up his quill, watching her face. Her mouth worked behind closed lips, but she forbore to speak. "What else?"

"The Little Chapel as well…" she hesitated now, plunking down her workbasket and beginning to fidget.

"What's this about the Little Chapel?" His gut tightened as he recognised fear in Eddy's eyes. Whenever a member of his father's household hesitated to speak up, it was to do with their master. "Mrs Edwards," he said quietly. "I would be most grateful to you for telling me what, exactly, has been going on at Clifton Hall while I have been away?"

The housekeeper shifted her weight. She would not meet his gaze.

Wil sighed, speaking in as gentle a tone as he could command. "If I can put it right, I shall."

"The Little Chapel has been let go entirely, captain. His Grace has not ordered anything done."

Wil did a quick calculation in his head. "I've been away some eighteen months. Roger—Lord Clifton—has been absent a full year." He sat back in his seat, staring at the duke's housekeeper. "*Nothing* has been done, you say?"

The housekeeper's voice coarsened as her emotions threatened to get the better of her. "The duchess… It is like she never existed," Mrs Edwards whispered, eyes downcast. Taking a deep breath, she lifted her head. "Many's the time I've considered giving in my notice, Master Wil. The Duke—well, he is no easy master, but I have others dependent on me." She swallowed. "My sister lives close by in White Chapel," she stood entirely still before him, all hauteur gone.

Wil knew what Eddy was getting at. The Little Chapel had, at one time, been the main place of worship for those employed on the estate. More than that, it was his mother's final resting place. The duke had a duty to his wife's memory—and to her children, however little he may choose to remember this.

He shook his head. "Say nothing of that, Mrs Edwards. Rest assured I will respect a confidence given to me with as much courage as trust. I shall tour the estate myself and do what I can. At least until Lord Clifton returns." Reaching for his cutter he drew a paper towards him. "I must find out when Lord Clifton will be with us. Roger is a personal friend of Brishen, you know. He must be made aware of the—umm, the state of things." He glanced up. "I will not mention names, Mrs Edwards. Roger will return if he can be spared. He is not the parody of a peer so many believe him to be." Just in time, he stopped himself from saying *like the duke*. He'd been bending his quill throughout the interview without realising until, quite suddenly, it cracked. He swore as ink spilled over the papers before him.

"*Language*, Master Wil, language. I taught you better than that."

Wil grinned, trying unsuccessfully to clean up the desk. "I formally beg your pardon, Mrs Edwards."

"Oh, get out of it," Eddy waved him away, drawing waxed cloths from her basket to mop up his mess. "Keep your linen out of the ink," she ordered, and Wil stood back, letting her do her work. "I shall take care of your guests, Master Wil," she sniffed. "Once I've set your room here to rights."

"Thank you, Mrs Edwards." Wil bowed his head slightly.

"Tish, it's Eddy. I shouldn't have told you otherwise except I was put out by your manner. There now." The housekeeper straightened up, tidying his paperwork with a critical eye. "You fetch Lord Clifton home, sir. It's high time he was back in England, same as you. Her Grace did not raise sons who forget their duty to the family seat." She made for the door as Wil resumed his place behind the desk.

Eddy cleared her throat. Looking up, he found her shrewd gaze levelled at his own. "I don't know what sort of accident could possibly fell a prince, sir."

Wil flushed. "Beg pardon, Eddy?"

"I've never known you to put a shot wrong, is all I'm saying." Eddy's gaze did not flicker. "However that there prince got hurt, we'll see you put it right. Only, don't get to thinking anybody believes he was shot by mistake. Not with yourself holding the pistol." Having made her point, Eddy hurried out the door. "It's glad I am you've come home, captain," she called over her shoulder.

Wil smiled after her. Eddy wouldn't betray him, and she'd ensure his guests were treated respectfully at Clifton Hall.

He spent the rest of the morning composing letters to the two generals his father had not yet offended. He also penned a diplomatic letter to his brother. Roger would not likely object to Brishen's presence at the hall, although Wil forbore to go into detail regarding the proposed duration of their stay. Eddy was right about one thing: Roger wouldn't believe in a 'shooting accident' at all. Wil wrote to him the complete truth, reminding Lord Clifton of his friend Prince Brishen. It was quite one of the most politic missives he'd ever crafted.

Chapter Eleven

On Captain Clifton's orders, the housekeeper showed Syeira to the guest quarters closest to her brother's. Mrs Edwards's opinion of Clifton's guests, and of Romany in general, was as plain to the princess Brishen as the sour look on the older woman's face.

To these English, her Romany were thieves, tricksters, charlatans. Like her brother, Syeira made a point of moving among the English whenever she could. To her mind, demonstrating her integrity in a manner that did not admit of a doubt was the most effective way to quell this type of thinking. There had never been so much as a breath of scandal to taint the dealings of Princess Brishen among the English, despite the many-varied challenges to her modesty, and her temper. Her brother, too, whatever his personal affairs, was scrupulous when it came to matters of congress between Brishen and the English. Syeira had seen for herself how much this sort of diplomacy benefited her House, and all the Romany in England.

"Might I venture a word, princess?" The chill in the housekeeper's voice was enough to bring back snow.

If the housekeeper sought payment for the use of the stillroom stores—well, Syeira's response to that might well see them depart the premises before luncheon.

"I am happy to hear anything you wish to say to me." Syeira gathered her dignity about her like a cloak.

The older woman swelled visibly in response. "I have prepared a place for the little gypsy boy in the nursery. Alongside Miss Lydia."

"I thank you, Mrs Edwards. Clifton Hall has been—most kind." She kept her voice even, looking the housekeeper straight in the eye. Did the woman's expression darken? *Impossible to tell.*

"The boy will have none of it, it seems." The housekeeper's voice sharpened. "He insists on sleeping in Captain Clifton—I mean in your prince's sick room. Like a lackey."

A lackey? Syeira checked her temper, recalling in time that the duel ought not to be mentioned. As far as the servants were concerned, Clifton's assistance was motivated from kindness alone. She studied the housekeeper more closely. Perhaps the woman did not know how to address a Romany royal. After all, such guests were hardly commonplace in English houses.

"We are so sorry to put you to any trouble, ma'am," she said patiently. "Janfri is *our* heir. He stays by Valkin's side to learn to be our leader if his brother does not heal."

The mention of Valkin's wound had an extraordinary effect on the woman. She seemed to deflate.

"I see," Mrs Edwards stared at Syeira and it was plain that she did not know what to do. When she next spoke, she sounded genuinely confused, all her anger blown away. "It is merely that... Well, princess, it is simply not done."

"If you please, ma'am, *what* is not done?" English niceties set her teeth on edge. Why could the woman not speak her meaning plainly?

"Why, to have a royal child sleep on the floor." Mrs Edwards seemed alarmed now.

Syeira rearranged her expression, taking a deep breath. "It is done among the Romany," she said quietly. "There is no need for concern, Mrs Edwards. Janfri is quite well where he is. I realise it is a little different, but for such a short while, can we not permit this?"

"I suppose it will have to be all right." Mrs Edwards said slowly, her indignation seeming to settle.

"Once again, I thank you for your kindness. It is greatly appreciated." Syeira grimaced inwardly. It was an untruth, certainly, but this seemed to be the way of things with the English. Manners at any cost. The price: honesty with nary an outburst of temper to disturb the ton.

She was tempted to laugh at the traditions these English considered important. Syeira was glad not to be an English girl, trained to politeness above all else. There were more than a few Romany traditions that would likely alarm the English. Like the education of marriageable Romany in the art and expectation of lovemaking. That one would have all the parlours and ballrooms of England in an uproar. Then again, the promise that held her life suspended was a Romany rule she wished was otherwise. It seemed there were always traditions worthy of change.

"I shall send a girl to call you for dinner," the housekeeper's voice broke into her reverie, but she left before Syeira could say anything further.

Syeira sighed. While the housekeeper's expression had not exactly warmed any, she was grateful the woman had brought the concerns to her and not troubled to lay them before her host. She was glad they'd reached an understanding. A moment later she revised her assumptions as a wide-eyed maidservant stepped far too cautiously into the room, bobbing a curtsey as she did so.

"Beggin' yer pardon, princess," the girl stammered. "Mrs Edwards said fer me ter see if there was anything ye'd be wanting."

Syeira arched her brows as the girl sidled along the wall, watching her narrowly. The princess read the intent in this, and the unsubtle insult. As if any Romany, much less the Romany princess, would steal from a host offering assistance. Anger flared before she remembered that this was not this child's fault. She was merely doing as she was bid. Her food and lodgings—possibly those of her family—depended upon it.

Pressing her lips closely together lest she be tempted to utter any one of the epithets now running through her mind, Syeira said, "Actually, there is, Miss—? I am afraid I did not hear your name."

"It's M—Martha, Martha Dale. Mrs Edwards said I was ter stay with yer, like. In case yer were in need of any help wiv yer dress."

"Thank you, Martha. There is something you can do for me. Please let Mrs Edwards know that the princess will not be stealing the family silver today." The girl's eyes grew wider. Syeira bit back a grin as she untied part of her bodice, baring her neck. "And would you be so good as to lay the fire? I wish to disrobe."

The girl scuttled towards the door. "I'll be gettin' that fire goin' for yer an'all, Highness." Dropping a full curtsey at last, the girl practically ran from the room.

This time Syeira did laugh, glad for once to be alone in a space where she could do so without causing offense.

In truth, Syeira could not change out of her riding habit at all. She had no other costume. Smoothing her skirts as best she could, she refreshed herself at the wash basin and tidied her hair, returning to Valkin's room directly. Janfri awaited her there, his face flushed with the exertion of what must have been a very rapid ride. He held out a large swag, which, on closer inspection, appeared to be one of her less valuable shawls.

"I have two fresh gowns for you, and new linen for Valkin and myself. It is enough?"

There was a chance Valkin's rib might heal easily. It wasn't a great probability in truth, but Syeira saw no point in raising undue alarm. Her little brother had seen enough this day. "You have been extremely prompt, my brother, my *prala*. I thank you." She kissed his cheek, relieving him of the swag. Examining the contents, her glance sharpened. Someone had selected her prettiest gowns to wear before the English. "You went through my gowns yourself?"

Janfri laughed. "What do I know about a woman's costume? Our sister Reyna chose for you. She says she hopes you are pleased to wear them before Captain Clifton."

Does she indeed? Syeira ignored the flush in her cheeks. "Reyna is young and fanciful," she replied. "You will please carry my thanks to her when you are next at *ker*." Anything Reyna knew about Captain Clifton likely came from rumour. "Now, how was your ride?" Putting aside the swag, she admitted to a twinge of jealousy. She would love to see this estate from horseback, with the moors past the fence line. Much as Syeira disliked being stuck at Clifton Hall, she had to admit the estate was happily situated.

Her brother grinned. "It is a wonderful estate to ride in daylight. Grygry made excellent time, taking all the low walls in stride."

"Walls?" Syeira's smile died. "Janfri, tell me you did not ride steeplechase to Camp Brishen?"

Janfri stuck out his chin like the child he was still sometimes permitted to be. "I do not see why this disturbs the English."

Folding her arms, Syeira did her level best to avoid sounding like an old crone. "*You* may not, Janfri, but I can assure you the English see their landholdings differently to you or I. That is, their lands are *theirs*. You must not traverse their property without permission."

He put his hands on his hips. "We are Romany. We do not recognise such laws."

"*We* may not, but the English do, and so do the local constabulary." Hopelessness rose within her again. Something akin to panic threatened to engulf her thinning sense of calm. "Janfri, I cannot spare you," she shot a glance at their slumbering brother.

"Valkin cannot." This would never do. Dropping her hands to her sides, she crossed the room and stood opposite her little brother. He was as tall as her and twice as stubborn. Placing her hands on his shoulders, Syeira met his gaze and held it.

"We remain indebted to Clifton Hall, and we need their help until Valkin heals. We cannot afford to offend them." She swallowed. "I understand, believe me I do. I too do not agree with all of the English rules but it is how they live, and we must live here with them. I do not have the resources to assist you should you be caught and accused of trespass." She looked down.

"I—I am not so skilled as Valkin at making trade with the English." It hurt her pride to admit this, even to her brother. "Do you understand, Janfri?" She paused, allowing him a moment to absorb her words. "I want your word that you will not trespass any English estates—"

"It is not trespass," her brother spoke over her. "You are asking me to waste hours."

Syeira lifted up both hands in surrender. "*Dosta,*" she responded quietly. "Enough, Janfri. Your word then, that you will ride to and from *ker* by the proper and direct roads only. That you will *not* cross the boundary lines of *any* English estates while Valkin is healing. Not even if Papa..." she could not finish. Tears pricked behind her eyes. She blinked hard. This was too important for tears. Her brother was too important. Could Janfri not see this?

Janfri opened his mouth to argue, saw her expression and closed his lips. He sighed and nodded.

Syeira's shoulders relaxed. Leaning forward, she kissed Janfri's cheek again.

"Thank you, Janfri. None of this is fair for the Romany. None of it feels like 'us', but Brishen House must show good faith. We need English goodwill now more than ever." She took up her swag and made for the door. "I am billeted in the bedchamber next door. I shall change for luncheon and join you here. I will attend the English captain in the dining room at dusk."

Janfri did not agree with this. "You will not have a chaperon."

Syeira grinned. "No? Have you seen how many butlers and footmen are present at Clifton Hall? If they will not suffice, I have also been allocated a *maid*." She shrugged, laughing at the scandalised expression on her brother's face. "What type of seduction do you believe our host intends in his own dining room?"

"And Valkin?" Janfri meant this as a challenge, but Syeira was not drawn. "I have not forgotten Valkin." Indicating the swag, she smiled at her still-scowling sibling. "Once again, I thank you. And Reyna."

***

"Mmmpft," the semi-conscious murmur from Valkin's bedclothes had Syeira beside him in a moment. Lifting his head, she helped him to drink the relief tea while keeping him as still as possible.

"Rest now," she soothed, arranging more pillows around his injured side. His repose was lopsided and less than comfortable, but Syeira was certain the cushioning was necessary until his rib knitted.

Probing his chest gently, she felt at least one break, and another softness. Syeira prayed this was simply a sort of body shock but she could not relax her ministrations yet. Instinct told her stillness and rest were the best remedies now. All she could do was keep faith, keep vigil, keep him immobilised—and wait.

Janfri sprawled across the chaise, a blanket twisted around him in sleep. Nearly spent coals burned low in the grate, like some kind of otherworldly warning. Syeira poked gently at the embers until a small blaze flared again. She moved closer to the heat. It didn't help.

Syeira paced Valkin's room so often she half-expected some kind of trace to form on the rug beneath her feet. She had no idea of the time, only that she could not sleep. It was strange. She was weary but felt wide awake. Tension coiled through her as she walked the perimeter of the room, then the diagonals. This was ridiculous. She needed her rest. Valkin's injury still had some way to heal and she could not spend her nights in restlessness like this.

Seizing her swag, she shook the contents to the floor. Throwing her shawl across her shoulders, Syeira lit the stub of a candle from the glowing coals. Making no sound at all padding across the rich rug, she exited the sickroom, finding her way to the main staircase by memory. She did not dare seek out a side door. She had no idea whether any servants were about, but she did not need to be caught moving furtively through an Englishman's house in the dark of night.

A rustling and an odour alerted her to the presence of several dogs, but they seemed too far into canine dreams to do much more than whine in their sleep. Even Mrs Edwards would be abed at this time. Easing open the great main door, Syeira crept out into the formal park. As soon as she was certain she was beyond anyone's hearing, she ran.

She ran and ran until her sides seized and her breath came in short, gulping gasps. Finding herself at the edge of the park, she leaned against the trunk of a great tree, panting, and looked up. There they were. The stars, the crescent moon and miles and miles of woodland. Open space at last.

Syeira shivered in the freezing night air. She smiled up at the spacious sky and the open air. This was one time the cold was welcome. She stood, breathing deeply until her hands turned numb with cold and her breath crystallised before her. A flash of guilt speared; she was not supposed to be here. Running wild and alone on an English estate was foolhardy. Hadn't she said as much to Janfri?

Still, the movement and the space were like breath to her after the closeness of Valkin's sick room and the proximity of their too-charming host, the sadness of his little sister and the coldness of his household. Syeira's need felt too great to regret escaping without informing anyone. Besides, she was alone. A few moments for herself wasn't too much to ask, was it? She'd be better able to face the coming weeks if she allowed herself some respite like this.

She jumped when she heard a clock strike a single chime, the echoes dying away over the moors. One o'clock and all was still. No wonder she hadn't met anyone in the hall. Syeira gazed at threads of grass silvered in the moonlight, formally clipped trees softened by the shadowed dark. Slowly, she turned her head back towards the walls she was so desperate to escape. Glaring at the too-solid stone building, she pulled a face at it like the child, Lydia, might do. Now that Syeira knew she must be here some weeks, she could not help disliking the English house even more.

Curious gold-green eyes stirred in her memory. How easy might it be to lose herself in such warmth? She shook her head. She must remember why she was obliged to remain here, not moon over an Englishman's eyes.

"I will stay," Syeira faced the implacable bulk of Clifton Hall. "I will stay, and I will nurse my brother, but this does not mean I will like it." Sighing, she turned back towards the Hall entrance. "Nor does it mean I will like *you*." Why she needed to utter this aloud she could not say. There wasn't a soul about who might hear.

Chapter Twelve

Wil woke from a restless sleep to find his sheets tangled and damp. *Damn.* Not for the first time in his life was he grateful for his valet. Hudson would ensure none of the maids were alarmed. Wil shook his head hard. It wasn't the dream that had woken him. Something else had disturbed him—a sound he'd not heard for years. He struggled to remember as he sat up, dragging back his bedclothes.

It came back to him. The door. The *great* wooden door of Clifton Hall. Its creak was unmistakeable, and he remembered it well. He did wonder that the pack of spaniels given free rein of the lower rooms at night did not raise any alarm. The silence of the animals alone was enough to make him uneasy.

Donning his dressing-gown he fumbled for a candle, lit it and padded silently out to the hall. Rounding the lower landing he cautiously peered out, but all was in darkness. Yet he knew he'd heard the door. Oak and iron and heavy as hell, it had been pulled slowly open—or closed? Someone was about. Someone who wished to avoid being noticed.

Making his way down the staircase, he held the candle high. The dogs *were* aware of the figure turning from the door.

"Who's there?"

A gasp, then, "It is all right, Captain Clifton." The princess's breathless treble stroked his senses. "It is only I."

"Is the prince worse? Is—is he..." He could not even speak the words.

"Oh... oh no," came the startled voice. "He sleeps. There is no sign of the sepsis."

"Then what the deuce are you doing?" He rubbed his face, feeling more than he might have done if he hadn't been dreaming of this very woman.

Closing the distance between them, he lifted his light to see her better. She wore nothing warmer than a shawl thrown hastily over the same gown he'd seen at dinner. He reached for her hands.

"You're freezing." Glimpsing the embers in the grate of the dog's room, he drew her through the doorway, stirring up the remains of an earlier fire. The animals surged around them in a subdued fur-pile, wagging tails and whining in delight as their ears were rubbed and their snouts fondled. One even lay at the princess's feet and rolled over, asking for a belly rub. At least the Clifton Hall spaniels delighted in his guest.

He caught a glimpse of Syeira by candlelight as she bent to pet all the dogs within reach. He couldn't be sure, but he didn't think she smiled.

"Are you all right?"

"Er, yes."

"Princess Brishen?"

"I beg your pardon, Captain Clifton. I have no adequate explanation for my conduct." She hesitated. Still holding her arm, he felt her tremble.

"Except, I—I had to get out. Some air."

Wil could not keep the astonishment from his voice. "Air?" He echoed. "At this hour?"

"Yes. I… I did not realise the hour. I have been tending my brother."

"All night?"

"I must. If his rib does not heal well, he—well, he will not be himself. He will not be able to lead House Brishen effectively. If—" she stopped speaking but her shivering grew worse. The princess's breathing grew shallow, then silenced. Her palms moved together for the first slow, quivering breath. Then another, slower and deeper. Finally, the third. The shivers stilled. Wil stood unmoving, acutely aware of each sensation rippling through his guest's slender frame. Her skin warmed beneath his touch as the fire brightened.

"I apologise if I startled you," she curtsied.

"Never mind that," Wil replied. "My concern is for your health. You will sicken without proper rest."

"I thank you, Captain Clifton. I do not take ill easily." She smiled shyly. "If you would please *not* mention this to Janfri, or to the Romany prince when he wakes?"

Keeping a secret from her brothers? Wil stared. "Why not?"

"It is not permitted to be outside alone without a chaperon," she admitted. "They would scold me."

"Perhaps you ought to be scolded," he replied. "Wandering outside on a winter's night in a strange place. Anything could happen, you know." He paused before repeating himself. "Anything." His suggestive baritone throbbed between them.

"I am not afraid of you," she said softly but surely.

You should be, he thought to himself, and he did not entirely believe her. Or was it that he didn't trust himself? She was so near to him now. So temptingly, terrifyingly close.

"Why should I be afraid of you?" she whispered, speaking his thoughts out loud.

"I may tell your brothers and you shall be scolded," he barely breathed, his voice a hush.

The princess stepped back a little then, considering him. "I do not think you would do such a thing, Captain." That shy smile appeared again.

Wil smiled back, clenching his fist hard against his thigh. Since when was his desire so troubling? Since he found his lips too close to her ear, her neck, those tempting lips he dreamed of this particular night. He should step away. Instead, he watched her eyes in the firelight, trying not to stare. Such depth there, such openness, framed by the darkest lashes he'd ever seen. He could barely stand it. This feeling... *What was it?*

He doubted the princess had any idea the effect she had on him. She was too carefully guarded from overt male attention. So focussed was he on ensuring his response to Syeira remained dormant that she was obliged to repeat herself, sounding faintly puzzled.

"I thank you for warming me, and for preserving my honour." She curtsied demurely. "Goodnight, Captain."

"Your honour is safe at Clifton Hall," he bowed. "Goodnight, princess." Wil watched her rapid, purposeful walk back to the second floor. Everything she did was sensible, practical. She wasted no energy in idleness or pointless activity. Each action had a clear purpose. Wil considered his own life as the duke's backup second. The thought came to him that there wasn't a great deal of purpose in that at all.

***

Wil sealed up the estate billings, addressing them to Lord Clifton. He eyed the pile of letters addressed to the personages in Whitehall he thought most likely to assist him in purchasing his new commission. There were no less than six, including the other two generals.

Having now spent his first few mornings home as industriously as he felt necessary, Wil thought to seek out his guests for a more congenial employment. *Guests, plural?* There was only one guest on his mind. He was fooling himself if he affected a like concern for her brothers. They were fine companions, true enough, but he spent little time thinking about them when they were not immediately before him. The same could not be said for their sister. Wil laughed at himself, wondering where on the estate Princess Brishen might be. She was not in her brothers' rooms, he knew. He'd looked in to see the herbs and tea powders all packed neatly away and the prince asleep, Janfri watching over him like a protective charm.

"Sir." The head butler knocked, entering the library with the morning's correspondence. "Mr Yates awaits you in the little parlour."

"Thank you, Oates. I'll not keep him long." Taking up the new correspondence from the tray, Wil grimaced and resumed his seat, shoulder muscles tightening anew. All the cares of the estate with none of the advantages. His thoughts strayed again to his intriguing guest. Well, there were *some* advantages to having the run of Clifton Hall while the duke busied himself among the brothels and gaming clubs of London.

Glancing over the letters he saw two, calligraphically designed by ladies in the form of *billet-doux* and as beautifully addressed, to *Captain Clifton, Esq.* The post marks were both from the continent. No well-bred English girl would make so free to correspond with a peer's son directly. Wil had never expressly objected to any of his French lovers writing to him, merely cautioning them not to depend on receiving any response. Only when he opened the desk drawer to add these to those already there, did Wil notice how embarrassingly large his collection of prettily directed stationery had become. Several epistles had arrived from London in the few months since it was known he'd been furloughed. Quite a number, too, from a persistent married lady currently residing in York. Wil registered with something like shock that not only had his responses slipped his mind, but he could not quite remember when he'd last visited her bed.

Somehow *all* these missives had gone unanswered, and somewhere in the midst of the scented and hot-pressed bundle was undoubtedly an epistle from Lady Gresham. Wil sighed. He simply did not have the heart for this sort of charade any longer.

Flipping through the rest of his correspondence, he took up the one from his brother, found his letter knife and broke the seal. Lord Clifton was returning home. He'd requested Wil forward all current estate reports to him in London. Rubbing his hand through his hair, Wil considered his response. From what he could tell, there *were* no current estate records. It was plain enough that the duke had not troubled himself about estate matters, while his sons campaigned on the king's behalf.

Wil had best draft a reply to Roger, and soon. Estimating the amount of work to be done on the estate might be the place to start. He stood up and hauled on the bell pull.

"Have Hudson ready the horses," he ordered the responding footman. "Ensure Mr Yates is ready."

A tour of the estate was well overdue. This was something both Captain and Lord Clifton undertook each quarter day, until the rude interruption of Monsieur Bonaparte. The steward could make note of any repairs or improvements which might be required. It would keep Yates on the estate for a week or two. This was the least Clifton Hall could do for the steward's long-suffering wife.

Wil began by reacquainting himself with Clifton Park, noting how easy it was to trespass on the grounds. The fences were in disrepair and in some cases had collapsed altogether. A fierce anger at his father's inattention flared, but when Wil recollected it had caused him to meet the princess, his anger fluttered into insignificance.

Attempting to focus on Yates's estate commentary but thinking of Syeira, his mind returned to the postscript of Roger's letter:

'PS: I received your note and have no objection to Brishen at the hall, but you'd best get them well clear before the duke hears of it from some other quarter. Be so good as to present

my compliments to Prince Brishen. I do not recollect the princess.'

Wil was unaccountably relieved at Roger's disinterest in the princess. Lord Clifton was always first when it came to women. *Why take the spare when they could have the heir?* He was long past petty jealousies, but being constantly reminded that he was never a woman's first choice left a bitter taste. Wil refused to look too closely at why he found his brother's lack of interest so pleasing in this instance.

He also refused to examine why he didn't seem able to turn his own attention from the princess with any success. He dreamed of her ripe mouth opening for him, her soft, sinuous flesh yielding. Her enticing body beneath his as he unleashed a fire he wanted to burn in for a long, long time. He woke up wanting her, the raging fire he felt refusing to be doused by wine or brandy, or any means he could devise.

He had desired women before now, but not like this. Not to the point where they invaded his every thought and he couldn't turn his mind to anything substantial at all. In the last few days he'd tried riding, walking, hunting and soothing his father's gamekeeper over the 'poaching by th' lake'. It was no use. Never before had he felt that strong, heated magnetic pull this woman seemed to exert over his senses so easily.

He occupied the guest room as far from hers as possible, keeping himself deliberately away from her chamber, three doors down from his own. Where she lay each night, alone. Without him. The princess Brishen lying there, magnificent midnight hair covering her inviting golden curves... with her brothers next door.

Wil refused to let his thoughts progress as he guided Nero along the western fence line, turning his attention resolutely back to the survey of the estate. Nodding at Yates's suggestions, he endeavoured to maintain focus on village and estate matters, doing his level best to forget the alluring Romany princess.

Chapter Thirteen

Wil doubted his uninjured guests slept at all. The princess was active in her brother's sickroom well before dawn and stayed in residence until after eleven at night, a fact he suspected the household staff found affronting, rather than complementary, in a guest. Indeed, Hudson was the one member of staff who made a point of appreciating how impressive the devotion of the Romany family to their prince seemed to be. It was he who informed Wil that the princess herself kept vigil over her brother for the first three days and nights following the duel. The deepening shadows under her eyes marked this as truth.

While the princess joined Wil and his sister for breakfast and dinner each day, Janfri hardly left Valkin's room. When he was not carrying messages between the Romany camp and Clifton Hall, the boy fixed himself on the chaise at the end of his brother's sickbed like a devoted servant. In the end, Wil ordered Janfri's food brought up to him and the Romany brothers took all their meals together. Their sister joined them there for luncheon.

"Are you worried?" Wil asked his dinner guest one evening as she nibbled her potatoes. "About the prince, I mean. He is healing, I take it?"

"Oh, yes." Princess Brishen bit her lips a little as she poured the tea. "It is only… if I do not take proper care how his rib knits, he may remain damaged, even if he heals. You will have seen this too when you served, captain—yes?"

"I did not spend too much of my service in the field hospitals," Wil told her truthfully, buttering bread as he spoke. "But yes, I have seen men who survived battle, only to remain permanently maimed in some way."

"It will make it difficult to return to their former occupations then," the princess observed. "This is so for the Romany as well."

"The prince has an occupation?" Wil could not help his astonishment.

She laughed, presumably at the puzzled expression on his face. "Yes. You are surprised?"

Wil shrugged. "His title is 'Prince'. I thought that was what he did. I mean, that he was just a prince."

"Ah, I understand you now. I will try to describe this." Princess Brishen paused, considering. "A Romany prince is not excepted from the work in a Romany camp. Valkin's title is part of the honour bestowed on the House of Brishen. Any Romany house can be deemed 'royal' if enough of the other houses choose to favour them with such distinction."

"Huh." Wil nodded slightly. "Your traditions are quite different." He imagined the duke's expression if His Grace's title was a gift bestowed by those living under his duchy, and only if they deemed him so worthy. His grin widened when he saw the princess's answering smile.

"Valkin trains the Brishen racing horses. It is physically demanding work and he cannot do it until he is fully healed. It is something all of my brothers learn from a young age," she continued. "The racing horses of Brishen are now well-known."

"Indeed, they are," Wil agreed. Romany racing stock was highly prized among the peers of his own acquaintance. "In point of fact, I believe this is how Lord Clifton came to know Prince Brishen."

"I am not acquainted with Lord Clifton," the princess replied. "I do spend more time among the English than other Romany women because I assist the prince in his parlay. It is still more Valkin's duty than my own. That is, it is the duty of our father, in truth," she fell silent a moment, her voice soft. Wary indigo eyes suffused with sadness as he watched.

Wil thought of his own father and felt only a dull sort of anger. "So Prince Brishen is responsible for the recent rise in racing prowess of the Romany stock? He is to be congratulated, princess. His achievements in this area are first class."

"I thank you. I shall tell him so when he wakes."

Janfri appeared in the doorway, clearly alarmed. The princess uttered a few words to her brother, rose and curtsied. "Please excuse me, captain. I am sorry to leave before the table is cleared but Janfri tells me Valkin is bleeding again."

"Of course," he stood, bowing as she exited. Janfri nodded at Wil and turned around, ignoring the meal entirely. The princess returned again directly, her agitation obvious. Wil rose again.

"Captain Clifton, I have a request, sir," she began.

"I will only grant it if you call me Wil," he teased, hoping for a smile, or at least another long look from those intriguing eyes.

She gratified him by smiling back. "You do not yet know what it is."

"Hmmm. True."

He watched the princess trying to maintain her solemn expression. Trying and failing to ignore the charge that sparked between them, even while her brother lay injured. She felt it too then, this attraction between them. Knowing this made it nearly impossible to direct his thoughts into cooler channels. Wil's smile warmed further as the princess shook her head and blinked, returning to her work.

"I have used up all my linen cloths, cap—I mean, Wil."

"There ought to be some in the nursery wing. Tend your brother. I shall fetch them."

The princess curtsied briefly before hurrying back up to the sick room. Wil followed a few moments later with the cloths he'd requisitioned from Lydia's governess. He knocked lightly. A curt command bid him enter. He saw the fire was blazing again, with steaming teapots and various herbal preparations in partial stages of assembly or disassembly. He was in time to witness her moment of reflection. With eyes closed and deep, slow breaths granting her calm and steady hands, she began.

"I like to say 'Wil'. It suits you much better," Princess Brishen murmured, her eyes on her work.

Her cheeks darkened as she spoke. Wil doubted her flushed face was entirely due to the enormous blaze in the grate. He wondered if she was aware of how deeply she blushed when she said his name. Listening to the way he sounded on her tongue, as though his name belonged between her lips, it was damned difficult to focus on what she was saying.

"The bleeding is heavier than I expected. It is as I feared. The rib is not mending properly. The bleeding is from the irritation of the bone."

"Oh." Wil did not know how to respond. He was not even sure he understood the anatomy. "Can you help him?"

His guest looked up, her face solemn. "I can slow the blood loss. I cannot splint his chest area. I must keep him still throughout the night."

She looked at Janfri, and even Wil could see the boy looked scared. The guilt within him trebled.

"*We* must," she amended. "Janfri and I must take turns. We shall watch over Valkin through the night until his bone begins to knit."

Wil felt ill at the thought of so little sleep for his guests. "How many nights will this be?"

Those fascinating eyes hardened. "We shall not disturb your household." Her fingers worked on the Romany prince in silence.

The stiffness in her posture and the hard blinking of her eyes did not escape him. *Now* what had he done?

Her next words clarified matters. "You wish us to leave?"

Her tongue stroked her lower lip as she looked at him, one palm steady on the place where, presumably, she monitored her brother's heartbeat. Another misunderstanding. *There have been quite enough of those.*

"You mistake my meaning, princess. I simply wish to assist."

The look of incredulity on her face was enough to tell him he'd read her right. *Finally.*

"Janfri must be well-rested if he is to ride safely. You, too, must not go many more nights without rest. Allow me to take a shift." He opened his palms in supplication and lifted his hands. "It's the least I can do."

He sat back, watching her choose. Or rather, watching her tongue slip across her lower lip. He tugged at his cravat, feeling suddenly far warmer than he ought. The princess did not seem to notice the heat. In fact, she was not looking at him at all. Having replaced the prince's soiled dressings, she was now addressing her other brother in English, which was obviously for his benefit.

"It is all right, Janfri." The princess's voice sounded less certain than it had at dinner. "It is a complication, that is all. I can remedy this." She reverted to Romany, issuing further instructions as Janfri gathered all the pillows he could find, fashioning at least one from a swag pile that appeared to be his own linen. Brother and sister nodded at each other. Once the prince seemed to be dozing again, Princess Brishen turned to Wil.

"Valkin has not been still enough—or I have not been vigilant enough."

He stood immediately. "This is not your doing. It is mine. I'll not have you bear the weight of it." Aware that his tone sounded harsher than he intended, he took a breath before closing the conversation. "I will watch over your prince tonight." Addressing himself to both of them, he avoided making it a request. Janfri smiled and shook his host's hand as he left the room, but Wil's attention remained focused on his sister.

Syeira stared at him curiously. "It is rare to meet an Englishman who shows compassion to my Romany. Thank you, cap—*Wil*." She turned back to the prince, removing her poultice.

"Don't thank me, princess. This responsibility is mine."

Watching her gaze warm and soften was thanks enough. His overheated mind conjured up several things he'd like to show the princess Brishen, and the gratitude would be his. *Compassion be damned.*

Wil cleared his throat. "Is there anything else you require to assist your work, princess?"

His guest offered a tight, brief smile. "I thank you, no, Wil, but I would be gratified if you would call me Syeira. It is only fair—yes?"

"Oh. Yes, I suppose it is." He seated himself on the chaise. "Syeira." His guest was already reapplying her salt-paste solution, as well as packing a fresh poultice onto the wound. The one that looked to clot the blood. Her fascinating tongue slipped in and out of her parted mouth as she worked, caressing her lower lip. Heat blazed along his thighs. This was maddening. The room was impossibly warm.

"Would it ruin your brother's health to open a window?" he asked hoarsely, keeping his voice low. He steadied his speech with an effort. Valkin was near dozing and Wil had no intention of awakening their chaperon. The heat within him intensified.

"It is better to keep the room warm," Syeira replied. "Better for drying the herbs too." She barely smiled at him, returning to her task. He removed his jacket and collar in silence, dispensed with his cravat, and loosened the top of his shirt. After all, the princess had seen him without both the morning of the duel, and this was usually his bedchamber. Not that she took any notice of him.

Her gaze darted back and forth, from her brother's dressings to her dried herbal preparations. She counted out leaves, ensuring readiness for future contingencies. He supposed she had to prepare for any situation that may befall a Romany cast among so many English. Her cautious glance fell upon him momentarily and softened.

The look in her eyes hit him like a horse's hoof to his chest. Was it a fleeting acknowledgement? A brief glimmer of respect and gratitude? Wil tried to think when he'd last seen anything in a woman's eyes beyond a cynical boredom and a calculation of his worth (not much while his brother lived). He hardly recalled the eyes of his last bed partner, and he'd hardly thought about bedding any woman in days. *Liar,* his conscience piped up again. Of course he'd thought about bedding a woman: *this* woman.

"May I ask you something?" Wil began, not quite sure why he needed to know.

"Of course." Syeira looked up. There was such depth of feeling in her gaze. Such a sincere interest in him, in what he thought, what he had to say. Wil felt his world shift. A woman who showed her emotion so clearly on her face, who was open to the world, was intoxicating, and then there was that mouth—

Wil realised she was waiting expectantly. "I thought Romany women married younger than eighteen," he said.

"It is the usual custom, yes," she answered, her voice lowering with every word.

"And you are not married?" Immediately, he knew he'd said something wrong.

The princess shook her head, pressing her mouth shut, holding herself in. She stood by the window, gazing determinedly out at nothing. Wil stared, aghast, before moving to her side. He turned her face towards his own with careful fingers that barely touched her. Syeira turned her gaze away from his, breath heaving. Her whole person shook as she fought for calm.

"Why do you want to know these things? It is not your business." Her voice faltered.

"I—I don't know exactly why," he glanced at the slumbering chaperon. "I want to know you, Syeira. I want to know more about you. I want to be with you. I want to spend time with you. I want... I want *you*." His voice was dangerously low now, the words wrenched from him unwillingly. He shocked himself with his own admission. Had he *ever* said that to a woman before? He didn't think so, could not recall. Honestly, he was having trouble remembering the other women he'd been with. A small voice inside him suggested perhaps this was a good thing.

Two tears spilled from her eyes. Eyes framed by dark, damp lashes. Wil wiped the tears away, skimming her golden cheeks with his fingertips. She stepped back automatically, as though his touch burned her skin. Wil watched her cheeks darken. His heart hammered faster until all he felt was heat, and her silken skin.

"I want you," he said again, and this time there was no mistaking the demand in his voice, or the husky tones of his desire. He stepped closer, holding her face between his hands. Raw desire moved through him in a wave. He could not move, could not breathe, could not draw his eyes away from her. He watched that delicious tongue moisten her ripe lips, and he was lost.

The first press of her lips yielding to his unleashed a searing heat as he burned with longing. His tongue slowly stroked her lower lip, teasing, probing, savouring before slipping inside her mouth and learning her enthralling taste.

Silken arms encircled his neck, drawing him in. He deepened his kiss, feeling his fiery response hard against her. His dark passion rose as she leaned deeply into him, one slender hand rubbing the bare skin of his neck and hovering lower, desperate to touch him, and oh, he wanted her to touch him. Her nipples pressed heat through his waistcoat, hot and tight under the thin silk. He ached to touch her. To take her ripe, sensitive flesh into his mouth, hear her cry out in pleasure. The mere thought sent his desire into a fever. His fingers fell through that incredible midnight hair. He left them there, not trusting himself to hold her shoulders or her waist or any part of her tantalising, golden body. His control was threading already, the heat in his loins a pressing ache.

Wil released her carefully, reluctantly, taking the longest possible time to draw his tongue and lips back from her own, because it was the hardest thing in the world to let her go. He breathed out slowly and inhaled again. Cinnamon, and wild roses. *Delicious.*

Syeira moved away from him, rubbing her hands over her arms. Wil's gaze travelled over her body and saw, in that moment, that she wanted him as much as he wanted her. Which made the sheen in her eyes even worse—gemstone eyes suddenly huge with pain and more unshed tears.

Shocked, Wil stepped away and sat. "Tell me."

Taking a deep, uneven breath, Syeira stared beyond the window, seemingly miles away. "I am… promised."

His heart tore in his chest. She was betrothed? Someone else would have her? Would take her to his bed? She could not want this. He did not believe it. Not after the way she'd kissed him. He stiffened, fists curled, suddenly furious. He'd never felt more murderous in his life. He opened his lips to speak, but she wasn't finished.

Chapter Fourteen

"My father promised me to the son of the *sher-engro* of an allied house," Syeira could not keep the hopelessness from her voice. "The alliance was to assist Brishen. I will not dishonour my family."

"Who is he?"

Syeira hardly recognised the ferocity in Wil's voice. All trace of gentleness was gone. The look on his face wild, savage, ready for any kind of fight, as though he would duel the entire House of Brishen if necessary. "I have never met him."

"So you don't even know to whom you are betrothed?" He sounded angry.

Syeira glanced with alarm toward Valkin. He slept on. Breathing out in relief, she turned back to Wil. "Do not waste your anger. There is nothing you can do," she continued. "His name was Stefan of the House of Besnik."

"But do you—you cannot *want* to be his? Wait, did you say '*was*'?"

Syeira smiled sadly at him. How she loved his fire, especially when it burned for her.

"I am certain I want the best thing for my family. Had Stefan lived, I would have been his wife. He was killed in a riding accident three years ago." She leaned her forehead against the window, willing herself not to cry. The Englishman would not understand.

"Then, you are *not* betrothed?"

A lump rose in her throat and she was powerless to stop it.

"You are free, aren't you?" he asked with an urgency she struggled to resist.

Perhaps because you do not want to? A small voice within fought to be heard, but hear it she did, and oh, how it hurt. *Why* did he need to know all this so badly? *And why are you telling him?*

"Are you?" That deep-voiced command again. Firm, gentle. *Impossibly determined.*

Syeira closed her eyes against the tears. She did not want to have to tell him. Especially *him*, this man who made her feel as though the burning ache within her had a purpose. As if he was reading her soul when he looked at her with smouldering, gold-green eyes. As though he might be able to offer her something she was honour-bound to refuse. She raised her chin, trying to speak. Her throat wouldn't work. She barely managed a whisper. Her gaze met his in the reflected windowpane.

"The vow," she began, and saw then that he finally grasped the truth.

She watched realisation crash through him as he crossed the room. Taking her shoulders between his hands, he turned her gently, swiftly.

"Do you mean—you mean, you are *still* promised to a dead man?"

Syeira nodded slowly. She couldn't bear to think about it.

His stunned tones unsettled her. The look on his face shook her to her core. Shock. Horror. Pity. The awful reality of her barren life laid bare sent a wave of scalding humiliation washing through her. His pity bit deepest. *Pity...* She shuddered, stepping away. She could not stand to feel his pity. Not anyone's, but especially not his. At least now he knew how far out of anyone's reach she truly was. Including his.

"There must be a way," he stammered. "Your father cannot want this—"

"None of Brishen want it," the voice came from the bed. Valkin was awake.

For how long? Syeira wondered. By the reddening in Wil's face, his thoughts were not too differently engaged. Her brother didn't seem to notice. He apologised in Romany for falling asleep, before returning to the subject at hand. "Our father believed Stefan and Syeira would love one another truly. He did not promise Syeira lightly. She is the pride of Brishen after all." Valkin looked about as unhappy as Syeira felt.

"It as I said, Captain Clifton," Syeira said softly. "There is nothing you can do. Papa's illness has been worsening for some years, much like your current king. He is no longer able to resolve my—my situation. It is to protect House Brishen that this information is not widely known." She stared unflinchingly at the Romany prince. "Captain Clifton—*Wil*—deserves the truth."

Her brother nodded in agreement. "Unlike the peers who assist your English king, we have no provision for the uncertainty Brishen faces now," Valkin continued. "We Romany do not go to war over these things, but Papa's vow is binding. The House of Besnik may take Syeira whenever they please. They may also never take her at all."

"But you *must* be able to—" Wil began.

Valkin cut him short. "I can do nothing until I succeed my father." Her brother's jaw tightened. "The promise is between him and *sher-engro* of The House of Besnik. I made no such vow and perhaps can parlay a solution when my father passes beyond, though even this is not certain. Until then," and here he glared at Wil, "it is not kind or clever or even pleasant to suggest any other kind of life for Syeira. To show her merely the promise of things she may never have. It may even be called cruel."

His meaning could not have been plainer. Wil flushed as the Romany prince held his gaze. He stared steadily back at Valkin, nodding firmly once.

Syeira turned away from them both. It was as though she had suddenly evaporated from the room. *How dare they?*

Mumbling an excuse even she did not find sensible, she retreated to the safety of her own room. With the door closed and not even the murmur of male voices next door to distract her, Syeira closed her eyes against the burning anger raging within. Heat twined through her, spinning from anger to desire as her traitor-thoughts returned to those moments before Valkin woke, when Wil's lips were on hers, his arms, his scent, his warmth, surrounding her. *His kiss. Oh, she had not stopped his kiss.* More than this, she had not wanted to. Even *more* than this, she wanted to kiss him again.

Dear God, she had not known, could never have guessed, that kissing a man could be like this. Like a gift to herself, a taste of what it felt like to be held by a man who wanted her. A man she chose.

A powerful, aching need to be with him filled her. She wanted his strong hands exploring the fire inside her, marking her with his touch, and with his undeniable passion. She'd pressed back into him, drawing his mouth to her own, giving him all that she could in a single, shared moment, wishing with every fibre of her being that it could be more.

She wanted to remember this, to remember *him*. The first, gentle press of his lips taking her by surprise. Her body responding of its own accord, mouth opening beneath his, his tongue moving between her lips, tasting her, teasing her. Warming her tenderly as his passionate lips nipped at her own. His heated touch still pulsed through her body. His words still echoed her thrumming pulse. *I want you,* he said. *I want you.*

Her father's vow was given and her family's honour at stake, but had she known she would be giving *this* up, would she have had the strength to endure it? She had never been tempted to break a promise to her family: Until now. *No wonder this is forbidden.*

***

Syeira's little triumph over the household staff hardly lasted their first week. Mrs Edwards's indignation knew no bounds when she found Syeira brewing herbs and coffee in the kitchens before dawn. The cook was thoroughly put out and the family's breakfast looked to be late. Syeira assured the kitchen staff that she had *not* taken anything from the stillroom. She had actually brought it all with her in her leather pouch.

"I will be as quick as I can, ma'am, but I must make certain my remedies are prepared," Syeira told Cook, aware of the fury on the older woman's face.

Next, she faced down Mrs Edwards. The formidable housekeeper arrived in the kitchen, having been sent for by one of the maids. Their collective glares burned holes in her skin. Syeira kept her eyes resolutely on her task, grinding more belladonna leaves into powder with her wooden pestle.

"The doctor arrives today from the village," she added.

"I am aware of this," sniffed Mrs Edwards. "However, Doctor Haydock will not arrive until quite late after luncheon. There are several local children who are quite ill." The housekeeper's tone altered slightly.

"Mmmm," Syeira agreed. "There is little local news that escapes Romany ears, ma'am." She hardly paused in her activities. Her medicines required precise preparations. The same plant may harm as well as heal if the remedy is prepared without due attention.

"Doctor Haydock says it is a kind of influenza," the housekeeper talked on remorselessly. "A contagion."

Syeira wondered if Mrs Edwards expected her Romany to flee the country at this news. No doubt the woman wished all of Brishen miles away, so things could return to normal at Clifton Hall. She supposed the hall was usually quieter than this. Quiet and cold and a little dull. No wonder Wil preferred the gaiety of London, but what about his little sister? Syeira tutted quietly to herself, crushing mistletoe berries savagely between two stones. It helped, a little.

She and her brothers were here at the invitation of the family. A Clifton had shot the Romany prince. Regardless of the circumstances (and Brishen's own hard-headed behaviour), Clifton Hall must play their part in his healing. Besides, the work she undertook today was not for the prince.

Laying aside her grinding stones, Syeira smoothed out the apron she'd pinned across the front of her gown, aware that the berries stained the fabric a bloody scarlet. Keeping her focus on her preparations, and her voice as calm as possible, she addressed the housekeeper.

"It is for this I am preparing my remedies, Mrs Edwards. My tonics will assist in reducing the severity of the fevers. Next, I will prepare some chest rubs to ease the breathing. It will help the children." Placing her mortar on the bench, Syeira began tearing at the last leaves from her spring stores.

"These are foxglove leaves, from a forest in Scotland. I gathered and dried them myself." She checked a steaming pot over the range and returned to her leaves. She waited a moment before adding the leaves, suffusing the kitchen with a refreshing scent.

"If any of my herbs can aid the village children, may we not at least try?" Syeira glanced up—and stopped.

The housekeeper was staring at her. Mrs Edwards wore the strangest expression on her face. Syeira gazed into the older woman's eyes for a moment before adding willow bark to a steeping tea.

Mrs Edwards blinked several times. The change in the air of the room was palpable. "Do you think your—remedies can truly help the children?" Her voice softened, all trace of thorniness vanishing with the scented steam.

Syeira sighed, suppressing her deep irritation at the impracticality of bigotry. She remembered her papa's profound distrust of Englishmen. Prejudice was not the sole purview of the English. She smothered her ire.

"I simply wish to help, ma'am. English or Romany, these are little children in pain."

Mrs Edwards sat down on the low stool usually reserved for Cook. "Yes. I know." She said nothing further for a long time, seemingly watching Syeira at her work. When she spoke again, her voice sounded troubled. "My nephew is one of the little children." Her eyes misted as she looked up at the Romany princess. "He is such a dear little boy. My sister is ill with worry and with her husband away at sea. He has never yet seen his son."

Syeira thought of her ailing father, her wounded brother. It had not been a good season for Brishen and she felt the weight of it. Impulsively, she took the older woman's hand in her own. When she spoke, her voice was full of warmth. "Then I will prepare something for your sister as well. She will need all her strength to nurse her son."

Mrs Edwards stared at Syeira as if seeing her for the first time. Taking the princess's other hand in her wrinkled one, she squeezed it hard. "Thank you, princess," she stammered. "I would like to apologise for my—my treatment of you. Your brother is ill. I have been…most unkind."

Syeira smiled faintly, glancing down at her spattered apron. "Mrs Edwards, we are not all the same. I know better than anyone that Romany take some getting used to, no?" Freeing her hands from the housekeeper's firm hold, she patted Mrs Edwards's shoulder.

"Losing family is a grief not soon recovered from. I would wish to spare you this if I am able. Now, I will get back to work."

Mrs Edwards rose with her, taking a breath. "You are too kind, Princess Brishen. I shall inform Cook that you are to have the use of her kitchen this morning. Would it assist if some few of the maids were to aid your preparations?"

"Yes, ma'am. If they will listen and can take direction exactly. There is little room for error if my preparations are to give relief."

"I'll see to it." The housekeeper nodded decisively. "I shall also announce that breakfast will be served a little later. The cause is good," she continued, "but it's as well His Grace is from home this Season. He would not countenance this."

"So I understand," Syeira replied, beginning to infuse her rosehip oil with nutmeg. She did not like the sound of the duke and pitied his family. In truth, she felt sorry for the entire household. Her Romany father may not possess any great understanding and he was as stubborn as the rock of Gragareth, but he was not knowingly cruel.

Chapter Fifteen

Doctor Haydock came at last. Wil was keen to hear the physician's opinion regarding the Romany prince, but it was some time before he could find the man.

"I believe he's with Cook, sir," Hudson reported when his master asked him to find the missing man. "In the kitchens."

Wil stared. "The *kitchens*? You're certain?"

"He's been down there some time, captain," Hudson said. "Closeted with the gypsy girl and several of the maids."

"Are you referring to the princess Brishen?" His valet reddened under Wil's stony glare, which was answer enough.

"Then you will please remember it. The doctor's ill manners are not Brishen's doing." He relented, taking the back stairs two at a time. "It is customary to greet one's host if one expects an invitation to dine, is it not, Hudson?"

"It is, sir."

The doctor was a short, barrel-chested man, possessing a hard-headed Scottish practicality and the dour manner for which his countrymen were well-known. Wil ran him to ground by the servants' passage off the second parlour.

"Good evening, doctor," he said pointedly. "How is our patient?"

The man had his hands full of bottles and jars, busily arranging them in his large black bag. "Oh, ah, Captain Clifton. I beg pardon for neglecting to pay my respects." Their visitor was *not* staying to dine it seemed. Indeed, he asked the butler to fetch his coat and seemed to be hurrying away.

"Prince Brishen is mending, captain. It is not a speedy process, but the wound is clean and well-kept. The risk of infection is but slight. He is in quite the most capable hands with that sister of his. She is, erm, most skilled." The doctor seemed to think he was required to say something more. "Most skilled," he repeated.

"Thank you. That is good news." Wil bowed. "Are you as well able to offer further news regarding the illness down in the village?"

The doctor responded with a firm shake of his head. "The illness is worsening for some of the children, captain, hence my haste. Thank you, I will not stay to dine." He put out his hand.

"There is no offense in doing your duty, Haydock. Rest your horse and take a carriage." Wil reached for the bell pull. "Do not scruple to send a messenger at any time, should you require any assistance from Clifton Hall."

Doctor Haydock hardly bowed. He truly did seem to be in the greatest haste. "I thank you. I will not wait even for a carriage to be readied. I once again beg pardon, captain. Princess Brishen has been kind enough to formulate these remedies for the children. I am anxious to deliver them where they can do the most good."

Wil remembered the leaf Syeira had given him on the morning of the duel. A headache cure was one thing, but fevers and infections? Could Romany medicines be trusted so far?

"The welfare of the village children is Clifton Hall's responsibility, Haydock. What has Princess Brishen dispensed for you? Is it all right?"

The doctor shot Wil a sharp glance. "I believe it is, sir. The curative properties of plants are known as far back as ancient Greece. I correspond a great deal with Doctor Withers on this matter. Princess Brishen is as dedicated as she is charming. While I have not made a study of this field as she has, I am not entirely ignorant."

"I should never have believed it so." Wil bowed. So, Haydock was impressed as well, was he? *As dedicated as she is charming.* The man was not wrong. The doctor hovered near the main hallway, haste seemingly forgotten.

"Is there something needful, Haydock?"

The Scot cleared his throat, looking sheepish. "Ah—"

His explanation was forestalled by the entrance of Princess Brishen herself, attired in her riding habit.

"Captain." The chilliness of her voice balanced the fire in her gaze too perfectly, indicating she'd overheard Wil's inquiries.

He hastened to apologise. "Princess, I—" but she cut him off. The cut direct, in fact.

The princess curtsied to the doctor. "Prince Brishen agrees to my attending on your patients. I will demonstrate my remedies before you." She moved swiftly towards the hall. "We are wasting time, Doctor Haydock."

The physician had the main door ajar at her command, even before Mr Oates had taken up his position.

The footmen scurried to take their proper places as Princess Brishen swept past them all, wearing an expression that in an Englishwoman might be called hauteur. Wil reached the door in time to admire her mounted seat as she swung herself up and across her animal's bare back.

The princess stared over the heads of both men, oblivious to the way the doctor gawped at her seat. Looking down, she directed her lethal glare at the stunned Scot. Haydock bowed, meekly handing up her bulging bag before mounting his own horse in a hurry.

"Thank you, Doctor Haydock."

There was nothing Wil could do but watch as Syeira galloped off in Haydock's wake.

Should he go after them? The villagers may treat the princess with the same suspicion as the staff at Clifton Hall. Drawing out his watch, Wil opened the case with an oath. He was overdue for Yates.

"Damn." Turning back into the hall, he narrowly avoided sending the housekeeper flying. "Beg pardon, Eddy. Do you know if Mr Yates is staying to dine?"

Eddy waved him away, steadying herself by the balustrade. "I was coming to tell you, Master Wil, that dinner will be late this evening, same as breakfast this morning. I was sure you'd await the princess's return, seeing as she's gone out into this weather to help the children."

Eddy rubbed her hands and blew on them, signalling for the main door to be closed. "Mr Yates awaits you in the second parlour." She hurried away, but Wil heard her say as she went, "I hope the princess took her shawl. Evenings are still crisp and no mistake."

Seeing as there was still some time before dinner, and the days were growing longer, Wil had Yates accompany him to the White Chapel village. They took note of the cottages fallen into disrepair. Wil met the tenants and apologised, promising to undertake the most urgent repairs immediately. The steward wrote down their names and a list of the required works before turning back.

"So soon, Yates?"

The steward indicated the lowering sun. "It's time I returned to the cottage, captain. It'll be dark soon, and there's rain on the way."

Wil eyed the fast-darkening clouds. There was a little more time, surely. "I wish to see the school house before we turn back." He hesitated, knowing Yates was needed at home.

"I've not been home for dinner time these three nights together, and the bairns are sickly still."

"Understood. Take the short road home, Mr Yates. I shall ride round by the school house on my own."

The steward nodded. "My thanks, captain. I'll call at the hall for eleven tomorrow. We'll be heading east."

"Very good." Wil turned Nero at a fast trot towards the White Chapel school. Glancing again at the rain clouds, he reckoned them an hour or so off, regretting his acquiescence regarding the carriage. Syeira might catch her death. The woman was stubborn.

Dismounting beside the schoolmaster's gate, he tied Nero to a post, rapped smartly on the door and was admitted by the maid. Following the servant upstairs to the nursery, he found Haydock seated on a child's bed, supporting the boy's body while Syeira rubbed a kind of minted salve over the child's arms.

"His chest now," the princess said softly, lifting the child's nightshirt.

Wil heard an audible gasp from the schoolmaster and his lady wife.

"Haydock, are you sure?" The schoolmaster quavered, his eyes bright and frightened. His wife looked at Syeira with fear and disgust.

"I'm sure." The doctor's soft brogue was firm. He met the father's gaze across the room and nodded. The whole room brimmed with tension. The looks they shot at Syeira tightened Wil's shoulders. He wondered how she bore it so calmly and saw her eyes flash only once, when the child's mother caught her gaze. Syeira sucked in her cheeks, giving herself the smallest of shakes. Wil doubted anyone could keep Syeira from holding her own child during illness.

Slowly, the princess applied the salve to the flushed little boy. The scent of liniment and lavender stole through the room. It even seemed to reach the child's parents. Wil saw the schoolmaster's wife sag against her husband. He squeezed his wife's hand. As they watched, the colour in the boy's cheeks lightened. His breathing eased. Syeira put the back of her hand to each cheek and nodded.

"It is better, yes?" She glanced at Haydock.

"Aye."

Wil had the distinct impression she was asking his approbation to ease the discomfort of the boy's parents. The princess clearly did not need Haydock's help. Next, she administered a teaspoon of liquid from one of her own vials. Haydock sat behind the boy, supporting the child's ruddy head to taste and swallow the remedy.

Turning to the mother and the maid, Syeira offered the vial. "A teaspoon, no more. Morning and before bed, ma'am." She stood there, by the bedhead of the child she'd treated, while his mother shrank away, nudging the maid forward.

The maid was doubtless a country girl. Superstitious, suspicious, and following her mistress's lead. She hopped forward, snatched the medicines from the princess and shrank back against the wall as though Syeira were infected with illness instead of assisting in its cure.

When the same pantomime was repeated with the salve, Wil had had enough. He entered the room, doing his best to level his temper.

"Good evening," he bowed to them all, turning more particularly to the princess. "I thank you, Princess Brishen, for your assistance here this night. Do you have your shawl?"

He heard the surprise in her voice. "I—er, yes, it is here, Captain Clifton."

She had not troubled to leave it with the staff downstairs. Or, more likely, they had not thought to take it at the door. To treat her as they would any other guest—she, the Romany princess. A muscle jumped in Wil's jaw.

Turning his back on the schoolmaster's wife, he had no choice when it came to her husband. "I am to tour the school, sir. At Lord Clifton's request." This wasn't quite a lie, and his brother's authority carried far more weight in this room than did his own.

The schoolmaster, in his turn, bowed politely back. "Very good, sir. You do not require my attendance?"

Wil shook his head. "It has been a long time since I walked the riverside path in twilight, but I believe I still know the way," he smiled tightly. "Princess? May I assist you to your horse?"

This evinced no surprise in anyone except Haydock. The doctor opened his mouth to speak but one glare from Wil shut him down. He held out his arm. The princess slipped her un-gloved hand over his own—more shocked gasps—as he escorted her from the room. His sole desire was to accompany Syeira out of that room, that house. Away from these people who accepted her help, but resented her presence. Who expressed gratitude in the same breath as revulsion and suspicion. These people he realised, these *English* people. People like himself.

"I beg your pardon." He bowed as they stood by his horse. "Are you all right?"

"I am perfectly well," she replied, her low voice a stroke. "Good evening, captain." She turned to her horse, at rest beside his own. Then she turned back. "May I accompany you to see the school house?"

"Of course." He offered his arm again but she seemed to prefer running her fingers along the tree trunks as the path sloped downward, more properly becoming the woody lane he remembered from when he was a boy. It was overgrown now and poorly kept. So much so that the ground was uneven in parts, and Wil did not realise how unsafe it was until they passed beneath the trees at a place where the path lay partially hidden by lengthening shadows. He stumbled and grabbed, missing his footing, and coming perilously close to pushing the princess into the Lune itself.

"I beg your pardon," he said, feeling foolish.

"I thank you." The princess stood aside, bracing herself on a willow branch. She too seemed embarrassed, if Wil was any judge of women at all.

"You seem most comfortable outside," he said, for lack of anything else to say. "Alone in the dark, on a chill spring eve."

"You need not concern yourself, captain." Her cool tone maintained its hint of challenge. "I am perfectly able to look after myself. Or is it your concern that I am planning a rebellion in your village?"

Sweet. Arch. Pointed and—accurate. Wil cleared his throat.

"When I spoke to Haydock earlier, I did not mean..." he stopped.

"It is truly exceptional," the princess said, staring at the last rays of sunlight blanketing the woods, "how often we say things we seem not to mean." She turned to look at him, all defiance and sadness. "You did mean it," she said softly. "You are only sorry I heard you say it. I do not like the way you English look at my Romany. At—at *me*."

"How is that?"

"As though I am here to steal something. Or poison you. Or harm your children. Or, or, or…" her voice trailed into silence.

Wil stood a moment, stunned, with no idea of what to say. How must this feel, day after day? How must this hurt? He blushed for himself. "I beg your pardon." Why did he always seem to be apologising to this woman? "If I've caused offense—"

"You have." Syeira replied solemnly. "I will never get used to it."

"Used to what?"

"Why do you think I agreed to leave with you while Doctor Haydock stays to dine?"

Wil scowled. "The schoolmaster requested you leave?"

Syeira sighed. "No, but his household is plainly discomfited by my presence. Their son is ailing. I have no wish to distress them further." Weariness tempered her tone. Weariness, but not resignation.

"You're tired, princess. Your attendance on your brother is taxing." *And now you attend the school children.* Syeira had a greater commitment to her work than anyone knew.

"I am tired," she whispered. "Tired of this treatment."

A frisson of anger darted through Wil at the folk who accepted Syeira's work but made their dislike of her plain. Although hadn't he thought much the same? Fancied himself liberal? Paternal, even? The scalding shame of it burnt his soul.

"I would never harm a child." Syeira spoke in a low murmur, as though she'd forgotten he was there.

"Of course you wouldn't." In the silence that fell between them, the echo of his earlier suspicion seemed suddenly loud. Somewhat desperate for a change of subject, Wil asked, "You desire children?"

"Yes." That shy smile again. "A foolish wish, no doubt." Again, she seemed to be speaking only to herself.

"Why is that?" He stepped closer. Put out his hand.

Syeira seemed to shake herself. "Shall we walk?"

"Er—yes. If you wish it, princess." Wil regained his balance and his composure. This was ground he knew, after all. He pretended not to notice the unanswered question.

Syeira's tone lightened. "I do wish to see the school house."

Offering his arm, and gratified she allowed it, Wil guided the princess towards the centre of the path, wondering how to ask her pardon.

He'd insulted her and she was angry. He should feel guilty. He *did* feel guilty. He also felt a sort of heady warmth. The quickening of spring reached into this moment. He could smell new-flowing sap coursing through the trees. Warming scents tanged the air. Simply being alone with Syeira was intoxicating. *Alone. Without a chaperon.* Wil's pulse picked up a little. He inhaled cinnamon again. Cinnamon and something irresistibly sweet. He glanced down at the slender hand resting over his own. Did Syeira feel it too? He wondered what this woman would do if he lifted those soft fingers to his lips. He felt her shiver and turned.

A moment later she broke away, running up to better examine a climbing moss growing along one wall of the school. "I've not had the chance to examine a school house so closely before." Cupping her eyes, Syeira peered into a small window. "What was it like?" She glanced back at Wil. "Attending school?"

Wil cleared his throat, determined to exercise a little more self-control. "Roger and I had tutors before being sent off to Cambridge. By then we were young men already."

"Young men? Like Janfri." Syeira turned to give him her attention. Then she stopped. "Do you smell anything, Wil?"

Wil was too engaged in watching her smile to be aware of much else. "What do you mean?"

"The air smells damp. Damp and decayed."

Wil inhaled deeply, recognising the scent of stagnant moisture, and something less than fresh. Spoiling vegetation perhaps, or rotten wood.

"You think this important?"

Syeira shrugged. "It may be so. Putrid water beneath the school may cause fever if the building is not sound."

Wil remembered the fences at Clifton Hall and closed his eyes. Could the duke be responsible for the illness among the estate children as well? *Dear God.*

"Would there not have been illness before now?"

"I understand from the schoolmaster that there was a fever last spring."

"Last year?" That would be right after Roger left with his regiment. A year, and the duke had done nothing. His fists curled as he took a breath. Syeira's words flowed back to him. *Do not waste your anger.* Wil wondered how long it took to let go of anger. This was something he might like to learn.

"Yates must look into this." No wonder the steward wished to speak with the schoolmaster. "The families shall have every assistance the hall can offer. Do you have any suggestion, princess?"

"It may have been ice that has now thawed. I am not an engineer," the princess said after a moment. She smiled at him, her tone gentling.

"But you are a…a…" Wil fumbled for the correct word as they returned along the path towards the schoolmaster's cottage.

This time the princess laughed. A genuine ripple that had Wil relaxed and smiling in a moment. "A healer. The Romany word for this is *drabarni*."

"*Drabarni*." Wil tried the foreign words on his tongue. He looked at her in the fading light. It was nearly too dark to see anything but the sheen of her eyes, and the last of the sunlight absorbed by her hair. "Did I get that right?"

Syeira nodded without smiling. "If I were a man it might be *drab-engro*," she paused. "It is the same word for poisoner."

"You are no poisoner, princess."

"Are you certain?" Her laughter came again.

He found himself wanting to grin in response, but he didn't. Not yet. Not until he was sure he was forgiven.

"I am certain." The words jammed in his throat again. "I've seen how you are with Lydie. I—I know your wish is to help. I was thoughtless. Arrogant."

"English?" Her chilly voice cut deep.

About to cover her hand with his free one, Wil dropped them both and stepped away, inhaling sharply. Was this a dismissal of some sort? A reminder of his secondary status? As if he needed reminding. An inheld breath cooled the air between them. The princess was waiting for something. Wil all but heard the impatient tapping of her shoe. Her sudden barb knocked him off balance. Such a tart response when he'd only been trying—*oh.*

"I suppose this is something like how it feels?"

"Yes." She thawed instantly.

Her laughter came again and he found himself grinning. Somehow, he'd been given a test and stumblingly managed to pass. It was a queer feeling. Never mind that he hadn't intended to hurt her. He'd been careless. Determined not to make that mistake again, he forbore to look too closely at why. Wil wondered if he'd feel as maligned at the Romany camp. Remembering his Mama, he doubted it was the same thing.

"Do you miss your camp?"

"Oh yes." The warmth in her response, the wistful tone, told him everything he needed to know.

He sighed as the princess swung herself up on to the Romany horse. Wil handed up her bag and bowed.

"I must take my leave," Wil said.

"Another English tradition?" She smiled down at him, her thighs clenched tightly across the bare back of her mount.

"I'm afraid so." Wil smiled, his pulse quickening as he turned away from her. "Are you returning to the hall?"

"I must take in another family on my way, but yes. This is no weather to be out."

"You must take care of your health as well, Syeira." He knocked on the schoolmaster's door once more. "I shall not keep you from your dinner long."

"Nor I, yours." She glanced at the lowering sky.

Even as the princess urged her horse to canter, lightning forked in the distance. Wil hoped they both arrived home before the storm hit. *Home? Since when did he think of Clifton Hall as 'home'?* Since he'd met Syeira? He mentally shook himself—hard. The princess Brishen belonged with her house. Besides, he was hardly suitable. He had his commission to make. Shrugging away further unsettling thoughts, he turned to greet the maid.

Chapter Sixteen

Syeira made her way to her room, hoping that her late arrival for dinner had passed unnoticed. She ought to beg Wil's pardon but felt unequal to the task. An icy, wet wind blew across her the whole ride back, chilling her to the bone, and she was beginning to shiver. It had been worth it though, to see for herself that more of the afflicted children were improving. Doctor Haydock was pleased, and most profuse in his thanks.

A soft knock at the door drew her attention to the maid. "Mrs Edwards seen you come up, miss." Martha curtsied. "She said to ask if yer might be after having a fire this day. It's that chilly."

Syeira smiled her agreement. "I thank you Martha, yes."

Once the girl had laid the fire and lit it, she left. Syeira removed her damp clothes, arranging them over chairs by the heat. Dragging the counterpane off the bed she curled into the armchair, as close to the warmth of the blaze as she could get. Outside, the sky rumbled and flashed. She'd been awake since dawn to see to Valkin, then visited the village children. A rest was in order, even if she had promised to join her host.

Another deafening crash sounded. Syeira jerked around as the door to her room thumped open in echo. It wasn't—it couldn't be Wil, was it? Another flash illumined the figure trembling in her doorway. A small figure—a child.

"P-p-princess Brishen?" The little girl's voice shrilled with fright. "Are you here?"

"Miss Clifton? Is it you?" Syeira cleared her throat. She could hear the whimpering from the tiny dog that accompanied the girl everywhere. "You may come in."

The little girl flew at her, almost knocking her to the ground with the force of her embrace. Her little dog wasted no time curling up before the fire.

"Oh, I am so glad." The child cried a few tears. "I saw the maid leave and I was so frightened all alone in the nursery. The thunder is so dreadfully loud." Another growl of thunder sounded and the girl shrank closer to Syeira.

"You do not like the storm?"

The girl shook her head violently. Gently, the princess led the child towards the centre of the room, away from the noise outside the window. "Where is your governess?"

Lydia's muffled voice was difficult to interpret.

"Come." Syeira took the little girl's hand, seating her on the chaise. "Sit here."

Instinctively touching her palm to the child's forehead, Syeira was relieved to find no sign of fever. She shook out the counterpane, tucking it securely around the little girl.

"Is that better?" She studied the child, who snuggled into the fabric and stared wide-eyed at the princess. Syeira repeated her question about the girl's governess.

Miss Clifton looked away. "Miss Lee is no longer my governess." Lydia lifted her chin, but her eyes remained downcast. "She is called to London by Papa."

Syeira sucked in a breath. The Romany were rarely surprised by the poor behaviour of Englishmen, but the princess confessed herself shocked. The duke truly did seem as bad as rumour indicated. He had no discretion at all. No wonder his son behaved the way he did—and no wonder Clifton Hall looked the way it did. As though the estate was improperly cared for or cared about. Like his family. Like this child.

"Would I be in your way if I stayed here a while, princess? U-until the storm is passed?" The child sniffled. "P-p-please," she whispered, shrinking further into her seat with each thunderclap.

"You may stay." Syeira smiled. "If you will call me Syeira." She sat beside Lydia, drawing the frightened girl closer, her arm a firm support across thin shoulders. "There now. You've no longer any need to be afraid. You are safe here, little one." Syeira hummed an old tune, until she was singing softly.

"Coin si deya, coin se dado?
Pukker mande drey Romanes,
Ta mande pukkeravava tute."

"That's pretty," the little girl murmured. "Is it English, prin— Syeira?"

"An old Romany lullaby I used to sing to my little brothers and sisters." Syeira whispered. "Hush now, little Lydia. Rest, child."

"Thank you." The girl's voice was soft. Calm and warm now, she grew sleepy. "Syeira," she sighed, laying her pretty head on her protector's shoulder.

Syeira held the child until she stopped shivering, and the little hand pinned tight within her own fell slack. Carefully, she gathered the girl in her arms, lifting her towards the bed. She was not a large child, but it was not easy either. Curling in around her young charge, Syeira strained her ears for any sounds from downstairs, but all indications of society were drowned out entirely as the heavens opened, pummelling all the land with a driving rain.

***

A weight shifted against her in sleep. One of her little sisters come to curl up in the night.

"Mmmm." Syeira opened her eyes slowly, savouring the last few moments before dawn. *Oh.*

Her gaze took in the stone walls, the windows, the four-poster bed. Glancing down, she recalled the storm, and the little girl running in for comfort. She smiled, gently easing herself from the bed so as not to wake Miss Clifton. Stepping to the wash basin, Syeira completed her simple toilette before moving next door to relieve Janfri.

Her younger brother needed no encouragement to head back to the camp with a list of requirements from his siblings. The storm was passed and the day promised fresh weather for riding.

"You will remain still today," she said, examining Valkin's torso. "It is healing."

"Mmmm," her brother agreed. "Perhaps, but so slowly."

"That, I cannot help." She handed him a tea she had left to steep overnight. He sipped it, making a face all the while.

Syeira shrugged. "If you will play by English rules, Valkin..." She let her sentence remain unfinished. Scolding could wait until her brother was healed. *If* he healed. She pushed the thought away. It did not bear thinking about. *I am doing everything I can.* She heard the words within like a prayer. *Everything you taught me, Mama. Please, let it be enough.* She swallowed and breathed deeply, hands clasped before her.

An hour later, Syeira rubbed lavender mint oil onto Valkin's wrists, watching as he fell into a light doze, courtesy of her tea. She ran her hands over her poultices, checking there were enough and that she had prepared them properly. She'd already done this a dozen times since sunrise.

The glass by the dressing room told too much truth as Syeira examined her reflection. She looked as she felt: pale and worn out. She'd been captive in this English sickroom for far too long now. The grounds of Clifton Hall, though unkempt, were very fine. Syeira longed to explore the woodlands during daylight. Spring was coming in. There was value in being among new green growth, and not merely for her spirit.

A muffled sound by the door made her turn. "Princess?"

Syeira smiled and motioned for Miss Clifton to enter. "Good morning, Miss Clifton. You are up and about early this day."

"Oh," the child blushed. "How early is it?"

Syeira glanced out the window. "Only a few hours past the dawn. Are you well?"

Lydia carried a sketch book and crayons under her arm. She stood by the fireplace, staring awkwardly at Syeira. After a moment, she remembered to curtsey. "I am quite well, princess, but no one else is awake yet." The child looked at her feet for a moment and seemed to take a breath. She pushed her shoulders back and looked Syeira in the face.

"May I sketch in here?" She spoke as though asking a magnificent favour that took all of her courage.

"Sketch?"

"I am supposed to sketch today. At least, this is what I would be doing if Miss Lee were still my governess. I am studying portraiture. I must practise if I am to improve." The little girl's words came out in a rush. "I would very much like to draw *your* portrait, princess." She fixed the full force of her pleading green eyes on Syeira, who could hardly resist. The Clifton charm was not reserved merely for the men of the family.

"I am flattered, Lydia. I am afraid I cannot sit so still this morning for I have much to do. Would you like to sketch the prince?" Syeira glanced between the child and her slumbering sibling. "He is certainly still enough at the moment."

The little girl's eyes went wide and she giggled. "Do you think he will mind it?"

Syeira leaned forward conspiratorially. "I think he will know nothing about it." She smiled. "He is dosed with quite a strong sleeping tea. He will likely sleep all morning."

"Then he is an ideal subject. Thank you, I shall." Miss Clifton settled herself in a nearby chair and began, humming quietly.

The girl's pale cheeks puffed out in concentration, those green eyes a little red. She'd been crying then, alone in Syeira's too-large empty bed. Lydia must be lonely. She might also be Syeira's solution this morning.

The herbs required to speed the prince's healing were nearly used up. And Syeira was restless. Janfri would not be back until breakfast time and she now knew where all the side doors were located. Slipping out for a breath of air would be easy enough. Looking again at her low herb stores, Syeira squinted at the sunbeams slanting patterns over the floor rug and made up her mind.

"I wonder, Miss Clifton, if I may prevail upon you to sit with the prince while I go out to replenish my bag?" Syeira held her near-empty herb pouch aloft. "Janfri will be back in a short while, but I have found the best time to gather some plants is the dawn. I am happy to trade you a morning's ride on a Romany horse."

Lydia seemed to actually glow at Syeira's request. "I am not a good enough rider, Syeira. But no trade is necessary. You may rely on me." Miss Clifton spoke with confidence, sounding a great deal like her brother.

"Perhaps a riding lesson, then?" Syeira grinned as she offered the trade.

"That will suit me very well." The child looked up from her work and smiled.

"It is a trade. I will be back soon." Snatching up a shawl, Syeira took but a moment to ready herself. She found the kitchen doorway and left from below stairs.

She was eager to explore more of the grounds than the park in front of the sickroom window. The Clifton Hall estate encompassed fully one-eighth of the county, including woodlands she doubted the family ever traversed.

Her shoulders relaxed the moment she exited Clifton Park. Slowing her pace to a walk, she strolled slowly, allowing the crisp air and the sight of trees and grasses to shift the shut-in feeling she'd endured since she began nursing her brother.

She wasn't sorry she'd agreed to do it. She was the most gifted healer in all of Brishen and the prince deserved no less, but was there any need for Captain Clifton and her brother to engage so effortlessly and charmingly? Did the duke's son have to offer them every assistance, naysaying his own household staff to smooth the atmosphere for his guests? His charm was as warm as his smile. It made his solicitous attentions to herself and her family difficult to resist, even if she wanted to.

Did she want to?

What was the matter with her? Was she ill that she allowed such ideas? She would not waste one more moment of this gloriously fresh morning air thinking about the Englishman and the way he kissed her. The way her pulse pounded and her whole body warmed when he stood too close.

The princess shook her head, shutting out further unruly thoughts and renewing her focus as she moved onto a pretty winding path. Here she would be able to gather the plants she needed in peace, with no chance of running into distractingly handsome *gadjo* captains. Her eyes scanned left and right, noting the wildflowers growing on either side. The path was less formal than most English gardens, although this did not seem to be from any calculated design. Rather, Syeira had the impression that the grounds were simply not well kept. Well, it may not be to the taste of her hosts, but she liked her gardens a little wild. Not all beautiful blooms did well when straightly trained. The unruly grasses and fernery delighted her vision. Spying some herbs near the roots of an ancient oak, she stepped aside to harvest them. Straightening up, she saw a handful of shrivelled berries left over from the winter snows.

"Mistletoe." She smiled, pleased at finding such an important ingredient so late in the season. Most gardeners cut it down for Christmas and burned it after the festivities, unaware that both the leaves and the berries had value in the art of healing.

Tapping the dried fruit with her tongue, Syeira pinched her face and wished for water. The tiny fruits were bitter, and poisonous in all but the smallest amounts. As a healing plant, however, and especially as a way to relieve pain, small doses could be added to tea or infused into oils. Dried berries were not as effective as fresh but they could be ground. Once powdered, this find would replenish Syeira's meagre stores. She also took care to cut the now-browned leaves from the magic plant, stowing them carefully away. Even dried, the leaves' medicinal properties were astonishing.

Stepping back from the great oak, Syeira looked about her. She arranged some leaves and sticks in a *patrin,* a sign to the rest of her house. The symbols were hardly noticeable to *gadjos* but Romany would see them, and they would know the value of these plants.

The nettle thorns she needed grew somewhere near the rundown fence they'd come through the morning of the duel. She also recalled a spire on the horizon. The pennyroyal plant often grew in churchyards and her supplies were running low.

It was a beautiful morning. Clear, crisp and even a little warmer than the past few weeks. Spring was coming. Lifting her face to the sky, Syeira could not help enjoying the day. At the Romany camp, family obligations commandeered most every moment. She was often called upon to nurse her father and other elders during times of illness. She had so few moments like this to herself. Joy filled her for the space around her now—joy, and gratitude for a morning spent in the woods among her beloved wild plants. Sunshine warmed her skin and she breathed deeply the scents of early lavender, mint and a hint of fungus. Oh yes, the woods were her safe place. No walls, no expectations, no traditions or customs to trip over.

By the time the sun had moved at least halfway above the horizon, Syeira had replenished her bag with plenty of the browned stalks from last spring's lavender and collected the nettle thorns she required. The church stood before her. It was no great establishment but in fact a small chapel meant, she supposed, for the Clifton family. As if prayers were solely for the nobility. Clicking her tongue in irritation, she walked the kirkyard boundary slowly, searching for the tri-shaped leaf she needed for her pain relief remedies.

Spotting a likely-looking greenish clump, she knelt down, taking care not to tear her skin. Someone—the estate gardener, she supposed—was in the process of removing what they must believe to be a weed. Indeed, the English name for this healing plant was 'bindweed'. She gathered up what she could before the entire patch was torn out. The sap was known to cause redness so Syeira proceeded with care, clipping patiently away at the shrubbery with her little silver knife. The work was painstakingly slow but rushing her harvest would achieve nothing.

She was still there some time later when she heard voices approaching. Focused on her methodical cutting, she did not look up.

Chapter Seventeen

Wil's tour of the estates proceeded smoothly, with Yates accompanying him to keep detailed notes. The news that the Easter celebrations would be returning to the Little Chapel mollified many of the disgruntled tenants. Mrs Edwards's sister had clearly been singing his praises as well. Wil remembered few of the older villagers but they all recalled his mother and her children with kindness. They said little about the duke, for which Wil was grateful.

If Clifton Hall was to be his home for the foreseeable future, he wished it to be kept in order, whether his father agreed with the expenses or not. Besides, the hall was the premier estate in the county, and the duke ought to remember it. The populations of some dozen or so hamlets and villages depended on Clifton Hall for their livelihood. It was these residents who grew the reputation of the estate. Their Clifton Hall preserves and Beacon Fell cheese receipts added much to the wealth of the Lancashire county seat.

Wil examined the south chancel of the Little Chapel, noting the mouldy and loosening stonework. The wrought iron was rusted entirely through. He shook his head at the duke's negligence.

"South chancel, right wing. Ironwork rusting through. Stonework in need of repair. Roof repair required," Wil announced. He waited while Yates completed the written notes. "That ought to be completed before Good Friday," he added as an aside. The entire estate attended Easter services at the chapel on that day and the roof needed to be secure.

"Noted, captain." Yates jotted it down.

Wil squinted up at the single, tiny oculus window. The artwork was ancient, depicting a Lancaster Rose above a lintel dating back to the fifteenth century, not that this could even be seen. The stained glass was spotted with soot and the filth of too many months' inattention. The men's boots clicked through the chapel vestry, examining the sandstone seating. The small building was beautiful but cold.

"Add a note for a supply of firewood to be made ready before Easter. His Grace cannot expect our villagers to show their devotion while shivering."

The tensions across Wil's shoulders tightened further. Easter was less than eight weeks away. How were they to ready this place in time? "Any idea as to how we clean that?" Wil jerked his head towards the oculus.

"Could the Romany not assist us, captain?" Yates spoke tentatively. "They produce quality ironwork and they are already on the estate."

Will considered this. The Romany had once been employed on the estate in such a capacity—why not now? House Brishen may require an equal trade of estate bounty to which they may help themselves. It was certainly a resourceful way to complete the necessary repairs without having to beg His Grace for access to the estate coffers. It might take months for the duke to notice the produce on his estate had been used as payment for its maintenance. Wil found himself smiling at this solution. "A clever thought, Yates. Thank you, you may leave it with me."

The steward nodded. "Captain, the arrangements for Easter," he continued, glancing at his list.

Wil ran a weary hand through his hair. The duties of a squire were never-ending. "If we can ready the chapel and see to the gardens then we'll be able to open the lower rooms. The villagers expect it and we cannot disappoint them. I must call on Palmer. The duke ought to have written him already, but it would be as well not to assume so."

"The curate is Evers, captain. Mr Evers," Mr Yates corrected him softly.

Wil stared at the steward. "What happened to Mr Palmer? How long has Evers been curate?"

"Evers is the nephew of a friend of the duke's. His uncle purchased the living on the estate while yourself and Lord Clifton served on the continent."

"Of course he did." Wil grimaced, his temper rising a notch. "Did the Duke sell anything else while Roger and I were at war?"

"Nothing else of which I am aware." The steward's diffident tone reminded Wil of the man's wife and family—and the duke's depravity. This did nothing to improve his mood. It was a wonder the family portraits still graced the walls in the Long Gallery. He made a mental note to check his mother's jewellery. It would pass to Lydia when she came out, if his father did not find a way to turn it to his own uses first.

He sighed and roped in his temper, a difficult task when he felt as though he'd not slept for several days. There was still much to do. All the burden of the heir with none of the entitlements. He silently chided himself. It wasn't Roger's fault that he was still campaigning in Cadiz.

The Little Chapel grounds were as unkempt as Eddy had indicated, although Wil could see that the gardeners had already been at work to correct this. It was one of the first orders he had given after Eddy's interview. There was one there now. He squinted at a body bent over one of the hedgerows – that did not look like a gardener. In fact, it did not look like a man. The figure turned. Wil started. It was a woman, and not any woman. His dreams of last night rose up before him. *He mustn't*. He had more self-command than this. Didn't he? His cheeks burned. *Damn*. He glanced briefly at his father's steward.

"That'll be all for now, Yates. We'll continue this after luncheon."

Following the captain's eyeline, the steward evinced no surprise at Wil's request. Mr Yates turned, bowing a discreet exit as he disappeared into the cooler dark of the chapel, presumably to exit out the main door of the church.

Keeping his gaze on the woman grubbing among the greenery, Wil quickened his step. "Good morning, Princess Brishen."

Syeira glanced up, nodded and returned her concentration to her hands. Her focus on her work was, as always, extremely dedicated.

"Is there something you require from the garden, Syeira?"

"It is one of my herbs," Syeira replied. "Your gardeners are cutting it away like a weed."

Wil looked where she was pointing. It all looked like weeds to him. "I do not know a great deal about the plants here," he admitted. "Are they removing healthy growth?"

"Do you remember the leaf I gave you on the day of the duel?"

"The one that cured my headache? Of course."

"That is from this plant. It is called aconite. I must gather it for drying before the gardeners burn it all."

Wil smiled. "They will not cut it down if I order them to let it be, princess."

"Then—then you do not mind if I gather further ingredients from your grounds?" Syeira asked, smiling shyly.

Wil sighed. "I requested that you stay until your brother is healed. Please, take what you need."

"Thank you, Wil."

He extended a hand and helped her up, tempted to press her fingers to his lips but she appeared wary of him, withdrawing her hand immediately as though he had the pox.

"There is no chaperon," Syeira reminded him.

"Of course," Wil stammered, stepping back, stumbling over loose stonewall and barely keeping his balance. Steadying himself onto more level ground, he repositioned against the wall, conscious all the while of being closely observed.

He looked up and saw her looking back. There was no pretence at coquetry, no feigned modesty or silly, sidelong glances. Only her face, curious and open, looking back into his. Those eyes of hers had a way of drawing him in. Perhaps that was it. An 'explanation' for the way he was beginning to feel each time he was around this woman. He needed an explanation from himself because this was not how he usually behaved around women, especially in his own home. Maybe it was the war. Perhaps it had affected him somehow. Any explanations he devised seemed so simple, and yet he had never felt *less* simple in his life. Wil wondered if being around a woman would ever feel simple to him again. He blinked, focusing on the one before him.

"You may have any herb on the estate you wish," he continued. "On one condition, princess."

Syeira stared at him. "A condition?"

"That we have no more quarrels about returning the 'favour' of Clifton Hall's assistance in this matter. The responsibility is mine. I insist on this." He watched a dark blush warm her cheeks. "How is your brother this day?"

"Improving, I thank you." Syeira smiled with relief. "The prince will soon be well enough to join us in the breakfast room. He may also be able to ride again in a week or two, if he is careful. We will be out of your way before Lady Day."

It was Wil's turn now to stare. "I thought your house would stay through the winter."

"Winter will soon be over," Syeira replied. "You have been far too kind, but the Romany do not stay in one place. I fear there are so many of us." She seemed to be considering something. "I am surprised you know that my Romany prefer to camp in one place for the whole winter, Wil." Her eyes flickered over him with frank curiosity, lingering on his mouth. Or was that his imagination?

"It is a lifestyle I admire. Mama counted many Romany among her acquaintance. She enjoyed the company, I think." He gestured to the Little Chapel. "This was one of her favourite places." He fell silent, remembering the duchess.

"I know this loss," Syeira said softly.

Wil studied her profile. The curve of her golden cheek, the ripeness of her mouth, and her defined chin. Her elegant neck... He stopped himself there.

"How old were you?" he asked, to distract himself.

"Fourteen."

He reached out a hand, tracing a line from her temple to her chin. "So young, princess," he said gently, surprised she did not flinch at his touch. Instead she smiled, looking down at her hands curled around a small silver knife.

"And your father?" he asked softly.

"He is unwell. We—we are not supposed to speak of it." Tears spilled from her eyes.

Wil fumbled for his handkerchief, but no more tears came. She was a strong woman. This was no plea for sympathy or aid. Not a wailing or a sobbing. A release. A revelation. An opening up. The princess had not been much older than Lydia when her mother died. *Fourteen.* So young had this girl stepped into the space left empty by her mother's passing. Learned to stand for her family and to move among the English, working with her brother on behalf of all the Romany. He watched the princess dab at her eyes before offering his barely soiled kerchief back to him.

"Keep it," he murmured, unable to draw his gaze from her lips.

He wondered how she could be unaware of how beautifully her shy smile opened up her face. Her cheeks warmed under his gaze, brightening her large eyes. She looked down at her hands, but the smile stayed. Wil smiled back.

The Romany do not stay in one place, their princess had said. Perhaps not, but they preferred not to travel until the spring thaw. Wil was not sure why this mattered so much. At least, not yet. All he did know was that the idea of House Brishen moving on caused a tightening across his chest and he did not like it. It was more than leashed desire then, this sensation inside him. More than mere lust for soft skin and violet eyes. He was not entirely certain *what* it was, but he wanted more time with Brishen and with their princess. More time and more...*what?* Wil did not know, but whatever this was, he wasn't ready to let it go. Yates's suggestion was good business. If Brishen accepted Wil's trade, they would remain on the estate. In all honesty, Wil wasn't thinking of Clifton Hall at all.

"Do you remember the duchess well?" Syeira seated herself on a low stone wall, her face alight with curiosity and genuine interest.

He could not resist such a pleasant companion, despite a great deal of the estate still to see today. She was so ready to listen. To help him remember. Seating himself by her, Wil told her what he could remember of his mother.

"She was one of the great beauties of her day. Lydia looks a good deal like her. My mother is buried over there." He pointed out a modest but beautifully carved tombstone beneath an evergreen.

"She is not buried with her own family?" Syeira looked shocked.

"We are her family," Wil replied automatically. He thought he understood what the princess meant though. His mother was buried where it gave the duke's family most comfort. It would have been far more generous to the memory of his gentle Mama had she been buried on her family estates in Tavistock, the property Wil came into if he ever acceded to the duke's wishes and married.

"Our traditions are different," he muttered, embarrassed for the lack of care this implied. "In any case, the Little Chapel kirkyard is Mama's resting place. I do not like it to look untidy, especially not at Easter."

"Oh yes. This is often a pleasant time for my house," Syeira said. "Brishen make the scented candles to trade."

"It was Mama's favourite day of the year. She made her own scented candles." Wil had a sudden, too-clear memory of his mother's slender hands lighting lavender-wax and reciting Good

116

Friday blessings in the Little Chapel. Her fair voice lifting to the vaulted ceiling as she sang:

Alas my love you do me wrong
To cast me off discourteously;
And I have loved you oh so long
Delighting in your company.

It was not the duchess's fault that the words she sang were more prophetic than anyone could have guessed. Wil remembered how hard his Mama had tried to shield Roger and himself from the worst aspects of the duke's character.

"Your mother—I think I understand from Martha—that she was a baroness as well?"

"Yes, she was." Wil fell silent then, lost in memory.

There was a powerful ache inside him. For a moment he missed his Mama far more than he ever had. The hall did not feel like home anymore. It hadn't, since she'd died.

He studied his guest. Being at the hall was not without compensations. His whole body hardened as he tried focusing on her conversation. It was damned difficult. She wore a simple wine-red gown with some kind of morning apron over it, but the silken cloth clinging to her soft shape made directing his thoughts elsewhere an impossible task. There were many other things he could be thinking about. The simple truth was that he preferred to think of her.

Even while she was immediately before him, patiently awaiting his response. Apparently, he had forgotten the art of conversation as well as self-command. Wil's cheeks heated again, not to mention the rest of his body.

"The baroness knew the way to make her own candle wax?" Syeira sounded impressed.

"Mama enjoyed doing things for herself. She told me once a Romany taught her how. She always had great respect for your people, as did her father. He was Baron Eliot."

"Baron Eliot. But he is extremely well thought of by House Brishen. Always a kind man, my Papa used to say. One of the few Englishmen with the power, and the will, to assist my Romany." She smiled. "Your mother was the daughter of Baron Eliot. I did not know this."

"It was she who encouraged Romany houses to camp on the estate during harsh weather. In return, the Romany maintained the estate through the worst of winter, when farmworkers find it difficult. Since Mama passed, the duke has not permitted this to continue. I am sorry for it."

"But we are here now," Syeira pointed out.

Wil inclined his head. "Indeed you are," he grinned. "And the duke is not. He will not likely be home for some time. Your brother may heal in peace." His Mama would approve. She, at least, had always had a strong sense of family—and a strong sense of justice. She would not have approved of the duel, Wil was sure of that, but she would have agreed with his attempt to set it aright.

Syeira returned her attention to the leaves she was plucking. "It is good of you to allow Brishen to remain camped here for so long, Wil, and for so little in traded goods."

"The pleasure is mine. Your family has brightened up the estate immeasurably," he replied, without ceremony. "I am enjoying the company a great deal." He watched her blush again when he spoke and did not offer up the reply he truly wished to make: That he could not bear to have her leave so soon, and that he would have traded the hall for her 'goods' if he could. But the hall was not his to trade. A fact he was never allowed to forget for long.

He wished she would look up. He wanted to see her eyes one more time, and her mouth.

Chapter Eighteen

Syeira avoided Wil's eyes. It was best not to align her gaze with his golden-green one. Her reaction would do her family no credit. If only he weren't so charming. *If only you were permitted to love.* She took a deep breath, releasing it slowly.

Looking up and away from Wil, her gaze swept the view. The rye grasses and vast, rolling green were in need of edging and a little work once the spring came, certainly, but beautiful. Here and there, tiny growths of snowdrops broke up the patchwork of greys, tans and browns that made up a winter palette. The kirkyard itself was dominated by the impressive evergreen. Syeira supposed it made a beautiful Christmas tree in December but it looked forlorn, lonely even. Like so much at Clifton Hall, it did not receive the care it deserved.

She remembered the little girl and felt a stab of anger at the duke. She hoped Lydia was able to have something to remind her of her mother.

"This is a lovely monument to connect you to your Mama. Does Miss Clifton visit here as often as you do?" Syeira asked.

"Lydia rarely visits this part of the estate. It is quite a ride from the hall and her health is not strong."

"She seems well enough to me," Syeira suggested but Wil wasn't listening. Instead, he frowned out at the chapel grounds, looking positively furious. He swore out loud, immediately collecting himself. "I beg your pardon, princess." He walked stiffly to the side of the chapel, mumbling. "This Little Chapel has stood since Norman times." He turned back to her, bowing briefly. "I will return to you shortly." His speech was short and angry. "I must speak with Mr Yates. Please excuse me."

Syeira followed his gaze, keen to learn what might cause his dangerous expression. The grounds were disorderly but the area was not large. The maintenance costs could not be great and had the grounds *been* maintained, they would not look so reduced. Syeira thought she understood Wil's anger now. Allowing this little area to get so rundown was disrespectful. Now it would be more difficult—and more costly, she supposed—to put the grounds to rights.

Syeira walked through the little kirkyard, breathing in the rich smell of rotted growth and mouldering earth. Touching her tongue to her teeth, she tasted decay. Though the area was damp and dank, thinning the greenery might let in more light. Warming the ground underfoot would encourage newer, more delicate spring growth without the fungus and moulds.

Threading her way carefully among the headstones, she reached one overlaid with a broken bell. With an artisan's eye, Syeira examined the iron ornament. It was not beyond repair. A little sanding, some oil and a few good, strong arms could return it to the bellcote if the clapper was undamaged. But what was it doing here?

Leaning forward, she pulled the brambles back from the headstone. The marker was not as old as some of the ancient graves but it was in a poor state. Scraping the lichen and moss from the carved stone with her little knife, Syeira leaned back a little to discern the inscription more clearly. She gasped.

In Memory of Catherine Maria Elizabeth Clifton
Duchess of Carston & Baroness of Bristol
Died this day 13th March 1799

It did not surprise her that the Little Chapel kirkyard held family graves. It was clearly intended as a private worshipping place for the family seat, but that Wil's mother lay buried in such a cold manner and her grave kept in such a state… Syeira felt tears on her cheeks and did not even realise she wept for the poor woman so dishonoured by her family. She checked herself. The duchess's son felt her loss keenly and certainly did not approve of the disrespect shown to his mother by her husband. Was this the reason he'd become so upset? It was no wonder. Gripped with a need to show her respect, to make things somehow better, she glanced around.

An entire meadow a lane's width from the kirkyard appeared to be in fallow. Syeira narrowed her gaze, squinting a little. She thought she recognised some of the weather-beaten stalk fronds. *Lavender.* Gathering these and the snowdrops from the edge of the walled-off field, Syeira deftly twisted a few stems, creating a delicate winter nosegay. Returning to the headstone, she laid her offering atop the gravesite of the highborn lady who had once been a friend to her Romany.

She heard the soft drumming of a horse's hooves as the steward trotted away. A noise sounded directly behind her. Turning, she met that green-eyed gaze she'd been avoiding so assiduously. The expression on her host's face indicated that her actions had not gone unnoticed. He looked…gentled, somehow.

Syeira held her breath, awaiting his response, but Wil simply held her gaze with his. Her heart shifted within her, as surely as the first sunbeam on her skin after frost. Indeed, her skin warmed beneath his deepening gaze and air sweetened with last season's lavender. She saw something in Wil's eyes she rarely encountered in a man. A kind of tender gratitude, a gentle strength that at last allowed her to glimpse his heart. To see his face in that moment, so full of love and pain and loss, was a gift. The man had depth, and she must turn away before she lost herself, lost her heart and cared more than she could afford. Nerving herself to adjust her gaze, she found she could not look away. The expression in his eyes held her.

It was Wil who moved first. Leaning past her, he placed a clumsy handful of snowdrops beside her own, keeping the space between them.

"Thank you, Syeira." He spoke thickly, as though his breath caught in his throat. His deep, strong voice made her feel as though they were too far apart. As though her knees were water and she must sit within the circle of his strong arms.

The scent of rich earth under snowy skies filled her lungs, curving her mouth upward. Turning, she saw Wil's gaze fixed upon her with an expression of such tenderness that she did not know where to look. Remembering his bare neck beneath her palm when they kissed, his hotly possessive mouth teaching hers, she shook herself—hard.

"Wil," she blushed, looking down at her hands. "What is it?"

"You," he said, and she wondered if he was quite in command of himself. "Simply *you*. You need not fear me." He maintained the perfectly respectable distance between them, holding her close with the heat of his gaze. "I will not approach, that is—" he smiled.

"It's… I wonder if you have any idea how beautiful you look in this moment?"

No man had ever said such things to her before. No Romany man would dare gainsay the Romany King. Wil kept his word and came no closer. She had not misjudged him. Her heart knew this man. *How* her heart knew him she could not say, but she was not Romany for nothing. The Romany trusted their heart above all else. *Even family? Even duty?*

Syeira turned her thoughts deliberately away from the pain of this. It truly did feel as though two different kinds of love were at war within her heart. Her spirit railed at the waste of it. There was nothing to be done, and nothing to be gained by allowing this desire for love to consume her. Right here, right now, she was nothing but content. It would have to be enough, and it would be. *Wouldn't it?*

Biting the insides of her cheeks, she took a breath, pointing at the muddy field not far away. "What is that space? Over there?" Syeira inhaled deeply. Her lungs seemed short of air today.

"They call it the 'Baroness's Meadow'. Each spring it blooms with lavender in Mama's memory. This is where she grew the flowers for Easter Sunday. The chapel smelled like her for a day. It was lovely." Wil wiped his eyes.

Without thinking, Syeira took his hand in her own, squeezing gently. Looking down, he seemed surprised to find her dark hand entwined so readily with his. He smiled, and Syeira thought she might have come as close as she ever had to seeing an Englishman blush. *This* Englishman: The son of Baroness Eliot, friend to her Romany.

Gently, he lifted her fingers to his lips, touching her skin to his mouth. *Oh, how long had she wanted to feel this?*

Her blush could light the church altar itself. "Wil, I—" she stopped, staring somewhere in the region of his chin, forcing herself to say past the clamouring of her heart, "With the worst of the winter now over, and Valkin's wound healing well, the House of Brishen will soon be moving on."

Wil dropped her hand. "You wish to leave Clifton Hall?" His voice, deep and soft, like sadness dipped in honey. *Oh, what a dangerous blend.*

Syeira shook her head, ignoring the bloom of tears pricking her eyelashes. "I do not, especially with both Valkin and Papa so ill, but

I think it is best to keep moving, no?" She swallowed, watching his face. "Most English landowners do not like to host a Romany house any longer than a week or so. Romany camps are noisy, busy places and the novelty wears off quickly. It is partly why the Romany do not stay in one place, Wil."

"I do not mind if you stay longer. In fact, I wish it."

"You do?"

"I do." Wil affirmed, then cleared his throat. "It will not be easy to find workmen to complete the repairs I need done before Easter Sunday. Not while sowing season is underway." He looked at her. "Mr Yates proposed I ask your house if they would do the work."

Syeira swallowed her disappointment. He wanted her Romany, not her. She gave herself another little shake. What was the matter with her today? She had a trade to make. Quirking her brow at him, she turned to business. "There is nothing the Romany cannot do, if the trade is fair. What is the work?"

Wil ticked the items off on his fingers. "We will need carpenters and gardeners."

"What is it you require our gardeners to do?"

"This is not how Mama's Chapel used to look. I would like the kirkyard to be..." Wil seemed to be searching for the right word.

"Tamed?" Syeira supplied it for him. "You wish it trained and formal. Like all English gardens." She kept her voice neutral. This was not her land and these were not her wildflowers. Her place was to make the trade for the good of Brishen. Nothing more. Studying Wil's expression from beneath her lashes, she saw uncertainty in his restless eyes. She already knew this was unusual for so decided a man.

"You do not approve, princess?"

Syeira shrugged. "It is a matter of personal preference. I enjoy wild woods and natural growth more than I do a formal garden. However, I am still able to direct Brishen's work to English tastes."

She watched him survey the Little Chapel grounds. Watched him take in the neglected tree line and overgrown grasses, saw his jaw tighten and his face flush, one fist smacking against his other curved palm. His shoulders dropped once his gaze reached the woodlands. A sigh escaped him as he uncrossed his arms.

So, the wild woods affected him too, did they? Perhaps training trees to militant angles did not reflect Wil's taste at all. Such artifice surely belonged more to the duke than his son. A smile warmed her face as her gaze followed his. The woods at Clifton Hall were truly beautiful. The more so for being untamed.

"A design less formal might suit." Wil thought a moment. "Mama had a penchant for wildflowers, you know. Especially those which grow in her woods. We will need a small army of good, strong labourers. A stonemason too, if Brishen have one?"

"Of course. There is always at least one stonemason in a Romany camp. The House of Brishen have three. We are camped in safety and can trade our work for time in your gaming woods perhaps? We will not need to wait until Lady Day." She stopped, considering. The exchange still felt uneven. She wanted access to those plants. "It is a great deal of work for House Brishen. There is a lichen in your woods I would wish Brishen to use as well."

"Lichen?"

Syeira nodded, attempting to formulate a botany lesson with her hands. "Yes. A yellow lichen. It is not good to have it so much on your elm trees but I can remove it with my knife. I have a use for it." She looked at him. "Lichen is a kind of plant, similar to a moss—"

"I know what it is," Wil interrupted, shaking his head. "Of course, you may take it. What on earth could you want with it?"

"We use lichen to dye our silks," Syeira explained. "Each Romany house has their speciality. Silken fabrics in unique shades is one of the other ways the House of Brishen earn our living. The dye we create with the lichen is available solely from Brishen."

"Your woods have many plants I would wish our women to gather for this purpose, if you agree. As well, we can better secure your northern boundary against trespassers. After all, who better than my Romany would know where a trespasser might take advantage?" Syeira grinned.

Wil grinned back. The only 'trespassers' in recent days were herself and her brothers on the day of the duel. He nodded. "The trade is fair."

The Romany princess extended her palm before noticing Wil's strange expression. "You will not shake hands with me to close the trade, Wil?"

Wil stared at her hand, clearly taken aback once again. "Are you not required to carry my request to your father or brothers?"

Syeira made a sound somewhere between a snort and a laugh. "Because I am a woman you mean?" She shrugged. "I am the eldest Romany princess and while I will never lead House Brishen, I am as entitled as Valkin or Janfri to make good terms for my house. All Romany children are taught *kin aley* from the cradle. That is our word for learning to trade like a Romany. We do not require our ladies to be silent and meek like you English."

Wil's eyebrows shot up and he bowed his head. "I meant no offense." He took her hand in his. This time, he forbore to release it.

"I am not offended, Wil. I will enjoy staying here a while longer." She patted her bulging herb bag affectionately with her free hand. "Your grounds are valuable to the Romany."

"I am glad you think so, Syeira." Wil looked at the Little Chapel. "It will be a fine thing to see Mama's Little Chapel full of softly singing voices for Easter. I do not think such a thing has happened at Clifton Hall since her passing."

Syeira's mood lifted noticeably and she smiled up at the sky, breathing deeply as she once again surveyed the spill of lands about her. Yes, it was lovely here, but in truth the smile on her face had more to do with the warm green eyes surveying the new Romany worksite all about her. It would not be easy to complete this trade before Easter but Syeira had faith in Brishen. Her house would see it done. There was something else she wished them to attempt. Timing would be important.

Syeira looked down. She was blushing again, too aware of her hand being held captive by the son of Baroness Eliot. She ought to command he release his hold of her, or draw back from him herself. She didn't. False modesty was not what she wanted. What she *did* want, was this. *Simply this.*

A little time, even a moment, to learn some part of knowing a man. To touch him with the gentlest part of herself, however briefly, was worth a little risk, wasn't it? Something stirred within her. Something like hope. *Is that what this is?* This feeling was somehow *more* than hope. Softer. Deeper. Warmer.

A slow heat spread through her as she savoured the strength in Wil's fingers, sensing him. Strength and gentleness—another dangerous blend, but Syeira finally knew enough of him now. She was not afraid of being alone with Wil.

His deep voice reached her. "It will be a fine occasion to celebrate Easter with your house. Mama always believed hosting the Romany at Easter heralded good luck."

Syeira released his hand, still smiling. "I cannot promise we will stay here so long. I *can* promise you Brishen's work will be satisfactory." Bobbing a curtsey she turned, one hand out to shield her eyes as she faced into the sun. "It is nearly noon and I have been gone from Valkin for some time now. It is truly a great pleasure to walk in your fine woods, Wil, but I must return to the hall." She extended her hand to him, savouring his lips against her bare skin one more time before she departed.

Dosta.
Enough.

Chapter Nineteen

Organising House Brishen into teams of workers around the Little Chapel meant spending more time outside than before, and Syeira felt a great deal better for it. It also kept her safely out of Wil's way, for which respite her head thanked her and her heart hurt. Her pride would not allow her heart to give way. Her duty to Brishen must come first.

She attempted to prove this to herself by fulfilling her trade with Miss Clifton. Watching the child gaze fearfully at Grygry, Syeira surmised the girl had serious misgivings about horse riding.

"Do you prefer to ride your own mount, Miss Clifton?"

"I do not have any pony of my own," Lydia informed her. "That is, I did so. Papa gifted my mare to Miss Lee. He says she is the better rider." Even her child's voice was brittle.

Syeira stiffened at this. Lydia was young, but she was not stupid, nor was she insensate. "I see."

Lydia turned from staring at Grygry, her gaze on her puppy. "What shall I do with Bony?"

"Here." Syeira fashioned a small sling out of her winter shawl for the little dog, then picked up the pup and placed him in it. "The pup will grow easily used to it. How do you like it, Miss Clifton?"

Miss Clifton laughed as the little dog pawed the air for a few moments before relaxing entirely. "Miss Lee would never have thought of that." She smiled up at Syeira.

"I dare say not." Syeira smiled back at her. "It is the Romany way to carry babies and young animals when we move our camp onwards. Now, let me see your mounting seat, Miss Clifton."

"I-I do not know how," the child looked on the verge of tears.

"Then this is where we begin."

As the girl seemed not to know how to mount a horse at all, Syeira assisted Lydia to leg up and position herself sideways, before taking a seat behind. Once firmly in place, arms around Lydia, she pointed Grygry's nose towards the wood, nudging him into a steady canter.

They slowed a little at the edge of the woodlands. Lydia's eyes shone. The girl's breathlessness matched cheeks pinker than Syeira had yet seen them. *Good.*

"I do wish for a pony of my own," Lydia sighed, watching Grygry's slowing hooves. "Papa said there is no need as I am not an accomplished rider. We do have three carriages. Do *you* have a carriage, princess?"

Syeira laughed. "In a manner of speaking. We do not use them to attend balls, Miss Clifton. I have my own *covo*. That is a Romany caravan. It is both my transportation and my home."

"You prefer to ride on horseback? Like this?" Lydia sat far too tensely in her sideways seat, which was precarious enough.

"I do."

"And you do it very well." Wil's deep voice interrupted them.

"Wil!" Lydia's excited squeal necessitated a tighter grip on the child from Syeira. Lydia gasped.

"I beg your pardon, Miss Clifton. Side-on is not a safe seat, especially without a saddle." Syeira kept her hold on the child to prevent her slipping off the animal's back. Turning Grygry in a tight circle to face Wil as he approached atop his own mount, she smiled.

"Good morning Lydie, Syeira. Have I interrupted a riding lesson?"

"I know how to ride, Wil," Miss Clifton pouted, not without another fearful look at Grygry's perfectly sedate hooves.

"Perhaps there is more than one way for a lady to ride, Miss Clifton," Syeira suggested gently. There was no denying their ride would have been far easier had Lydia sat as she did, Romany-fashion.

"It is not safe to gallop in a sideways seat," Wil agreed.

His sister scowled, then half-jumped, half-fell from the bay horse to the ground.

"Lydie." Wil made his dismount in alarm.

"I *can* do it, Wil. I am not such a little child," his sister retorted. Turning to Syeira, the child curtsied before lifting her little dog to the ground. "I did not mean to deny you a gallop, princess."

"Nonsense. I enjoyed our ride." Syeira shot Wil a well-practised look.

The little girl's cheeks were scarlet with mortification. With that unerring instinct children have for truth over lies, Miss Clifton simply raised her brows at both of them and shook her head. The dog trotted towards the woods before pausing to look back at his mistress as if to say 'Well? Are you coming?'

"Where are you off to now, Lydie?" Her brother's tone tightened. "Eddy expects you at the Hall for luncheon."

"I shall gather a spring posy for Eddy then," Lydia called back, dented dignity forgotten as she ran after her pup beneath the new-greening trees.

Syeira was left alone with Wil. She looked down at him, astonished to find his face so close to her thigh. Assailed by a sudden urge to slip off her horse and into his arms, Syeira closed her eyes in momentary horror at herself. She looked away, barely noticing Wil returning to his horse.

"I would be happy to show you the lake, Syeira," Wil said, mounting up again. "That is, if you still wish a proper ride."

Did she imagine the deepening of his voice? No doubt the man meant to sound courteous, and he did, but the way he asked the question had her blushing. That voice of his, so deep and full of heated intent. A thrill of wicked desire ran through her at being alone with him, in this moment. It had been too long—far, far too long—since the Romany princess had ridden steeplechase. She chose not to mention chaperons. Surely seduction was not possible on a horse—*two* horses, come to that. None of her *camello* had taught her so. What harm could there be in a spirited ride?

Still, the lake…

"The lake? Where my house is camped?" Her tongue worried at her lower lip.

Wil blinked suddenly, looking away. "The *other* lake. Where no one is camped. It's rarely visited by anyone except me. I check the fences there each quarter when I am at home. I assure you it is quite secure from any trespass. Brishen have already seen to that. Eddy packed a picnic for my luncheon. It is a pity to picnic alone on such a fine day." He grinned, already positioning his horse as though for a race.

"You do not wish Miss Clifton to join us?"

"Lydia is safer closer to Clifton Park. Besides, she cannot ride so far. It *is* quite a ride, if you're up to it?"

Syeira thought she saw him smile as she gripped her mount's mane and tossed her head. "Try me," she grinned, racing after him.

How she had missed this. The thunder of hooves beneath her, the racing of the blood beneath her skin. The powerful sensation of all that strength and energy urging her forward. It was momentum, it was breathing, it was freedom. She heard laughter on the wind and it was her own. This was her release, and Brishen, Clifton Hall, Papa's illness—even Wil's stolen, heated kisses seemed something she could outrun for a few moments. Her eyes shone and her breath caught. She knew it and laughed again, as Grygry chased the tail of the thoroughbred stallion before him and Syeira smiled until her cheeks hurt.

She arrived at the lake laughing, hot, and out of breath. Wil was there before her, having given Nero his head. He had their picnic laid under an obliging willow by the time Syeira rode up. He rose, but before he could assist with her dismount, she kicked up her skirts, swinging one leg high up over the other to leap lightly down, giving Wil a momentary view of her booted calves again.

She bent down, buttoning the slits that hid her legs from view. Her companion uttered a disappointed sigh, turning to stare at the lake. The rushes and boggy grasses were enough to tell her that this was a natural lake. It was rarely used. Old logs furred with moss served as seats and willow trees shaded the water lapping at a little beach, no more than two or three feet across. The sand afforded access to the water over a small estuary.

Syeira squinted at the distant roof of the hall. They were on the other side of the woods. No one would disturb them here. "Beautiful," she declared, smiling at Wil. "I thank you for showing me this lake. It is special for you, yes?"

"Roger and I learned to swim here as boys," he explained. "We preferred it to the trout lake because its distance from the house meant we could usually avoid our tutors and our relatives."

And avoid the duke? Syeira wondered.

"We used to sail model boats here with Mama. She enjoyed eating outdoors." Wil gazed around him, his face suffused with memory. "Yes. Yes, I suppose it is special."

"This is something you still like to do?" Syeira asked him. "Eat out of doors?"

Wil frowned. "I don't think any of the family have been here for some time," he said quietly. "Truly, I had not considered it. Perhaps I can arrange something for Lydie. She isn't averse to model boats."

"Miss Clifton will like this, I think," Syeira said. "She misses you. And your Mama."

"Yes," Wil agreed. "She is yet a child."

"She is growing up," Syeira said. "If she were a Romany girl, she would be coming in to her betrothal perhaps this year."

Wil seemed horrified by such an idea, actually choking on his scone. He banged a fist into his chest and coughed. "I beg your pardon," he offered.

Syeira suppressed a smile. "I simply mean that she is not a little girl any longer." She nerved herself to speak her mind. "And she is becoming desperate for someone—anyone—to notice this. To see she is becoming a woman."

Wil was silent for a long time, staring at her. So long in fact that she thought she'd offended him.

"Thank you," he said finally. "I shall try to remember that." The look he gave her then made her gasp. A kind of intense speculation. As if he knew that she, too, understood something about desperation. May, in fact, be familiar with a feeling akin to it himself. Was it something everyone felt at some point? Or only when someone like this man stared at them with eyes like molten fire? She stared back, watching his face. Wondering about the angle of his jaw and how it might feel to touch him again. He turned away suddenly, a muscle in his jaw tightening.

Syeira realised she'd been looking at him too long to notice a detail as intricate as that. Sipping at her small beer, she couldn't be sure, but she thought he turned back to her, watching. Learning. She shivered in the spring sunshine, shivers that had nothing to do with the weather. She so rarely had the opportunity to sit still. To feel and take in the moment. Moments could be powerful. *Timing matters.*

"It's warm today," Wil said, removing his jacket and loosening his cravat. He eyed the cool waters of the lake.

"Do you wish to swim, Wil?" Syeira spoke slowly, feeling languor seeping into her skin. Glancing shyly at him, she smiled.

He grinned back at her, leapt up and began tugging off his waistcoat, dragging his feet from his boots. He paused, watching her watch him. "Is it permitted for you to swim as well?" he said then swallowed hard.

Syeira wondered if she dared swim. She gulped a little air, like a fish. Swimming was permitted with a chaperon present. But there wasn't one, and the glimpse of Wil's hard, masculine lines beneath his shirt sent heat flooding through her body. It wasn't as if he were naked after all. He had on his breeches, his shirt…his dazzling smile. Watching him swim seemed like another gift she might choose for herself. Like his kiss. *His kiss.*

She stood up and nodded, motioning Wil to avert his eyes. He closed them obligingly, still smiling.

Diving in ahead of him, she revelled in the cool, silken touch of water on over-warm skin. The temperature was not quite freezing. She splashed at the chilliness. "I am already wet, Wil," she called out with a laugh.

Wil turned, opening his eyes at her voice, laughing in amazement as he shook his head and approached the lake edge. "How is it?"

"See for yourself," she replied, ducking down to luxuriate in the coolness as he began his dive.

Chapter Twenty

Syeira's head came up again as Wil surfaced, the dark mane weighing heavily behind her as she tilted her head back, smiling up at the sky. Onyx lashes framed her wild eyes with water and sunshine. Her mouth glistened in the sunlight. Wil didn't think he'd ever seen anything more beautiful.

They swam out further until he could barely stand. She could not and faced him, treading water. He moved closer, lifting her hair off her face, failing utterly not to stare at her mouth. She did not draw away. In fact, she drew nearer. Slowly, he balanced himself on the lakebed, cupping her cheek with one dripping hand. He bent his head, brushing her lips with his. It was hardly a touch: feather-light and softer than silk.

"Is this allowed?" he murmured against her lips. His eyes were closed. Part reverence, part restraint. Both seemed right.

"Mmmm, yes, this is allowed." Syeira seemed hardly conscious of speech at all.

Pressing his lips more firmly to hers, he rested there so they were breath to breath against each other.

"And this?" he whispered huskily.

"Mmmm," she said. "Yes, I think—"

He caught her lips with his as she spoke, sliding his tongue inside and beginning a warm, slow exploration of that lower lip he'd been dreaming about. Feeling her slip, he swept her into his arms, holding her tight against him without releasing her mouth. His hand cradled her bottom through the wet silk, his other arm across her hip. Syeira looped her arms around his neck, leaning into the crook of his shoulder.

Wil pressed his brow against hers, his breathing ragged. *To kiss her, but not to take her. Could he do this?* He wasn't at all sure it was possible. Even now he wanted nothing more than to be inside her, feeling her fire surround him. Watching her eyes dilate with pleasure as he sank himself into her dark, wet heat. Her palm slid over his chest, reaching for his waist. He shifted—if she touched him *there,* he'd lose all restraint. He groaned as she turned her head, glorying in the sensation of her tongue seeking his, pressing herself into the hardness of his body, her hand behind his head now, holding his mouth to hers.

Wil touched every part of her through the thin silk. The water made sliding his fingers over her too smooth. His lips moulded firmly to her ripe mouth, moving only to penetrate her warmth more deeply. Stroking her cheek now, sliding his wet palm across her throat, slipping his hand down to rounded breasts, he softly rubbed her tender nipples, savouring small whimpers of desire.

Running his fingers across her body, he felt her quivering need burning for him the way he burned for her. As his feather-light caress moved over her centre, she shifted slightly, her lips parting further. Growling low in his throat, Wil deepened his kiss, tasting every inch of her warm mouth. Sliding his fingers beneath the silk, he caressed the moist curls he found there, probing her tender flesh, seeking the molten fire that burned at the very centre of her.

Ignoring the ferocious heat from his groin, Wil stroked his fingers over her hot liquid core again and again until she jerked her mouth away from his and cried out, whispering tangled words in Romany and English. Hot liquid rushed over his fingers as he held her, crushing her body tightly to his, taking her mouth again as her pleasure came in waves. Catching her cries in his, he rested his lips on hers.

Rivulets of lake water dripped down his face trickling onto his collar, his hair spiking a little. His princess raised a shaking hand to touch his face. Wil breathed so hard he was surprised he didn't drop her. His whole body shook. He smiled, his hungry gaze looking right back at her. The softness in her eyes almost broke him. He moved his mouth against her ear, whispering fiercely. Soft words from deep within his throat, soft kisses all over her face, soft lips yielding to his, soft skin beneath his fingers…anything, anything to drown out that hard, driving, pounding heat he fought to hold back.

"Syeira, Syeira, my sweet, sweet love." He shuddered with passion then, moving closer to the lakeshore. He had to let her go. Now. Before he…

As soon as he was certain she could stand safely, he released her, moving back into deeper water. "I take it that is *not* permitted?" His voice rasped on a whisper.

Slowly, she shook her head.

"All right then," he attempted to clear his throat. "You dry off and eat. I'll stay here until—" *Until what?* Until he could sit beside her while she wore a clinging silk gown that outlined her every delicious curve, and calmly eat a picnic? *May as well stay here forever then.* "Until later," he finished distractedly.

He saw everything now through eyes glazed with desire, with need, with a fire that burned for her. His gaze followed her careful walk, saw her pause, and he knew she was drawing the strings that released her sleeves and skirt. He watched her rise from the water and sit. Spreading the silk skirt around her, Syeira leaned back on her hands, drinking in the warmth of the spring sunshine. She arranged her hair in order that it might dry as rapidly as possible.

Wil stared in amazement. He'd half-expected steam.

Chapter Twenty-One

Syeira closed her eyes as much to block out the sight of Wil soaking wet as to appreciate the sunshine. She had only a few more moments and would not be staying to eat the meal so efficiently packed by Mrs Edwards (who would, undoubtedly, raise her hands to her face in holy horror at what had occurred moments ago). She would not sit beside this man on this intimate little beach and enjoy what remained of this fine spring day but instead, would mount Grygry and ride back to the hall to relieve Janfri.

Her eyes remained closed. Closed, because she did not want to look at Wil and see regret, confusion or even dismissal in his eyes. Syeira did not want to be in this moment 'after'. She wanted the one before, the one where her whole body shuddered with pleasure when his touch explored her soft, damp centre.

Where, barely breathing, she whimpered low in her throat, pulling him closer, unable to do anything but respond to the flood of heat and fire and passionate flame he awoke within her. When her breaths tore through her as she moved her thighs apart, feeling intense need building inside her, like nothing she'd ever known. When Wil's gentle, teasing fingers slid lower, and lower, slid right inside her, touching in the most sensuously intimate way. When she gripped his shoulders and held on, feeling as though she would go up in flames at any moment. When she cried out, and he held her, kissing the shout from her mouth—and she let him.

This was the moment she wanted to remember, imprint and hold within herself forever. If she opened her eyes, it was lost. It was *past,* and for the first time in her life, she knew the pain of momentum. The jolt of a forward movement that was neither desired, nor looked-for, nor wanted. It was merely expected. *Expected, expecting, expectations.* Syeira felt the weight of them all pressing in on her. If she opened her eyes, they would crush her.

If she opened her eyes, she would see his eyes, his remorse, *his* expectations. They would come with apologies. With regrets, backward steps and a relinquishing of the bright warmth that filled her now. Of course they would. English or Romany, no one was exempt from expectations. *Ugh.*

She kept her eyes resolutely closed, her face turned up to the sun. A moment later, the yellow light behind her eyelids seemed to darken. Syeira flinched as a drop of too-cold water hit her cheek, dripping slowly down her face, like a tear. She shivered.

He was out of the lake and come to apologise as expected. She would not look at him while he expressed his regret and made his excuses. As he took his giant, English step backwards. She would not let him see that she did not regret it at all. That she wanted to swim right back out there and touch him again, and more.

"Syeira?"

"Wil." She sighed his name on a breath, her eyes closed.

"Open your eyes, Syeira." That deep command she felt deep within. "Look at me."

With infinite slowness, Syeira raised her eyelids. She raised her head, following Wil's clinging breeches over his rider's thighs. She kept her gaze moving upward in a straight line, not pausing, not skimming and quite deliberately not avoiding the bulge she'd felt pressing against her belly in the lake.

Then his belly, his torso so well-outlined by the soaking linen. His strong, broad, shoulders and his bared neck. That well-formed chin, sensual mouth, narrow nose. She paused *then*. Breathed in, held it—and met his gaze.

She nearly closed her eyes again in shock. There was no apology there. No regret. She stared into eyes that radiated nothing but barely leashed desire. For her. For *her*. *Oh.*

"Syeira." He said her name again, and it sounded like a prayer.

Syeira was on her feet in seconds, one hand curled reflexively into Grygry's mane, her leg lifting ready to mount with a jump. In one more moment she would not be able to leave. She would not want to. She *did not want* to leave this moment.

She did not need Wil's assistance to mount her horse. Nevertheless, Wil lifted her in his arms as she jumped up more slowly than she ever had in her life. So slowly that she fell partly backwards and only his bracing of her body prevented it. His hand on her thigh held her a moment in mid-mount. Hands that ought to have been cooled by lake water in late March were not cold at all. His touch was fire on her skin. Her entire body flushed as she took her seat.

She wanted to glance at his hand on her thigh. To hint at its removal so she could manoeuvre her horse. She couldn't. She *could not* look away from those eyes whose heated radiance had never, for a moment, altered nor failed to stare back at her. He understood though, removing his hand without so much as a blink. He did not step back as she nudged Grygry forward, turning him instinctively. Wil stood right there, almost, but not quite, in her way. She still had room. He still held her with that look.

At last, she looked away. She must, in order to leave.

"I—I must go," she whispered. Then, kicking Grygry into a canter, she did exactly that.

***

"Good morning," Wil stood by his chair while Syeira rose and curtsied.

She noticed he did not breakfast immediately. Instead he seemed rather to feast his eyes on *her*. Oh, this would never do. If he continued to look at her like so, and she responded with the same kind of blush now creeping over her cheeks—well, discretion was hardly to be hoped for. She looked at her plate, out the window, turned repeatedly towards the door through which she expected Miss Clifton at any moment and knew it was all, all perfectly useless indeed. She did not see anything but Wil's heated gold-green eyes. What Wil chose to focus on she dared not guess. She had not courage to meet his eyes again, though he seemed to gaze a great deal at her mouth. In fact, so fixed was his eye on her lips that he did not immediately notice the important missive beside his plate.

Seizing her opportunity, Syeira said, "It seems you have a breakfast correspondent."

"Correspondent?" He blinked in surprise. "I do not recognise the seal." He broke it anyway. "It may be regarding my commiss—" he broke off, smiling as he read. "Hmmm," he said aloud, rising to a bow as his sister took her place. "I'm summoned to the stables this morning, Lydie. I don't suppose you know why?"

His sister's over-bright eyes betrayed some awareness but she shook her head vehemently and could not be drawn. "I shan't, Wil," she repeated two or three times over. "I shall not utter even the smallest of inklings." But she grinned at him for so long that his shoulders shook with laughter. Clearly, some sort of mischief was afoot.

Syeira smiled as Wil showed her the note. "Shall we all eat a few moments later and satisfy his curiosity?" she asked Lydia.

Lydia's enthusiastic agreement decided the matter and she offered to race them both. Syeira shook her head, wrapping her shawl more tightly as they left the room.

"Lydie, it is still too damp to run," Wil called, but his sister was already racing ahead. Wil strolled beside Syeira to the stable gates. "She needs a turn in the army to keep her in line," he commented.

Syeira raised one dark eyebrow, shaking her head again.

"I see you do not agree."

"I do not, Wil." Following Lydia's deft leap to one side as the girl avoided a muddy patch of ground, Syeira said, "Miss Clifton is a lively young girl. Spirit is no bad thing in a child."

"In a child, perhaps not. Her coming out is a few years away yet," he shook his head. "Impetuosity is not highly prized by the society in which she is expected to distinguish herself. She will be required to comport herself as a young lady of the ton."

"I have not been among these ladies but I comprehend your meaning. I am sorry for it though," Syeira shivered again, tugging at her shawl. "And sorry for Miss Clifton as well. It will be a shame to see her spirit so reduced."

"I am not sure of your meaning, Syeira," Wil said. "Do you think there is something else I ought to consider here?"

"Most certainly," she replied. "This is difficult to explain, Wil. Especially to a man." She sighed. Could no one at Clifton Hall see what this child needed? Syeira felt a sudden, powerful burst of gratitude towards Mrs Edwards. She wished with all her heart that Miss Clifton might find some mother-like comfort there. Or even a friend. It seemed obvious that the girl was lonely. Syeira, of all people, knew how it felt to be surrounded by family and yet still so alone.

"A girl learns to be a woman from her Mama," Syeira said slowly. "The Romany have other family to supply this learning if a mother passes. Aunts, cousins, sisters." She spoke gently. The duchess's death was a tender area for Wil as well, but Lydia's need cried out to her. "Robbing her of her governess was cruel."

Wil flinched, swallowing visibly. "I wish I could make some objection." His reply was low. "Our traditions are different."

Like herself, Wil had doubtless heard this all his life. That did not make it less hollow. Syeira's voice softened. "A tradition is only a habit that too many people have."

Wil stopped a moment. "That sounds less empty to me." His tone was one of dawning wonder. He smiled at her. "Is that a Romany belief?"

"It is my own thought. I merely mean that all traditions must begin somewhere. It is a Romany tradition that keeps me where I am." Syeira shivered as she spoke, acutely aware of Wil's silence. She'd not meant to speak again of the empty promise that bound her. Wil's warmth tempted her, and oh how she wanted it. Wanted *him*. She shivered again, rearranging her shawl. "Spring may well be on its way but I still find the mornings too cold for my liking. I hope the weather improves."

"Take my coat?"

Syeira shook her head. "I thank you, but then you too will be cold."

"The glass is rising. I shall see about a warmer wrap for you after breakfast."

"There is no need, Wil. Janfri can fetch one from the camp, or I may visit there myself. Valkin is much improved," she spoke rapidly now, wary again.

Wil sighed. "Nonsense. You are my guest. It is my honour to supply all your wants."

The moment the words left his mouth she felt it: that heated connection between them again, a warming flame from the inside out. Any more of his gentle consideration and she might actually melt, chill or no. She might lose herself as well, in this strangely alluring energy between herself and Captain Clifton. *No*. This simply *could not* be. She shook her head again.

"Why won't you let me help you?" he burst out, stopping before the stable gates.

Wil's face reddened and she suspected he hadn't meant to say that out loud. Syeira looked around but they were alone, Lydia having disappeared somewhere towards the ponies at the back. He blinked as Syeira took his hand in hers. "I am not sure what you mean, Wil. Do you mean my—my situation?"

"Well, yes and…and everything. All of it. I wish to ensure you are comfortable but you will accept nothing." His gaze caught hers with such intensity in that moment that she gasped.

Syeira stepped back, furrowing her brow. "I am taught to trade for everything, and also, I do not wish to cause offense but I have been taught never to be in any debt to any Englishman. As a Romany, it is unsafe. As a Romany woman it can be—much worse. Wil, I…" She hesitated. "This is why I must always offer a trade."

"You do not trust me." Disappointment softened his voice.

Now she wished again to close her eyes. The look on his face sharpened the ache inside her too suddenly, twistingly cruel. The man had a point. Wil had not pressed his attentions on her with any force. She had merely told him such attentions were prohibited, not that they were unwelcome. And why had she not asked him to stop?

The memory of yesterday rose up all around her, and she knew: She had not asked him to stop because she did not wish it. The gentle warmth of his mouth claiming hers, his passionate possession that spoke of tenderness thrumming through her skin. No, she did not want this sensation gone. She did not want it drowned out by duty and all the demands to which the Romany princess felt bound. Like all Romany, Syeira prized freedom. Until this moment she had not understood that the freedom to love is the hardest to attain in life by far, and therefore the most precious.

Dropping her gaze, Syeira blushed. "I am caught up in my traditions as much as you, it seems. I would not trade with you if I did not trust you. I have not been taught to trust an Englishman, is all. Do you understand it, Wil?"

"I do, Syeira."

She watched him take a breath, and then another.

"Do you see who *I* am?" he asked finally.

Could any request be more gallant? Syeira nodded slowly. "I did not mean to give offense. If—if you wish to gift me a wrap," she said, looking down, unable to meet his gaze, "I am sure I am most grateful to be so honoured."

Wil lifted her hand to his lips and smiled. "The honour in gifting anything to a lady is always the gentleman's." He kissed her hand, lifting her chin with his finger so she had to meet his eyes again. "I am no exception, Syeira."

His voice warmed. The heated look in his eyes deepened. Her skin felt far too hot beneath his fingertips. She blushed, standing so close to him now. Far too close. Gently, tenderly, she leaned up to kiss his cheek, as his palm curved around her waist, and stopped. Stopped moving entirely, her lips resting against his skin. She inhaled him. Sandalwood and coffee, the musky aroma of him. Breathing in, she held it, leaning back to take him in. Those eyes again. That look. Wil seemed frozen in place.

"Lydie." He cleared his throat, removing his hands from her waist and stepped back.

Glancing behind them, Syeira saw they were in full view of the hall. Loosening her shawl a little more, she decided not to discuss her 'situation' under a rising sun that haloed Wil's golden head like a crown. In any case, it was a Romany matter. He could not help her even if he wanted to. *But that he wanted to…* Her blush deepened as she stood there, struggling to keep her breathing steady. So close to a man she—what? Cared for? Wanted? Loved? *Loved.* There. She'd said it to herself. She need not admit it to anyone else. There was nothing to be done about it, after all.

The day was warming up. The strangeness of the empty stable yard distracted them. The grooms worked the horses early. The stables should be full of activity around this time. Today, the yards were deserted, which was decidedly eerie.

"I am starting to wish for my service pistol," Wil muttered as an arm came across his neck from behind in something like a wrestling hold. Quick as lightning he issued a shout, heaving the attacker over his shoulder in one swift movement. The larger man landed none-too-gently in the opposite horse stall, which, fortunately, happened to be empty. Or empty of horses anyway. It was, however, full of manure.

Syeira grinned and Wil did not even bother trying to hold in his belly laugh when he saw Lord Clifton's reddened face among the hay-wisps and horse dung.

"Damn you, Wil, it was supposed to be my April Fool for you." From where he lay, Lord Clifton looked up and burst out laughing. "How do you like it?" He put out his arm.

"I like it very well," Wil grinned, hauling his brother to his feet and brushing him down. "Welcome home."

Lydia flew at both of them, giggling with delight. "Roger, I told you I could keep your secret."

"Yes, Lydie, yes child. You kept it superbly." Gently, Lord Clifton disengaged himself from his sister's effusive greeting and shook hands with his brother. "We are both of us home for a little, Lydia. How are your studies coming along? Is Miss Lee making much progress?"

His sister pouted. "I do not wish to discuss Miss Lee. I want to know what it was like in the fighting. Were you dreadfully frightened? Did you meet the Marquess of Wellington? Is he as brave as you wrote in your letters?"

"Yes, I did, and yes he is. Bony is quite the scared little game cock to our fine commander's foxhound." Roger suddenly seemed to notice Syeira by the stall door.

He bowed. "Have I the honour of addressing Princess Brishen? Good morning. Wil wrote me your house is in residence. How is Prince Brishen this day?"

Syeira curtsied in response, wondering when she'd ever seen two siblings so contrasting in appearance. Where Wil was tall and fair, with a measure of slow movement that might be called grace, Lord Clifton presented completely differently. He was as tall as Wil, but far broader. His hair was as dark as Wil's was blond. If it were not for his height, he might be mistaken for Romany himself. He looked far more like a man of Brishen than an Englishman.

"We have been looked after far too generously by your brother, my lord. I thank you for your inquiry. Prince Brishen is a great deal better. He moves with some stiffness now, but the movement is an improvement in itself."

Lord Clifton smiled at her. "Excellent." He turned to Wil. "Is there breakfast?"

"Of course."

"Excellent," repeated Lord Clifton. "I arrived for sunrise. I wanted to surprise you."

"You certainly did that." Wil grinned. "I did think your furlough had been granted along with my own. How long can it possibly take to visit your—ahem—that is, to gain your passage?"

Syeira glanced at them both, not forgetting their little sister. Roger, she noted, had enough grace to flush faintly.

"It wasn't all pleasure and delight in the rooms of London you know." Lord Clifton's voice conveyed his derision. "I was summoned before the duke. He had someone 'suitable' for me to meet."

"Ah," replied his brother. "Did you go?"

"Of course I went. You know how His Grace's requests are much like commands."

"I do, Roger." Wil grimaced. "Did you inform the duke about—?"

Lord Clifton snorted. "Of course not. What sort of brother do you take me for? You should know however, that His Grace plans to return to the hall by Easter."

"So he says," Wil countered.

"You don't believe it?" Roger lifted one shoulder in a half-shrug. "Well, you may be right. He has a new—well, that is, the man does not lie straight. Now, how are the school children of White Chapel? Is the illness contained?"

"The news from the village is good," Syeira spoke up before Wil had a chance. "Doctor Haydock has found my tonics effective and the little ones who had breathing troubles are mending now. There has also been no further incidence of fever," she reported, before catching Lord Clifton's gaze. Her voice faltered at the look in his eye.

Roger stared. "I...see." He seemed to have temporarily lost the power of speech. "Ummm, actually I don't. But I will." Turning his head slowly, he fixed his gaze on his brother.

Chapter Twenty-Two

"It was under Haydock's direction," Wil offered and saw Roger relax. No need to tell his brother that in truth, Haydock had ministered under the princess's instruction. Wil worked to keep his face expressionless. He doubted that Roger would have taken such a decision in his place, but he had not been in Wil's place and Wil would never be in his.

Roger's tone was decidedly cooler when he next spoke. "I thank you, princess, for your aid in this matter. Wil, we will discuss this further at a more suitable time. Now, tell me what else is going on."

They discussed estate matters all through breakfast, with Wil outlining the maintenance issues he had come across. He explained the arrangement with the Romany. "Do you approve?"

Roger's response was far more considered than Wil expected. "I approve the *trade*," he said cautiously.

Wil suppressed a smile when his brother caught the princess's death-glare. Her voice was already rising, sultry eyes darkening in warning.

"You do not trust Brishen? The trade is made, sir. The work is already begun. I will not stand to see Brishen treated unfairly in an already-sealed agreement."

Roger raised his palm, meeting Syeira's gaze. "Peace, princess. I agree the trade is fair. It's not that at all," he said levelly. "My acquaintance with Valkin is of some years' standing. I am sure the work Brishen do for the estate is unexceptionable. I am simply offering a cautionary hint to my far-too-responsible brother. I am the heir, but let us not delude ourselves. The duke could *not* approve such a scheme and he is very far from being dead, ma'am." He returned to his breakfast.

"The trade may stand?" Syeira leaned forward, relaxing back at Lord Clifton's nod.

He cut a piece of ham, placed it on his tongue, chewed and swallowed before he spoke again. "Seeing as it is unlikely, no matter what he says, that the duke will be favouring us with his presence, my acquaintance shall join us for Easter. We will fill Mama's Chapel if nothing else." He grinned with an exaggerated shudder. "It will unfortunately exclude the young lady with whom His Grace insisted I ingratiate myself."

"I'll inform Eddy," Wil said.

"Already done," his brother affirmed. "You have taken great care here since your return, Wil and I thank you. I am in residence now, though I have acquaintance to attend."

Wil made no response other than to nod. Directing estate matters was not his place but damn if he apologised for it. He examined his brother. It was fully ten months since they'd last parted in Spain. Roger appeared slimmer. He looked weary and a little worse for wear. It was not only the duke who'd delayed his return, then. Wil wondered what else ailed his brother. A demirep in Cadiz or Paris was the most likely explanation.

"Is your valet with you?'

"Carter arrived with me, yes." Lord Clifton cleared his plate in record time, winking at his sister. "Now, who's for a ride after I've paid my respects to the prince? We'd best go this morning. The glass predicts rain after luncheon."

"A ride, oh I do long to ride again." Seated between her brothers, Lydia clapped her hands in delight. "Princess Brishen took me riding yesterday. I have forgotten so much and am determined to improve."

Wil smiled at his sister. "It is quite a distance to the river side, Lydia, but I will take a turn in the park with you if you wish it." Shrugging when she puffed out her cheeks, he turned to the princess. "Princess? Will you join us?"

Grinning at Lydia's evident joy in having her two brothers home again, Syeira rose, nodding as the gentlemen did the same. "You will excuse me, Lord Clifton. It is a fine day for a ride to be sure, but I must return to my brother."

"Indeed?" Lord Clifton responded. "This is a pity, princess. Still, I hope you will both join us for supper and cards this evening. I have acquaintance arriving from York. Will the prince be enough recovered?"

Syeira laughed. "I've never seen yet the shot that could keep my brother from your card table, my lord. I, however, am bid to the village with Doctor Haydock. There is more work to do there still. I will join your game if I am in time."

Lord Clifton bowed. "A great pity, princess," he replied, watching her go.

Wil watched his brother staring after Syeira. He knew that look, and he knew Lord Clifton. *Damn.* He cleared his throat. "The cottages closest to the Lune, Roger?"

His brother turned, blinking at him. "Yes?"

Wil explained some of the problems the thaw may have caused. His brother poured them both coffee and waved his words away. "Yes, yes. Yates will no doubt take me through it. I assure you that the tenants' concerns will be addressed." Roger glanced again at the door through which Syeira had departed.

"So the princess Brishen does not ride?"

"Oh, she rides." Wil's wistful tone was obvious, even to him.

"Wil says Princess Brishen has the finest seat he's yet witnessed in a woman," Lydia chimed in.

Wil groaned inwardly. That child and her effervescent mouth.

"Is that so?" Roger sharpened his gaze on Wil. "That's quite a claim."

"She's—ahem—quite a rider." Wil ignored the heat rising into his cheeks. Roger merely appeared cavalier. In truth, he was no fool.

"Have you seen her mount?" Lydia went on.

Wil leaned his elbow on the table, sinking his face in his palm. He did not need to see Roger's face to know what he was thinking. His brother's acute focus speared him across the uncleared table. Without raising his head, Wil addressed his sister.

"Lydia," he began. "If you've finished your breakfast, perhaps you'd best change for riding?"

Lydia smiled sweetly, helping herself to more ham.

Wil cleared his throat, determined to avoid further conversation about the princess. "Which acquaintance arrive from York today, and when do they come?"

Glancing at Lydia, Roger eyed Wil in a way that indicated his inquisition was merely postponed, and said, "The well-behaved ones. The better behaved, anyway. Horsham and his friends.

Maynooth will be glad to see you. He accompanies his wife and her cousin. Are you acquainted with Lady Maynooth?"

Wil shook his head. "Not at all."

"Her cousin is said to be quite the musician."

"I'll take your word for it, Roger."

"Her father is a general's aide, Wil."

That got his attention. "Her cousin is…?"

"Lady Maria Huntingdon. Just out, and quite lovely."

"Thank you for the hint."

"Even the duke could not disapprove." His brother glanced again at the empty doorway. "Lady Maria is eminently suitable, you know. No doubt she is as keen to be allied to the duchy as any daughter of the ton."

Wil's appetite evaporated. He'd rather the army than wedlock. He had no need to be shackled to both, and the sooner he followed up his commission the better. He pushed his breakfast away and stood, bowing to his sister.

"I must see if I've any letters regarding my commission. Meet me in the hall in a quarter hour, Lydie." He smiled stiffly as she clapped her hands again. "I'll take you round the park myself. We'll ride to the edge of the woods if you're up to it."

His sister's squeal of delight followed him all the way up the stairs. Fresh air and exercise were a good idea for the both of them.

Chapter Twenty-Three

Wil thought to breakfast alone with Syeira on Maundy Thursday as Roger and his guests rarely rose early, and Lydia had begun an early morning riding practise. Syeira had not yet made an appearance by the time the covers were brought in but his expectations were forestalled in any case, by Lady Maria Huntingdon rustling in to join him.

"Good morning, captain." She curtsied, allowing him to see to her chair.

"Lady Huntingdon." He bowed. "How do you find Lancashire?"

"A little wetter than I had anticipated, captain, but the company quite exceeds my expectations." Here she turned to face him directly, offering a tight little smile and a cryptic nod of the head. "I have written to Papa on your behalf. I understand you shall hear something in a day or two."

Wil swallowed. "I thank you. It is generous of you to think of me."

The lady waved his words away as though they were so many dust motes. "Nonsense. Lord Clifton's recommendation is enough but even if it were not, you very nearly have all the *right* connections here. Evidently you ought to be a major, and the sooner the better if you ask me."

"I am keen to return to the army."

"Most commendable, captain. Once you've your new commission perhaps you may consider more—permanent—changes in your life." She smiled.

There was something about that smile. It did not reach her eyes, but before he could study it further it disappeared, as though fleeing the young lady's face forever. Wil wondered at her intentions. She must know he had little to offer, other than his rank.

The oak door creaked and Syeira rushed in from the entrance hall rather than the stairs, smiling and out of breath. She paused, curtsying to her companions before smiling again at them both.

"Good morning, Lady Huntingdon, Captain Clifton."

Lady Huntingdon hardly rose. Wil stood, losing the thread of his conversation with Lady Huntingdon entirely.

"You've been out already? I thought you may be taking some well-earned rest, Princess Brishen."

Syeira laughed, shaking her head. "I do not like to be so still indoors all the time. I rode Valkin's horse to the village to visit with Doctor Haydock. I stopped also by the Little Chapel to see that we complete your trade on time."

Wil shook himself slightly to banish the image of Syeira mounted and riding into a rising dawn. "How does the Little Chapel look?"

"Trade?" Lady Huntingdon asked, and Syeira explained how the trade had come about.

"There is some delay in works after the rain so I am assisting Brishen with the gardening. I think you will be pleased." Syeira took her seat. "Would you care to ride over with us, Lady Huntingdon? We go to pay our respects to the late duchess."

The mention of the Duchess seemed to galvanise Lady Huntingdon. She actually sat up straighter. "Of course. I shall be glad to accompany you all." She said this with another of her little smiles directed at Wil. Wil suddenly found himself far less keen on the idea of such an outing.

Syeira did not seem to notice. She had more important news to impart. "The prince will be well enough to ride with us on Holy Saturday, if he takes care."

"This is excellent news," Wil swallowed, trying for cheer amid his dismay. With the prince healed and the estate back to rights, was it time to let Brishen go? "It's wonderful your brother is so well-recovered. You are highly skilled, Syeira. Brishen House is most fortunate."

"Indeed," breathed Lady Huntingdon, staring between Wil and Syeira as though confounded by a puzzle.

"I thank you. I am pleased to assist all whom I can." The princess smiled gently, a quiet, inward curling of her lovely lips as her pride showed itself to him softly for perhaps the first time.

Lady Huntingdon began speaking again and Wil turned to grant her the smile and attention she must be expecting. It was no use. A moment later, his gaze turned back to Syeira. He read her blush and the glimmer of pride in her startling eyes for what it was. Well, she ought to be proud. Achievements such as hers were no small thing. He opened his mouth to say so, and prudently closed it again without speaking. There was something to be said for listening to one's instincts.

***

That same afternoon, Wil stared out his window at Clifton Park. Originally designed as a formal garden, it now looked the part, having been pruned assiduously over the past few weeks. The Brishen were skilled artisans and knew the correctness that would best please the English. There were no more wildly growing weeds in this reclaimed garden. Neat little beds of pansies and Sweet William studded the richly turned earth, bordered by snapdragons, marigolds and columns of Lancaster rose bushes that did not dare bend. Wil imagined these plants tied tightly to attention and thought of the duke.

His Grace's topiary was once again clipped into shape and the sandstone paving had been scrubbed. Despite the recent rains, there was no sign of staining. Not even a browned leaf dared appear. Wil allowed his gaze to drift up to the figures in the garden and stopped pretending to admire the skill of the Romany gardeners. Lord Maynooth and his wife could be seen whisking out of sight behind a fountain. Her cousin seemed to be elsewhere, presumably with her 'great friend', the Earl of Horsham.

Wil hardly noticed their absence. His attention was rather more fully engaged in watching the princess Syeira walking Clifton Park—on the arm of Lord Clifton. True, the Romany prince walked with them, leaning a little on Roger's arm, but Wil still did not like it. He liked it even less when there chanced to be a slight change. Prince Brishen seated himself on the prettily placed iron bench, clearly done in for the moment, while the princess and Lord Clifton walked on.

"Do you think this wise, captain?" Hudson asked as he laced his master into his fencing jacket. Forcing himself away from the sight of Syeira laughing with his brother, Wil inhaled sharply, turned back to his valet, and shrugged.

"That is the third time you have asked me that." He spoke without irritation. When Hudson pushed a point, he had a reason.

"Yet you have made no answer." His man completed Wil's toilette and handed him his épée mask. "Lord Clifton is an excellent challenger."

Wil tested his épée, lunging lightly at his valet.

Hudson very properly did not move, though his lips twitched a little.

Wil shook his head, replaced his weapon, and tested the balance of the other blade. "Better." He turned back to his valet. "Lord Clifton has agreed to the bout. It has been too long since we have had the pleasure of challenging each other."

He lunged again, smiling at his valet. Hudson did not smile back. Instead, he nodded in the direction of Clifton Park. "Is it your intent to duel Lord Clifton this morn, Captain?"

"There is a storm incoming," Wil replied. "Have the fire ready-laid in the princess's rooms, if you please, Hudson."

"I shall speak with Mrs Edwards about laying a fire, Captain," Hudson replied. "Would you not rather a game of billiards?"

Wil glared. "No. The billiards room needs airing."

"Oh—er, does it, captain?" His valet's voice was far too disingenuous.

"And the felts need replacing," Wil added. Besides, he was terrible at billiards. Roger would be sure to win.

***

Syeira listened politely as Lord Clifton listed the plants in Clifton Park and how the garden design had been completed with paving stone from York. She chose not to mention that her host confused two species of flower and mispronounced one of his roses. Englishmen did not like to be corrected; they had this in common with Romany men.

"I understand you enjoy riding as much as your brother?" Lord Clifton smiled at her. It was a similar smile to his brother's but somehow not as warm. It did not quite reach his eyes. There was something far less open about Lord Roger Clifton.

"Yes. I enjoy a spirited canter, my lord." She did not wish to misunderstand anything. Speaking with Roger felt far less…truthful. *Was that the word? Did the English* have *a word for a man who seemed so intent on insincerity?* Conversing with the duke's heir seemed a sort of game. Syeira already knew Lord Clifton was good-humoured, and witty. There was still something amiss in her estimation.

Still, Clifton Hall was his domain even more so than his brother's, and he was doing his best to charm her. His talk was entertaining enough, but Syeira did not feel at ease in his presence. She sighed inwardly, careful not to let Lord Clifton see her *ennui*.

The princess looked back at her brother, turning into a paved pathway to keep within his sight. Their host was not going to succeed in flattering his vanity today. Syeira had not spent her time among the English for nothing. She recognised worn-out charms when she heard them, and the way to tell a genuine smile from a calculated one. Lowering her shoulders, she smiled back at Lord Clifton, as expected. She was grateful when the young man appeared by the archway to the park, calling to them.

"My lord?"

Roger turned, his tone altering to one of impatience. "What is it, Carter?"

"Captain Clifton awaits you in the larger lower room. With épées."

A slow smile creased Lord Clifton's face, warming his eyes properly for the first time since he began their walk. "Excellent. Tell him I shall be with him directly." He turned back to Syeira. "Would you care to join us, princess?" He rubbed his hands together in evident delight. "It seems Wil has challenged me to a bout."

"A 'bout'?" Syeira repeated. "Is this some sort of fight?" They had reached her brother by this time and the prince rose to his feet.

"A bout of fencing, my sister, my *pen*." Valkin accepted Lord Clifton's assistance as they made their way back to the Hall. "It is a sport of great skill and quite something to watch. It is a pity Janfri is not here. I should like him to learn the sport."

"I should be happy to show him at any time," Lord Clifton replied. "What say you to a wager?"

Valkin laughed. "Name your terms."

Syeira said nothing. There were some traditions she believed ought to be left behind. English or Romany, this fascination men had for pointing weapons at each other in the guise of 'sport' still made no sense to her. Nevertheless, as the sky lowered and the wind blew up, an afternoon indoors seemed a sensible course. She followed Roger's other guests to the lower rooms where Lord Clifton's valet assisted him into the required costume. Lord Maynooth called for his purse and even his young wife asked about the odds. The Earl of Horsham made a later, but ruddy-faced, appearance with Lady Huntingdon.

"A guinea on Clifton," he said.

Hudson stepped forward, clearly used to such dealings. "*Which* Clifton, m'lord?"

Syeira watched the valets moving from guest to guest, even approaching Valkin.

"Princess?" Hudson bowed. "Would you care to place a wager?"

Syeira stared at him, about to shake her head. She had no coin of her own, and Romany women did not gamble. She watched as her brother placed a small amount on Roger to win, something Valkin had clearly done before. She took a deep breath and closed her eyes briefly. Did she dare? Opening her eyes to find her brother's attention too fully engaged in charming Lady Maynooth, Syeira made up her mind. The Romany prince always enjoyed himself among the English. Why should his sister not do the same? Slowly, carefully, Syeira removed two full silver pins from her hair, handing them to the valet.

"May I wager these?"

Hudson examined them minutely, straightening up immediately once he'd decided. "Certainly, princess."

Syeira noticed that Wil's valet did not need her to declare which Clifton she trusted to win. Once both men were suitably attired, and their guests gathered, the exhibition began in earnest. Syeira's nerves tightened as Carter stood between the two masked figures.

"*En garde. Prêts?*" He returned their nods, stepping well back.

"*Allez.*"

The odds altered as soon as Lord Clifton lifted his blade, the valets moving among the guests to adjust the wagers as demanded. Syeira barely noticed. Her focus remained on the action itself, and the danger. In the back of her mind she felt her fear. Saw a man fall from his horse, a mother dying, an ailing father with a diminishing mind. Her brother collapsing on an open field, the scent of cordite, and again, she wished to close her eyes. She felt ill, faint, a thousand other nervous ailments for which no remedy existed because this—this fear—was the other side of love. It is what you face when you love someone, and she faced it now. Syeira swallowed, keeping her eyes resolutely open.

The two competitors moved so often and so quickly that she was soon uncertain as to who was whom. The sky outside flashed and growled. Soon she felt Miss Clifton seated beside her. The little girl clapped and squealed at certain moments, solidifying Syeira's opinion that this sport was not entirely safe. Each time the blades struck torso or limb, Syeira felt her nails score her palms until she was certain she'd drawn a little blood. Soft sounds of fear fell from her lips as the feeling in the pit of her gut worsened, anxiety coiling and uncoiling until she was nauseous, and still she did not turn her head.

At one point, Lydia leaned in to whisper, "If Papa was here, my brothers would be forced to take this game out of doors."

As one of the challengers almost toppled an ancient shield (Wil? Roger? She could no longer tell the two men apart), Syeira was for the first time in agreement with the formidable incumbent of Clifton Hall. This did not improve her opinion of duelling for sport.

The clink of blades punctuated the flickering lightning outside. Syeira felt Lydia's hand creep into her own and she held it fast, squeezing until the child gasped in pain. She released Miss Clifton without an apology or even a turn of the head. All her focus, all her attention remained fixed on the men with the blades, watching each challenger thrust forward as his opponent parried while swiftly shifting position.

The momentum accelerated along with the rhythm of the game. It was something of a dance and, given the grace such a sport required, she thought Wil might have the upper hand. She imagined him to be the slightly taller figure who made more of the successful thrusts. Soon she was watching the flashing glint of this blade as eagerly as she urged her brothers' Romany stock to victory at Appleby. Each time his blade was parried, she sighed. When he was hit, she winced. Her heart hammered at her ribs and she bit her lower lip so hard she tasted blood.

Looking round briefly, she noticed that Hudson had stationed himself in the doorway, staring at the two challengers with a rather severe eye. Perhaps he did not share her confidence in his master's ability, and surely Wil's personal valet would know more of this than she. Syeira grabbed Lydia's hand again, squeezing in response to another flash outside the window. Another attack on the torso of the man she loved.

Finally, the taller figure all but disarmed the other, holding him at the point of the épée. The defeated player surrendered his blade, raising his hands before coming to attention with a bow. The victor removed his mask first. Lord Clifton's ruddy-faced delight lacked his brother's grace of manner, but he had clearly won and it had not been easy.

"You about had me with that last cutover," he grinned, clapping Wil on the back.

Captain Clifton removed his mask slowly. His disappointment was fleeting but Syeira saw it. "I am no match for you, Roger. I enjoyed the challenge though." He smiled at his brother and shook his hand.

"As did I." Lord Clifton turned to their guests. "Did he not acquit himself well, gentlemen?" Then, addressing Syeira, he continued, "What did you think of the game, princess?"

Like the others, Valkin was warmly effusive but his sister remained silent. As Roger's other guests gathered around the valets to settle their wagers, Lydia excused herself to return to her drawing. Syeira glanced at Wil, standing there, his mask in hand, watching her.

"You did not give us your opinion," Wil persisted.

Syeira glanced down. "I do not think there are any here who would care to hear it." The heat in her cheeks burned and this time it was not from desire.

"I am not the best exemplar of the sport. Roger is far more skilled," Wil faced her then, with a determined, penetrating stare. "This is not why you did not speak your mind, is it?"

Syeira took a breath, looking up at him. "If you truly wish to hear my opinion, I will give it," she answered. "But I do not think any sporting Englishman will like it."

"Nevertheless, I am curious to hear it."

"Then you shall have it." She met his gaze and spoke her mind. "I thank you for your exhibition. It was most impressive." She swallowed. "I still do not see the point of playing so many games."

Wil's eyebrows rose so high they disappeared into his hairline. "Games?"

"Pistols, cards, duels—all these games you *gentlemen* play." Syeira did her best to keep the indignation from her voice, fearing she failed because she simply could not see sense in such folly. Not when there was clearly a chance of injury.

"Are not wars enough for you? I enjoy a good contest as much as anyone, but the risk to yourselves... It is worth this for you, Wil?" Her voice broke and she closed her mouth, lest she expose herself entirely, but not before uttering a final few words.

"You could have been hurt." Her shaking whisper tore from her throat. Turning away in earnest, she practically ran from the room.

Chapter Twenty-Four

Wil stared after her. He did not miss the slight tremor in her voice, or the fear looming in her dark eyes as she turned away from them all. He was distantly aware of Lady Huntingdon laughing with Prince Brishen, Horsham and Maynooth counting their winnings, Lady Maynooth fluttering between them. Roger holding court, dissecting every thrust. All of it faded somehow to a distant buzzing. Syeira's words echoed in her wake, as though he could see them in the air.

You could have been hurt.

She'd been worried. Concerned and scared something could have gone wrong. Scared for him. *Him.* He felt suddenly unequal to standing and looked vaguely around for a chair. Hudson tapped his shoulder, whispered information. Wil took back the silver pins and handed his purse to his valet, making as discreet an exit as he was able.

He had to find her. His first instinct was to call for his horse, but Janfri had taken the Romany horse, so where would Syeira go? It took him a moment to realise something was tugging at his ankle. Biting, actually. Looking down, he saw the spaniel pup attempting to chew the soft leather of his fencing shoe.

"Stop that." Lydia rushed in, catching the little dog up. "Wil, what on earth did you say to the princess?"

"You've seen her?" He did his best to sound nonchalant.

"Of course." Lydia frowned. "Though why she'd want to be outside in a storm makes no sense to me." His sister gave him a look that rivalled Princess Brishen's.

"The storm?" Wil flicked a glance at the window. It looked as though all the oceans of the world were pouring from the skies above Clifton Hall. Above Clifton Woods. *The woods.*

Wil creaked the main door open. Shrugging in against the blinding, freezing rain, he faced the walk across the estate the way he'd faced his commanding officer. *Quick march.*

He found her beneath the old cypress tree in the Little Chapel kirkyard. Though it was difficult to hear anything above the pounding rain, he detected murmuring. A steady stream of Romany words, most of which he was fairly certain were curses. Wil shivered where he stood.

"Are you all right?"

She did not reply. Her eyes were closed, her brow pressing lightly against the tree trunk. The drumming rain increased in volume. Or her silence made it seem that way.

"Syeira, are you—"

"I heard what you said," she shouted without turning around, crying aloud to the sky as much as to him. "Stefan falling from his horse, my Mama succumbing to illness. Papa cannot help the feebleness of his mind now. Valkin's ribs and now you—you. *You.*" She swallowed, clearly doing her best to rein herself in, but there was no stopping this now. "You play at tragedy like it is nothing." She wiped uselessly at cheeks that would be wet anyway, even without the rain, and it was then that Wil realised: Syeira stood with her back turned to him, wet through and getting wetter—and *crying*.

"Why are you crying?" His voice was as gentle as ripples on lake water. Like ripples, it had a calming effect. "I *assure* you, there was no danger."

"You misunderstand." Syeira sniffed indelicately. "I am crying because there *was* danger. There was clearly a chance you could be hurt, and you do not care. You care less than I do and that is wrong. *Wrong.*" She sucked in a breath. "It is like everything in this place. The games matter more than the people, and I—I cannot learn such careless ways to live." She stopped then and seemed nearly to sway. "I *will* not," she affirmed and Wil only heard her because he was attuned to her voice now, taking in each word. She did not turn, did not even look at him.

Reaching out, he touched her shoulder. She jumped. Started, actually, whirling around as though ready to unleash another cyclonic scolding.

"How could you?" she said next. "How *could* you?" Her voice, when she spoke, was quiet now in a sad and frightening way. Like the hush before battle. A heartbeat later she launched herself at him, beating at his chest with all the strength she had in those slender, skilful, wonderful hands now balled into fists, weapons and utterly,

utterly useless against the thickness of his fencing jacket and his soldier's strength.

"Syeira. Stop it, Syeira. There was no danger." He tried vainly to capture her flailing fists and then gave up, letting her beat out her fear over his well-guarded heart until she stopped, exhausted and worn out with the frustration of not reaching him. Not touching him.

She sagged into him as though he were an oak. An oak with arms that came up automatically to hold her against him, as though this was always supposed to happen to him, and she was always supposed to end up pressed against his chest, and Wil stood there, utterly at a loss and amazed.

"There was no danger," he repeated, holding her fast as tremors shook through her. Fear, fear for *him*, and he was no less astonished now than he had been that day in the lake.

"Syeira, I—" He stopped because she gave a little whimper, holding him tighter and turning her face into his body. Breath heaving, face streaming with rain and tears and God-knew-what, she stepped back, staring at the dirt. Again, she would not meet his eyes. So, he tipped up her chin, turning her head resolutely towards him. Wil saw her face then, her eyes.

"Ah." That furious rage he remembered from the morning of the duel. This time, he did not step back from her anger. This time, he understood that the anger was not anger, but fear. A fear for those you loved. He thought of Lydia and Roger and his dear Mama.

"It was not my intent to hurt you, Syeira."

"What was your intent?" She stepped back, removing herself from his hands. Keeping him at bay with the force of her glare alone. "Why would you risk yourself so? In front of your family?"

Wil shifted uncomfortably on the spot. His challenge to Roger suddenly seemed the act of a far younger man. He tried to look rueful, fearing he failed. He was soaking wet and freezing cold, but a scalding heat broke across his body and he must have turned red.

"I—honestly, Syeira, I do not know," he replied, shocked by his own admission. "It is what we do. We are sportsmen. Games are sport. Surely the Romany—well, I know Brishen race horses. That's a game of sorts, is it not?"

Syeira exhaled and nodded. "Yes, but—"

"But nothing," Wil broke in. "There *was* no risk. It was only Roger. In any case, I can look after myself." He paused. This was not about the fencing. Or even the wagers. "I regret anything I have done to pain you, Syeira, but I do not understand."

"I know." Her low voice was audible only because the driving rain had stopped. The drip-drip as water tipped from leaf to leaf and branch to branch seemed loud in the sudden quiet. Nothing settled, and everything did. The storm was over, and in its aftermath, a serenely sad silence lay between them.

"I am sorry you lost your pins," he said then, to use up the silence. To fill it and perhaps bring a smile to her face. It didn't work. The sky remained grey.

Syeira shook herself as the wind came up, staring at him as though he were far away. Wil could only imagine how cold she must be now.

"Oh Wil, do you not see?" She looked suddenly ill and he felt the first stirrings of alarm.

"What do I not see?"

"Love." Her voice broke and she stopped speaking.

"Love," he repeated, breathless, the word as foreign as pain-relieving leaves, as new as this sensation currently invading his chest. He stood still enough to have been the work of stonemasons himself. He could not think what to do. What to say. Every part of him so utterly still. Then he took her hands in his. They were freezing and shaking as he lifted them to his mouth. He kissed them, pulling her in close again. So close he could feel the pounding of her fiercely magnanimous heart all the way through his thickest fencing jacket. He touched his lips to hers so tenderly. As though she were made of porcelain and he had, indeed, been careless.

A strange tolling sound made him start. The Little Chapel bell ringing in four o'clock. Tea, and the arrival of more guests for Lord Clifton.

Syeira pushed against him reluctantly. "Lord Clifton expects Prince and Princess Brishen to greet his guests. I must change." Her voice sounded rusty, as though it had been an age since she last spoke. "You ought to attend Lady Huntingdon in to dinner."

Wil smiled humourlessly. "Is that an order, princess?"

"It is good sense," she responded softly, sadly. "Is it not?"

She would ask nothing of him. Not even the silver pins in his hand. Wil dropped his arms, releasing her, and it felt like a betrayal. A crime. He watched Syeira walking determinedly away from him towards the hall, weighed down by the wet silk. Nevertheless, she held herself ramrod-straight, reminding him of an infantryman returning to battle.

Love. He barely felt the wind whipping around his thoroughly wet costume. He ought to feel it. He ought to be chilled to the bone, but Syeira's words seeped through him, warming from within, pooling in the pit of his belly even as he recognised the recklessness of such a feeling. Of such a love. The princess Brishen had no place scolding anybody for careless behaviour when she—*when she what?* Spoke to him of love and walked away from it? A shiver raced down his spine and he closed his eyes, placed his brow against the cypress tree and swore. *Love?* Since when was love enough?

By the time Wil reached the hall, the wind was turning and the rain blowing back around again. Hudson met him in the drive, brandishing a letter.

"The seal is from Whitehall, captain."

Wil took it up, breaking the seal then and there and perusing the few scrawled lines in a daze.

"Is it your commission, captain? Are you made?" Hudson asked, almost hopping in place. Wil glanced at him, and the man stood still.

"It is, Hudson. I may purchase in General Wallis's regiment, if I am able to close by the end of the quarter." He smiled as a queer feeling took him over. It wasn't quite elation. At least not the elation it ought to have been.

"This is excellent news, Sir. Congratulations."

Wil permitted himself a half-smile. "It is, Hudson, I thank you. Where is Lord Clifton?"

Roger exited the door as two carriages came to a mud-splattering stop and Wil hauled himself and his valet out of their path just in time.

"You've had a wet journey," his brother was saying. "Come in, come in, do. There's a warm fire and some refreshments awaiting you in the parlour."

The doors opened, the footmen arranged themselves and clouds of muslin and taffeta swirled round him. Men shook hands and offered their arms, inquired after each others' birds and all the usual things. At the centre of it all was Lord Clifton, his charming, ebullient self. Wil followed the crowd, keeping to the back.

He stood a moment at the foot of the ancient stone steps leading up to the great oak door, amid the swish of cloaks and grumbling of maids and footmen as they were forced to move around his stillness. Then the heavens opened, the downpour began again and Wil stood there, feeling the pressed paper from Whitehall coming apart in his fingers until it was nothing but a soggy, inarticulate mess. He had his commission, his way to leave the hall, and it brought him no comfort at all.

Something else pressed sharply against the skin of his palm. Looking down at the mess that had been his letter, he realised he still held two solid silver hair pins—and then he knew. He did love her. He must. And there was absolutely nothing he could do about it. The exquisite pain of the realisation brought a pricking sensation to his eyes.

Roger reappeared and stared at him. "Wil? What the deuce are you doing? You're wet through, man." He glanced behind him. "Lady Huntingdon awaits you. Are you ever going to change for dinner or do you intend another bout over the meat?"

Attending Lady Huntingdon in to dinner suddenly seemed reassuring. Wil shook himself, taking the steps to the huge oak door at a run. He'd best get inside before he drowned.

Chapter Twenty-Five

Lydia and her little dog waited in Syeira's room. The princess had agreed that stormy nights necessitated such sleeping arrangements, even while Syeira attended on her hosts for dinner. Besides, having the little girl sleep in her room felt so much like Camp Brishen that Syeira found herself quite as grateful for the arrangement as Miss Clifton.

"Oh, princess." The girl flew at her and Syeira found herself caught up and tightly clasped by her second Clifton for the day. At least this one was safe from foolish challenges with pistols and swords.

"Good evening, Miss Clifton." She clasped the girl tight for a moment before stepping back to curtsey, stumbling a little in the heaviness of wet silk.

"Oooh, you are wet, Syeira," Miss Clifton exclaimed. "You cannot appear at dinner so."

Syeira smiled. "Thank you, Miss Clifton, I am aware of this." Drawing out her three other gowns, she laid each out on the enormous bed. "Which do you think most suitable for cards?"

Lydia leapt upon a deep burgundy silk with many Romany ruffles. Tiny silver threads woven through the fabric enhanced the shimmer when the cloth moved under the light.

"This one. Oh, wear this one, princess, *please*." Lydia stroked the ears of her little dog. "It sets off your colouring."

Syeira could not help laughing. "I thank you, Miss Clifton," she nodded. "Burgundy silk it is." Stripping off her soaked dove-coloured gown, she arranged it near the fire. Her shift was wet through.

"Hmmm," she mused aloud. "I do not have another." She placed it before the fire as well.

Lydia leapt off the chaise and all but ran for the door.

Syeira turned in astonishment. "Miss Clifton, child. What is wrong?"

"You—you are changing your dress."

"Of course. I must. Even if it were not Lord Clifton's card party tonight, the other is wet through." Syeira's brows rose. "There is no need to race out of here as though all the armies of France were after you."

"Oh." The child stared. "Miss Lee orders me out of the nursery wing when she tries on gowns. Do you not wish me to go away too?"

Syeira sat down on the chaise, patting the space next to her. "Listen to me, Miss—*Lydia*," she began. "We are going to have a talk about Miss Lee, and about you and I. *I* say, you may stay." She looked the young girl in the eye, her expression serious. "As you know, I am a princess. If I say it, this must be so. Do you understand it?"

Miss Clifton nodded, a small smile creeping uncertainly over her face.

"You will find, I think, that I am not like your governess at all," Syeira finished.

Lydia's smile widened. "No, you're not. You're much prettier. And you let me stay." This was clearly the most appealing part for Miss Clifton.

Syeira shook her head to hide her smile. "At the Romany camp, I often dress in the same small space as my sisters."

"How many sisters do you have?" The girl's face lit with curiosity.

Syeira pretended a grimace. "Three younger sisters, and three brothers younger than Valkin. You have met Janfri?"

Lydia nodded. "He played bowls with me and Bony."

"Very sporting of Bony, I'm sure. Your pup may stay with you in here tonight while I attend the card party. He is not to sleep in the bed if you please."

"No indeed, Syeira."

On this particular evening, such child's chatter was as welcome as the blazing fire in the grate. Syeira had no wish to be alone with her thoughts. Not now. Possibly not ever. Still, she would not be sorry for speaking the truth. Not to Miss Clifton and not to her brother. She turned to the glass and studied her hair, remembering only one style that required so few pins.

With Lydia's help, she began work on her braids.

"You have such beautiful hair, princess." Miss Clifton seemed to enjoy dressing it. "And such lovely pins. Wherever did you find them?"

"I traded for them," Syeira explained. "Many years ago, when I was about your age."

"There, now." Lydia twined the last braid around itself and tucked it behind another. "You do look lovely."

"I thank you, Miss Clifton." Syeira kissed the little girl who settled down comfortably enough in the enormous bed while she visited next door to assist her brother.

She knocked once, entering on Valkin's command.

"There you are." Valkin smiled. "Are you all right, Syeira?"

"I am quite well, Valkin, thank you." Stepping in to check his wound, she saw the puckered skin pinking up nicely. "Hush now." She tapped at his ribcage, feeling for softness. Valkin seemed to know she did not need silence to check his ribs.

"You disappeared after the fencing exhibition."

"I needed some air," Syeira replied stiffly.

"In this?" Her brother pointed to the rain-lashed window.

"Do not move so," she ordered, taking his arm and touching his ribcage gently. "I can take care of myself, Valkin." Her tone softened when she saw his face. "Any pain?"

"No. Some stiffness though." Valkin held himself as still as possible while she completed her examination. The rib was healed, no question about it. The bone had knitted well, and apart from a small irregularity in his symmetry, Valkin appeared to be whole.

Syeira smiled with relief. "It is good, Valkin. It is healed. The stiffness is to be expected after so long a time of inactivity." She looked up at him, seeing his shoulders drop. "Please, take care for a few more days when you ride or run or shoot with the English gentlemen. How do you feel?"

"I feel like myself again." He reached for his shirt. "Restless. Strong. Ready to ride again. I have missed my horses." He beamed at her, bowing. "I thank you my sister, my *pen*."

Syeira watched him move with pride. "Is there pain when you bow?"

Valkin shook his head, bowing again. Syeira curtsied. Her brother took her hands, swinging her lightly in a few steps of one of the Scottish reels she knew a little.

He laughed. "No lasting harm at all. It is quite wonderful. Thank you." His gaze brightened as he took in her appearance. "And you look wonderful, Syeira. Truly."

"As do you, Valkin. A true Romany prince, from your hair to the toes of your boots. Papa would be proud." Kneeling, she tied the ceremonial sash around her brother's hips, checking his dress as he had hers. He was magnificent. Bright, proud and darkly handsome.

A teasing smile rose to her lips. "Lady Maria Huntingdon will be enchanted."

Her brother shrugged. "Perhaps. I think it far more likely she is enchanted with Captain Clifton. Or the duchy at any rate. I understand that Lady Huntingdon has persuaded her father to find Wil a new commission. I should think he'll be leaving Clifton Hall with the rest of us."

"*With* House Brishen?" Syeira could barely speak the words. The sting of it hit her low in her belly and she gasped. One heavy, low, guttural sound was all she allowed herself. Blinking hard until the sensation of imminent tears rolled back, she swallowed a pain more bitter than belladonna powder, clenching her teeth as she bit it back. *So, this is love.* Love and pain. Giving up everything you want for the happiness of another. She scowled once, briefly, and her brother saw.

His voice was a gentle thing and his words carefully chosen. "Syeira. You must know, my sister, my *pen,* that the English will never—" he stopped himself. Took a breath. "Captain Clifton cannot remain in the service of the king with a Romany wife." He spoke the words slowly, with infinite regret. "The man must keep himself, Syeira. What else would you have him do?"

"Nothing." Her voice was clipped, cold, and so unlike her usual tones that Valkin seemed alarmed. Answering his look, Syeira shook her head. "There is nothing else he can do, Valkin. His commission—well, it is what he always wanted. I am—I am most pleased for him."

Her brother's eyebrows rose. "You might consider rehearsing that a little more before we go down," he said dryly. "Or hope the English cannot see through such poor Romany acting."

Is that so? Syeira glared at him with all the fire she could muster. To her surprise, Valkin smiled back.

"That's better," he spoke softly, seemingly aware that more talk on this matter could only hurt her further. "Spirit is better than sadness, Syeira." He paused again, looking at her carefully as though he too were afraid she might shatter. "Any pain?"

"None that the English shall see." Straightening, Syeira turned to the door, smiling a wide, large smile entirely unlike her own. *Oh yes, Valkin. Pain for days my* prala, *my brother. Pain for days.*

"Your bravery is appreciated. Brishen will not forget it," he vowed. "You are also a terrible liar."

A soft laugh fell from her mouth as she turned to gaze at her brother. "No doubt I shall improve." There was love here. It was not the same love her heart desired for so long, but this was family. This was Brishen. This was love *too*.

Gathering her courage, she exhaled and adjusted her stance. Bringing her hands in front of her, she saw Valkin do the same. Once, twice, three breaths for calm. For love. For the family of Brishen. Syeira completed one more. For herself. For luck and a last evening with their hosts. She released this final breath slowly, tasting goodbye.

Valkin held out his arm. Syeira placed her hand above his. His other hand closed over hers as though he were, indeed, holding her in place for all of Brishen. She looked at him unflinchingly. "We are ready."

"Ready for what, Syeira?"

"To meet Lord Clifton's guests, of course."

To say goodbye. To return home. To let go.

***

Dinner was a lively affair, with too many courses and too many people. Romany party guests were unusual, and many of Lord Clifton's friends were simply fascinated. They pressed Syeira and Valkin for more details about the places they'd travelled and the strange sights they'd seen. To these inquiries Syeira responded with pleasure. Lord Clifton held court and Syeira found she could avoid Wil quite well if she simply sat beside her brother and assisted him with introductions.

"I simply adore your silk," Lady Maynooth smiled graciously. "May I inquire as to its origin, princess?"

Syeira smiled politely back. "Of course, Lady Maynooth. It is a unique Brishen tint. The colour is fitting for Michaelmas, is it not?"

The lady's eyes went wide with delight as Syeira discussed fashions and styles, the colours of the silks Brishen had in process, and began her trade. Straightening her shoulders, she reminded herself that she was here for Brishen as much as Valkin was. They had not yet secured a place to camp for the winter. The familiar conversation soothed her as she fell back on competence, conversing for her house with confidence.

Beside her, her brother traded shares in his racing ventures for permission to hunt on the well-stocked Boscowan estate in Derbyshire. English dinners were social events for their hosts, but they were always business for Brishen.

Wil barely glanced at her. He sat beside Lord Clifton, deep in conversation for most of the meal. Lord Clifton glanced across to Valkin about as often as Lady Huntingdon did. Roger seemed intent on maintaining a whispered monologue directed at his brother. Syeira wondered what they could be talking of so earnestly, until she saw Lady Huntingdon listening closely to every word. Of course— his commission. The one thing Wil truly wanted, and with which Lady Huntingdon was willing to assist.

Syeira swallowed, wondering again about Wil's desire to place himself in harm's way. Giving herself a little shake, she blinked and turned her full attention back to the Maynooths. While no announcement had been made, Syeira noted the signs in Her Ladyship's looks and steered the conversation around to her remedies and their efficacy during the early weeks of pregnancy. She now had his lordship's attention as well. Both the earl and his countess were on the cusp of deciding that having Brishen camped nearby towards the end of the year may be of assistance 'when the time came' to paraphrase his lordship, when the princess let them know she had had a similar offer from Derbyshire.

"Oh no," Her Ladyship said sharply. "That will never do, my dear Princess Brishen. Your house must come to Holderness and that is all there is to it. Charles insists upon it, do you not, Charles?"

It was plain enough that Lord Maynooth insisted on nothing but his wife's approbation. He smiled easily and shrugged, addressing himself to the Romany prince with an outstretched hand. "If you would be so good as to bear a Yorkshire winter, Brishen, I shall be pleased to show you over my woods."

"I shall be pleased to shoot with you there." Valkin shook him firmly by the hand and grinned. "Well done," he whispered in a low voice by Syeira's ear.

She allowed herself a small smile of triumph. Still, it was a long evening. Syeira was grateful for the weariness of the English ladies, most of whom retired early in consequence of having arrived that day. Her heart twisted as Lady Huntingdon slipped her arm through Wil's, walking with him from the dining room. Clearly, that lady had no intention of retiring early.

Turning away from the sight of Wil and a match that would no doubt delight his father, Syeira met his gaze once. She tried to offer a polite smile, something coolly proper, and curtsied low. Wil bowed, his expression unreadable. It was a fitting end to her evening. Her face ached from smiling and her spirits from a surfeit of 'politeness'. She was not sorry to return to her room, curling in around Miss Clifton's little frame with relief.

Chapter Twenty-Six

Wil was once again woken unceremoniously by his valet, his man gripping him by the shoulder, shaking him hard.

"Captain. Sir, please."

He came alert at once, opening his eyes as he sat up, pulling himself out of Hudson's none-too-gentle hold. "Yes, Hudson, what is it?" Rubbing his face, he glanced at the window. Though the drapes remained drawn, it was not yet light. Grateful that his head was quite clear this night, Wil swung himself out of bed, reaching for his dressing gown. "What's happened? Is it the children? Is the prince bleeding again?" Despite Brishen's assurances, Syeira's early retirement last night had also concerned him for her health.

"It's Miss Clifton, captain." In the dim light of the candle on his nightstand, Wil could see little, but the alarm in his valet's voice was obvious.

"*Lydia?* Is she ill?" For the first time since the battlefields of France, Wil knew true fear. He dropped the dressing gown and found his linen. Dressing quickly, he focused on keeping calm. With all the strangers at the house recently, Lydie could easily have caught an infection. Her health was not strong.

"Are the grooms about yet? Never mind. I can saddle Nero myself. I'll fetch Haydock." He was already pulling on his boots but his valet hadn't moved. Wil froze in his action.

"What is it, Hudson?"

"She isn't ill." Hudson looked as worried as his master felt. "At least, I do not think so, captain. The scullery maid this moment looked in to the nursery as she does most days on her way below stairs. Miss Clifton is not in her bed. Her cover is not turned down."

Wil felt his heart stop. His little sister—missing? "The pup?"

"Also absent."

Wil swore audibly, completed his dress, and stood. "Where is Lord Clifton?"

"I cannot find him either, sir."

"He'll not likely be in his own quarters after last night. Wake Carter."

He was not terribly surprised to learn that his brother's valet was also not in his own bed. Wil strode to the window, pulling back the curtain. Driving rain splashed up against the glazing. The downpour had not stopped all night. Could little Lydia truly be out in this? He turned to see Hudson hesitating by the door. Acrid fear shortened his temper. "Spit it out, man."

"It's about the gypsies, Sir."

Wil eyed him. "What about the Romany?"

His valet flinched. "Ought we not to visit the camp and see if Miss Lydia has—well, I mean, what if she is with the gyps—I mean Romany? What if they have somehow taken her to their ways? It's been known to happen, sir."

Wil pinched the bridge of his nose between his thumb and forefinger. "I have addressed this already with Eddy. Brishen camped on these grounds for decades while the duchess lived. With*out* incident," he added, his tone tight. "I appreciate your concern for Miss Clifton. I ask you also to remember that Prince and Princess Brishen are our guests and if I hear that cow-slaver repeated, the person who does so will regret it. You will please ensure this information is understood below stairs. Do I make myself clear?"

His man nodded.

Wil cleared his throat. "We are losing time."

Lighting his candle from the stump of the valet's, Wil opened the door. "Lord Clifton must be told," he continued, as though the previous exchange had never occurred. "Find Carter first. Let him disturb my brother."

Roger had a temper when he was drunk, especially if anyone disturbed him in bed with a woman. Wil saw no reason for his valet to bear the brunt of his brother's behaviour. He glanced down the hall. A few servants were scurrying here and there, shivering in the pre-dawn light but all was otherwise silent. Wil grabbed up his dressing gown again. When they did find Roger, it was a sure bet his brother would need clothes.

"She can't have gone far," he reasoned. "Not in weather this foul. We'd best go door to door."

"Sir?" Hudson sounded appalled.

"We are looking for Miss Clifton, Hudson. Not permission." Leading the way to the nearest door, he proceeded to knock none-too-lightly. No response. Carefully, Wil opened the door and looked in. "Lady Boscowan," he whispered, leaving aside the name of her lover. "Dead to the world." No Lydia.

Following his lead, Hudson worked his way along the rest of the east wing. All the rooms were occupied. Even those guests who had not intended to stay so long forbore to risk both their health and their carriage wheels in such formidable weather.

Wil located his brother in the third room he tried. Waking him discreetly, Wil handed him the dressing gown and waited outside. He deigned not to notice the two lovely creatures entwined as gracefully with his brother's bedclothes as they were with each other. *No wonder Carter chose to take his leave.*

Lord Clifton rubbed his hands over his face several times as Wil explained. Shaking his head once, hard, Roger seemed to gather himself. Without a word, he tied on the gown, moving towards the other wing of the house.

Wil took the stairs two at a time, nodding as he passed more of the household staff in the hall. The drapes were open now, dim slants of amber light pooling in the upstairs hallway. The storm was passing over, but there was still no sign of his sister. By the time the men reconvened, even Roger looked worried.

"Where the bloody hell can she be?" he exploded.

Hudson shook his head, shrugging.

Wil ran a hand over his jaw, gut tightening with fear. Where might Lydia go? Who *could* she go to? It came to him then, and he turned from the others so fast that their exclamations barely registered.

Wil raced up all the stairs, pausing outside the door to his bedchamber. Hearing a girlish giggle and Syeira's robust laugh, he almost swayed with relief. Hudson's theory had not been so far-fetched after all. Lydia did seem to have been charmed away by the Romany princess. He knocked firmly.

"Come in," called his sister, giggling again. Entering the room, his gaze took in Syeira busily mixing coloured dyes, as well as something less herbal than usual bubbling in a pot over his fireplace.

Valkin was sitting up on the chaise fully dressed, preparing a palette with a pen knife.

"Lydia," Wil exclaimed. "We've been searching the rooms for you." He strode across to her, barely restraining himself from shaking the little idiot.

His sister frowned. "But—but I was frightened of the storm. With Miss Lee sent away, the princess said I could sleep in with her, and—"

"It is not Miss Clifton's fault," Syeira spoke up. "I should have told someone she spends stormy nights in my room. Although, I did not think it would cause anyone too much concern." Her face flamed dark crimson as she heard her own implication. "I mean, where else did anyone think such a little girl would go on her own?" She shook her head, whispering a Romany word that made her brother start.

"Syeira."

"I am *not* little," Lydia interjected.

"Perhaps not, but your brothers worry about you. As do others." Wil spoke in a tone that brooked no argument. "Hudson and Carter are also searching for you. You ought to tell them you are found, and Roger too."

His sister reluctantly relinquished her stirring spoon, positioning him by the hearth. "When it bubbles a bit more, remove it from the hook," she instructed.

"There will be no occasion for disturbing Roger's guests, mind," Wil added as an afterthought, tentatively poking at the lurid pink mixture. Lydia was far too young to know what went on in some of those rooms.

"No, Wil." Lydia sighed, stooping to gather up the little dog dozing on the chaise. "Come, Bony." The dog wriggled in her arms until she let him down, smiling at the way he trotted along beside her.

"Bony?"

"Yes," his sister replied over her shoulder. "He seems to be afraid of Englishmen, so I have named him after the French usurper."

Wil opened his mouth to reply and promptly shut it. His sister was still young and would learn to curb such a lively mind in time. He returned his attention to his offended guest. He stared at Syeira until her gaze met his, her dark purple eyes already flashing fire.

"I am not come to accuse anyone, princess. I merely wished to ask if you knew where Lydie might go." He bit back a grin. She really was a most striking woman, especially when she was roused. "The query was raised and as summarily dismissed. By myself. Are you satisfied?" His body heated as her gaze softened into a smile.

"I thank you," she blinked. "And it is Syeira." Her voice lower now, a small smile. "Or have you forgotten?"

Forgotten? Her name? Her fire? The power of her kiss? *Not bloody likely.* Wil felt the prince's eyes burning into him from behind. He cleared his throat, hoping for any distraction. At least two dozen eggs rolled about a partially wrapped swag.

"Eggs?" he inquired.

Syeira smiled at him again. "This is something Valkin is doing as he heals. We thought to divert Miss Clifton. She was so unhappy about missing her father at Easter," she explained. "We paint the eggs, then we roll them for a race." Syeira touched her tongue to her lower lip. "I hope we did not cause any trouble."

Wil's mouth fell open. They would do all this for his little sister? He felt an odd sensation behind his eyes and looked away. No one in his family had ever gone to so much trouble for another before. He was deeply touched. "Of course not, and I thank you. Lydie will be enchanted." He was enchanted too, at the simple scene of a brother and sister spending a morning together taking such pleasure in each other's company. He suddenly had no wish to leave this happy room. "How may I assist?"

Syeira's eyes warmed as she passed him a palette and a fine brush. They worked together in silence, Syeira smiling politely as Wil showed off his painting.

"It is—nice, Wil." She wasn't one to pour out false flattery then.

"Come, I must have your honest opinion," he pressed, wondering what it would take to make her smile at him again.

Syeira solemnly examined his egg before putting it aside, a smile twitching her lips. "It's very nice for a blob."

"I was attempting to paint a bird," Wil replied.

Syeira ducked her head and made a sound that *may* have been a small laugh. Wil set his brush aside to study her work. Simple flowers adorned all her coloured eggs, each one completed with painstaking care. He could even recognise a daffodil from a buttercup, and a lavender flower from a lilac bloom. Smiling, Wil took up another egg.

Chapter Twenty-Seven

Holy Saturday dawned overcast again. Wil watched as Eddy, under Syeira's direction, marshalled the gardeners in a manner that would have done no disgrace to Wellington himself. They were sent off to various groves of the woods and little-tramped corners of Clifton Park, with neatly written lists and large baskets.

Roger arranged a gallop for all those guests who wished to pay their respects to the late duchess. Lady Huntingdon slipped her arm through Wil's as a groom brought the grey mare round for her. Smiling coyly up at him, she put out her hand. "Would you be so good, captain?"

Wil placed his hands around her tiny waist and lifted her into the side-saddle. "Are you comfortable?"

The heiress smiled, tilting her head as she adjusted her skirts. "I'm not much of a rider," she confessed.

"Do not worry, Lady Huntingdon." Syeira stepped up to stroke the long nose of the mare. "It is not far to the chapel, and Valkin will be pleased to ride beside you."

Prince Brishen was already seated on one of Roger's hard-won hunters, quietly escorting Lady Maynooth the length of the park. Syeira called out something in Romany and the pair turned back, her brother wearing an expression of deepest chagrin. Syeira smiled at Lady Huntingdon, turned to greet Grygry, nodded to herself and did not look at Wil at all. Twisting her hands into her horse's mane, she took her seat.

Wil heard his brother's incredulous shout as they mounted their horses. Lord Clifton and the earls stared open-mouthed after the Romany princess and her horse's vanishing tail.

Wil raised an eyebrow at their looks. "Is there any problem, gentlemen?"

"She rides..." Lord Clifton's face registered his surprise—and his interest.

"Indeed," Wil scowled, guessing his brother's thoughts.

"It's…" Roger seemed at a loss for words. "Damnable."

It was so rare to witness Lord Clifton robbed of the power to complete full sentences that Wil grinned, shaking off his tension.

Lord Maynooth recovered first. "She rides well."

"Indeed." Wil sent Nero after Roger's mount, squinting into the sun as the Little Chapel came into view.

When they arrived in sight of what had been the Romany work area, Wil halted his horse and simply stared. Looking across the kirkyard, he nudged Nero closer, moving slowly as if in a dream.

"My God," he whispered.

The modest headstone marking the duchess's resting place was no longer lichen-spotted and forlorn. The stone lettering was once again discernible and a large, blooming lavender bush had been planted there.

Syeira had already dismounted. Shading her eyes with her hand, she peered up at him, smiling faintly. "A tribute to Baroness Eliot from my Romany. I found some living plants in your woods." She gestured towards the lane way, her dark gaze full of tenderness. "The living lavender bush? I thought it better for her—yes, Wil?"

Nero's reins slipped from Wil's fingers as his palms touched his pommel. He didn't feel the leather beneath his fingers or hear his stallion's soft whicker. Indeed, he sensed nothing outside himself. For this moment, he felt *stopped*. So still he could barely manage a nod for his princess. It wasn't enough. He knew it wasn't enough, yet he could not speak, so completely, utterly, and entirely overcome, his pulse beat harder in his throat. His mouth dried as the blood sped beneath his veins and his breathing hitched, lifting until his lungs moved too fast.

A touch at his knee. He looked down. Syeira's hand rested there. She looked up at him, searching his face. His gaze met hers and stayed there. As if all his senses were pitched to precisely the same frequency at exactly the same moment, a music no one else could hear playing through him, and the sound was golden. Golden and soaring and worth the strange expressions he saw on the faces of those around him. Clifton Hall had always been a place of such pain, and now–he hardly dared believe this was no longer the way of things. Change was possible after all. Possible, and even desirable.

Acutely aware of all eyes watching him now, he could *do* nothing. He wanted to—oh, God so badly did he want to—sweep this woman onto his horse and ride away with her. But there was nothing he could do but breathe into this feeling, as dusk-opal eyes stared into his.

His knee beneath her palm. Her hand, on his knee. Where it was not proper to place it. Wil blinked, intensely aware of Roger's stern gaze. Prince Brishen too was staring at Syeira as though he had something to say. Wil did not move a muscle. He *wanted* her palm there. Wanted her hands on him. This was not about Roger *or* Valkin. He sought Syeira's face. Her eyes. The slow, shy curve of her mouth. Deep purple warmth drew him in. Her generous smile held him there.

The flurry of movement as the others rode up barely registered. He dismounted in a kind of dawning daze. There were hands to kiss and flowers to arrange over his Mama's grave. Lady Maria Huntingdon offered him a gleaming gloved arm as she leaned in to place a large bouquet of Lancaster roses over the lavender bush.

"There now," she said loudly, with a forced little laugh. "Isn't that better?"

"Better than what, Lady Huntingdon?" He gazed at the lavender bush that would bloom and grow here at Clifton Hall in a way his Mama never had. "It's too lovely."

"Isn't it?" Lady Huntingdon replied. "I had my maid rise early and make this up for me this morning. She was compelled to travel into the village and wake up one of your farmers. Hardly found what she needed on the estate. So few flowers in residence, Captain Clifton?"

"So few, Lady Huntingdon." Wil kissed her golden glove, aware, as he straightened, that her gaze remained staring fixedly over his shoulder. Without turning, Wil knew Roger stood directly behind him. *Ah.*

"Sometimes one flower can be everything." he surprised himself by speaking aloud.

"Tell me, captain, when did you decide so?" Lady Huntingdon's giddy laugh came out beautifully unconvincing.

Today. In this moment. Now.

Lady Huntingdon's gaze remained trained on Roger like an archer measuring the distance to his bullseye. Wil shook his head ever so slightly. So, her assistance with his commission was about the duchy. A tension he did not even know he'd been holding slid from his shoulders.

Leaning past Lady Huntingdon, he adjusted the position of her over-large bouquet so it no longer obscured the lavender bush. Placing it below the flowers from the Maynooths, and the simple arrangement Mrs Edwards had added, he stood back.

"Sometimes, Lady Huntingdon, you simply *know*." Without waiting to hear her response, Wil walked over to the Romany.

***

Once the Easter Sunday festivities began, Wil could not fail to be touched by his sister's delight, or Syeira's smile. From across the lawn came music that drew all eyes to the Nutter's Dance. The procession pranced, leaped and jogged across the park, featuring traditional characters from the Noble Youth to the Soldier Brave. One of Syeira's sisters was even dressed as the Lady Gay. The Old Toss-Pot teased the children with its pretend tail so successfully that even Eddy could not contain her laughter. The actor must certainly be Janfri. Valkin strummed an instrument that bore a closer resemblance to a lute than anything Wil had yet seen. His gaze lingered on Syeira as she clapped and smiled with the children. The players all performed to banging Romany tambourines while the children clapped in time and stamped their feet. Then Princess Brishen was granted the honour of judging the winner of the egg rolling. To Wil's great delight, Lydia won the Easter egg roll, although she confessed that Janfri had helped her practise all week so the win wasn't *all* hers.

Afterward, the parade of pace-eggers made their way over to the giggling group of children, collecting all the broken eggshells, lest the old legends come true and witches return to Lancashire.

Tea was served on the lawn of Clifton Park. Wil, Roger and a myriad of newly arrived guests joined the children for fresh-baked Easter buns and ginger beer, with several of the Romany children joining in. The children sat to watch the mumming play before chasing after the pace-eggers who led them all in a lively parade across the grounds, calling all present to follow. Syeira extended her hand, and before he knew what he was about, Wil took it, Lydia running to join them on the princess's other side.

Somewhere up ahead of them, the Little Chapel bell called all to Easter service. The estate workers appeared, attired in their festive best to honour the late duchess and they all trooped across the estate together. Roger brought up the rear, preferring to ride rather than walk. Straightening his best waistcoat himself, Wil looked down at the slender, womanly hand clasped in his. *Happy Easter indeed.*

He relinquished the hands of both ladies only when Hudson caught them up with Nero and the Romany horse in tow. Syeira curtsied to his sister before swinging herself up and on to her mount. With an acknowledged tilt of her head to the Clifton brothers, the princess cantered the last mile ahead of them both, seemingly moving in time with the tolling bell.

Glancing behind Nero, Wil saw the pace-eggers proceeding with admirably energetic haste towards them, leading the gangling band of children in a sort of jig. If such a ramble did not wear out Lydie's excitable little companions, he did not know what would.

A grunt sounded behind him as Roger reined in his horse. "Beautiful," Lord Clifton breathed, but he wasn't looking at the chapel at all.

Following the line of his brother's gaze, Wil's reins slackened in wonder. There in the formerly unkempt field beside the tiny churchyard, was the Baroness's Meadow. The broken wall around the field was no more, replaced by a border of tall grasses and a fence of rushes. The grasses were trained without severity, with flowers blooming in a celebration of spring. The little paddock offered up a sea of greens and purples with lavender, lilacs and semi-wild violets all blooming together and waving in the breeze. The scent of lavender drifted across to him. Wil turned to his brother.

"Does it remind you—?"

Roger nodded. "It does. You have my thanks, Wil." Lord Clifton trotted his horse forward while Wil slowed Nero to a walk, admiring the purple and green field beside the now-picturesque Little Chapel that had been so dear to his departed Mama.

He arrived in time to hear his brother's words in praise of the work accomplished.

"...cannot express my gratitude more warmly, princess." Roger's smile was too knowing, one Lord Clifton wore too well and succeeded with far too often. Wil did wonder at Roger's manners though. The Romany were not servants, and it was not respectful to address them from so high a mount, especially on Easter Sunday. Wil dismounted before shaking each member of the Romany house by the hand. He stopped to greet the princess, who was trimming a few herbs from the edging that now bordered the little flowering field.

"Happy Easter, princess," he said quietly. Syeira extended her hand, allowing Wil to kiss it briefly. He noticed Roger watching him narrowly. Raising his head, he met his brother's gaze with a levelling challenge of his own. *This is how it is done, brother*, but Lord Clifton merely looked back at him, apparently feeling no need to comment.

"Roger is quite right," Wil said. "The trade exceeds all my expectations. I thank you, and all of Brishen." He gazed again at the purpled meadow. "However did you get the flowers to appear in such abundance? Yesterday they were not yet in bud."

Syeira rewarded his interest with that shy smile he had grown to value. "Ah, that is a secret, Wil." She blushed as she extended her palm. A small, well-crafted lavender boutonniere lay in her hand. "A gift for you. To remind you of Baroness Eliot's Easter celebrations. May I?"

Wil nodded, allowing her to pin the arrangement into his lapel. He looked down when she was done, at the lavender flower sewn from dyed silk. No doubt Syeira had made this herself. Glancing again at the field, he wondered how many of the flowers were created rather than cultivated. Brishen, and their princess, must have worked all night to complete this surprise.

Tenderness overtook him again, that overpowering sensation he'd felt earlier. How long must this have taken for Syeira to complete? While she also visited with the recovering village children and took care of her brother? No wonder she woke before dawn. He touched his gift lightly with one fingertip. He wanted to take her in his arms right there and then, even with all these people. He caught her hand in his, bowing as he lifted it to his lips once more. "My thanks, Syeira."

She smiled back at him, curtsied, and handed a similar creation to Roger who accepted it with alacrity.

"Shall we?" The prince bowed them all towards the church as the children walked up, led by Mrs Edwards, the maids and the ebullient pace-eggers.

Wil stood a moment at the nave entry, gazing at the chancel, breath caught in his chest. The Little Chapel was so well restored it seemed the whole place glowed. All traces of mould and lichen were gone, the stone whetted and brushed. The building gleamed richly in the soft sunlight, giving it a shining, golden look. From the efficient tidiness of the sanctuary space to the neat altar linen, Syeira's attentions were everywhere. The simple warmth and gentleness showed her touches in each aspect. Even the merry little fire behind the altar was tidily laid and brightly warm enough for the day.

Small, Romany-embroidered cushions positioned here and there enhanced the comfort of the stone pews for those dedicated to worship. The russet and lilac colours matched the light, and the scents from the Baroness's Meadow outside. Amber sunshine poured down through the coloured oculus design, lighting the flagged stone floor with scarlet reflections. The light glowed like jewels among polished honey-gold warmth, glinting on ironwork with a deep glow made warmer by the dozens of lavender-wax candles lit and flickering, like angels guarding this place that had once been so dear to his Mama.

For a moment it seemed that the altar rails were aflame but it was only that they were newly carved and oiled to a brightly burnished gleam beside the dozens of tiny flames. Even from the still-darkened doorway, Wil could make out the carved blooms and the crest. The crest of Baron Eliot of Bristol, not of Clifton Hall. No doubt the duke would be furious, but this was no longer about him. The Little Chapel had been the duchess's favourite place and her son felt the rightness of this tribute.

Wil breathed it all in, the scent of lavender soothing his burgeoning senses. Lydia stepped up beside him and stood there, open-mouthed. "Oh," she breathed, hands over her mouth. "It's *beautiful*."

Wil looked down to see a tear tease the corner of her eye. How like their mother she was. His heart shifted in his breast with that sense, again, of awe and wonder. As they took their seats, the feeling he could not quite name rose within him so strongly as to be virtually palpable. How he breathed, he knew not. Blinking, staring, he was grateful services began and silence was now expected. Had he been asked to utter a sound, it would have been quite beyond his power.

"A happy Easter to you all." Mr Evers stepped in from the other entrance and took his place on the dais. "Restoration and resurrection, m'lord." The curate bowed to Lord Clifton as Roger escorted Lady Huntingdon to the front pew. One by one, the Cliftons and their guests filed in and sat to hear Mr Evers read Easter services. Wil barely heard a word, his whole attention focused on the transformation that had taken place here. The gentleness of heart that understood what this meant to him. His eyes would only rest on the dark head bending down beside his sister's fair one, and the warm hand that Lydia held so tight.

After church, the guests made their way to the lower rooms of Clifton Hall, and Wil withdrew to the library, smiling when he caught the sounds of children's play coming in from the lawn. Seating himself at his writing desk, he looked for what seemed like the hundredth time at the sodden mass of paper that had been the general's letter. He'd still not penned his response. He stared at the smeared words for a long while, a trimmed pen and the ink before him. The note was short and to the point. Did 'Captain Clifton wish to purchase a major's commission in Wallis's regiment?'

With the sale of his own commission added to his winnings at cards, Wil had the resources on his own. Entirely and powerfully on his own, Lady Huntingdon's introduction to her father notwithstanding. This was a connection in which Roger had undoubtedly had a hand, and in which Wil was expected to participate.

A month ago, this would have been enough. A month ago, nothing would have pleased him more than a flying visit to Clifton Hall, enlivened by an illegal duel where he bested Haversham, bid good day and farewell to his sister in a single breath, and departed for parts unknown with a major's commission in one hand and a *billet-doux* from Lady Huntingdon in the other. A short interlude with a lover in love with the duchy would have satisfied him a month ago. A month ago, he wanted for nothing more. *And now?*

Now that he realised there *was* more? That *he* was—and could become—more than Roger's second and the duke's spare? A month ago, Wil had not realised the satisfaction in learning to make Clifton

Hall a home. Learning to behave like a family, instead of like a Clifton. A month ago, his life was different. *He* was different. So, what did he want *now*?

"I don't yet know," he murmured and realised this was all too true. He suspected he'd also learned to make important decisions with consideration instead of haste. Life was not, after all, a survivable sport. He thought of his Mama. There was most assuredly danger in making choices that were grounded entirely in tradition, and not at all in love. His mind shifted then, to the last person who had looked him in the eye and dared to utter that word. The tears she'd shed over him. Over *him*—it was not easy to forget.

Wil slid open the drawer to his writing desk, as though afraid to tip a precariously balanced weight within himself. Amid the piles of unanswered correspondence from lovers in London and abroad, he stowed the fragile paper from Whitehall. The end of the quarter was some weeks away yet. He had a little time.

A knock at the door made him close his drawer with a bang. Lydia came rushing in as the last carriage wheels faded down the drive, her wooden spoon with its tied-on purple egg providing no end of temptation for the delighted Bony as both egg and spaniel trailed behind her. Throwing her arms around her brother, she rested her head on his shoulder.

"Oh, thank you, thank you, Wil," she squealed. "I've had an absolutely marvellous afternoon."

Wil laughed at her, planting a kiss on her cheek. "I'm glad, Lydie. The credit truly belongs to Syeira and her house. You have remembered to thank the prince and princess Brishen?"

"Well, I tried but the princess will not let me thank her. She won't even let Eddy in to see her. It's why I came to find you. The princess declares she will not attend the assembly tonight. You do *want* her to come, don't you?"

"Of course." Come to think of it, he hadn't seen Syeira since tea time. He'd noticed Janfri running here and there with the other children, but of the princess, there'd been no sign.

"No, Bony, stop that." His sister raced off after her errant dog without a backward glance.

Wil shook his head as he left the library.

Knocking softly at the door to Brishen's room, he found Syeira kneeling to tie the prince's ceremonial sash as he dressed for dinner, taking care to move his recovering torso as little as possible.

"Allow me." Wil knelt beside her to produce the correct knots while Syeira smoothed her brother's formal dress. It brought him close to her again. Clenching his jaw, he exhaled heavily, endeavouring to control his body's inevitable response. Clearly the prince intended to attend Roger's dance.

"I hope you will both join us this evening?" He followed Brishen, surprised he did not lead his sister in.

"I am accompanying Lady Huntingdon." Valkin preceded him down the stairs. When the princess turned toward her room, Wil doubled back, alarmed at the quiet sorrow he saw in Syeira's eyes.

"Are you not joining us, Syeira?"

She shook her head, looking away as she reached her chamber door.

"Has someone offended you?" Wil gazed at the top of her head. "Some of Roger's acquaintances can be —"

Syeira made a kind of choking noise. "It is not that. I—I do not know your dances, and I believe Mrs Edwards meant well when she sent the maid to dress me for this evening with the impractical under-things. But it is not what our women—well, it is different." The princess blushed so deeply she appeared briefly feverish. "I do not wish to offend Lord Clifton, or yourself Wil, by appearing...*wrong*." She shuddered.

Oh. Wil stood speechless, stunned. He'd never thought of such a thing. What, then, did she wear under her gowns? Against her warm, dark-honey skin? Was it more than the women he knew? He remembered her riding her horse. Less, it must be less. How much less?

Never mind.

She did not want to offend *him* in front of his friends? He thought of his friends. Rowdy, boisterous, often drunk and riotous. Then he thought of the way she held herself like a queen beside her proud, loyal brothers. She could descend the stairs naked and his friends would still be some way behind when it came to modesty, grace and manners. He ran a frustrated hand through his hair and cleared his throat.

"There is no possible way you could embarrass either Roger or myself, Syeira. You may wear whatever you choose. I am humbled and honoured to host the royal House of Brishen at Clifton Hall this Easter night." He inclined his head.

Syeira gazed at him, her hand poised to open her chamber door. She smiled. "I shall join you as soon as I rearrange my dress, Wil." She lifted her gaze to his, smiling again, sighing. "I thank you."

Wil nodded. *Those eyes, that smile.* Turning resolutely away from her bedroom door, he walked slowly toward the stairs.

Chapter Twenty-Eight

Wil stood by the drawing-room fireplace, scowling into his brandy. His friends—all the gentlemen at least—seemed to be competing to seduce the Romany princess. Valkin sat nearby, apparently oblivious as he engaged in a card game with three young ladies who simpered and giggled at him. Shouldn't the prince be chaperoning his sister?

Wil watched as Syeira opened the dancing with Lord Clifton. Thank God Roger had requested one of the more traditional reels. Still, it was plain the princess was having a little trouble. She blushed and blushed again as Roger struggled to lead her. Wil felt an absurd satisfaction at Syeira's continued confusion, and his brother's mumbled apologies.

He returned his attention to Lady Huntingdon, who did indeed look extremely pretty in a new gown and stays undoubtedly from Paris. Wil could imagine those stays plaguing the life out of her lover, whomsoever he may be. He'd already decided one thing. It would not be him.

"You dance extremely well, Captain Clifton."

"As do you. I must compliment you on your arrangements, Lady Huntingdon."

A little laugh escaped her then. "You may call me Maria."

Over her head, he caught a glimpse of Roger's delighted countenance as he passed them. A month ago, that might have been enough. *Now?*

Wil smiled tightly, shaking his head. "Perhaps when we are better acquainted, Lady Huntingdon."

"Or better suited, captain?" His dance partner's voice sharpened a touch.

Wil smiled faintly, shrugging. Then he told her the truth. "I do not know."

He had not failed to notice the direction of *her* gaze as she, once again, unfailingly followed Roger's every move. No amount of military charm could eclipse the duchy, it seemed. Thankful of this fact for once, Wil returned Lady Huntingdon to her cousin once the set was over, swapping dancing for wine and taking great relief in the trade.

When the reel set was complete, his brother directed the musicians to play the waltz, and Wil about crushed his wine glass as Syeira stepped back, looking alarmingly around for assistance. She appeared to have no choice but to step in to Lord Clifton's arms. With no gloves and no knowledge of the steps, Syeira seemed defenceless. Handing off his glass to a steward, Wil moved but Valkin was there before him.

The prince smiled, cutting Lord Clifton entirely. Wil exhaled, offering his hand to Lady Maynooth for the rest of the set. She declined, preferring to take such a scandalous turn on the arm of her husband.

Returning to his wine, Wil watched Syeira relax as she moved more easily around the floor, allowing her brother to lead. Or was she leading? He studied them a moment then grinned; they were clearly taking turns. Siblings and teammates together. He laughed inwardly. No wonder Roger had had trouble directing her dancing.

Speaking of the devil, Roger appeared at Wil's side, instructing him to entertain their guests in the cards room. As Wil moved away, he couldn't help but look back at Syeira as she danced with her brother. She was magnificent. Her hair was tightly braided and pinned up in an intricate coiffure. His gaze followed the line of her cheek, the soft elegance of her neck, taking in a pair of slim shoulders with the barest hint of her cleavage. A hint was more than enough for Wil. He dared not approach her too often in such a crowd, and for such a dance, but that merely enhanced his awareness of her.

As he walked across the room, nodding and engaging with his other guests, he felt her presence. A flame on the edge of his notice, continually raising his body temperature. He let out a breath, smiling absently as he joined his brother's 'friends' for euchre. He hoped his civilities appeared more attentive than his attempt at cards. He couldn't focus on the pretty heiress beside him, or the one opposite.

Everywhere men laughed, leering at dowried ladies with each feigning ignorance of the intentions of the other. The lower rooms of Clifton Hall contained more than mere arrogance tonight. Cynicism abounded. Even Prince Brishen did not scruple to resist the cooing sympathies from several muslin-clad quarters. He was adept at adopting English manners among English company. According to Wil's information, Syeira's brother practically specialised in bedding married Englishwomen. He flushed as he realised Syeira likely knew this. What might she then know of Wil's reputation? He pushed his glass aside. The last thing he needed right now was more brandy. He was afraid to look too closely at what he did need. Knowing what he wanted, but could never have, was pain enough.

Suddenly the restrictions of his position were stifling and the company around him barely tolerable. His glance kept shifting, his eyes restless. No matter how much he attempted to deny it, his focus would not hold still until it alighted on the princess's elegant face. Intricately worked silver rings and necklaces caught the candlelight as Syeira laughed with a young laird from Scotland she seemed to know slightly. Wil wanted nothing more right then than to take the boy apart. She spoke to Roger as they danced again and he noticed the way his brother looked at her. His own *brother*, for God's sake. Roger's reputation was worse than his own and far more well-deserved. Lord Clifton went some way towards rivalling their father. Only the Romany princess held herself apart. Pride paired with honour—it commanded his respect. When had he last felt anything like respect for a woman he wanted to bed?

His eyes sought her out again, and he gave up his feigned interest in his companions and the pretence of playing at games. He was losing anyway. Wil shifted, ready to rise. Belatedly, he noticed the lace fan lying over his latchets, entwined with a heraldically embroidered handkerchief. He glanced up, suddenly awkward. He had no idea to whom each favour belonged. Both pouting, painted faces spoke to his great offense and he could not summon even the barest flicker of interest to redeem himself. He had no stomach to indulge in pointless flirtations tonight, even with his fan-thrower and her admittedly prettier young 'friend'. Signalling an under butler with his eyes, his servant returned the ladies' accessories with a bow and whispered absolutely nothing in Wil's ear.

"I beg you will excuse me," Wil rose, bowed, and smiled, lifting his eyebrows as the young laird took the spare seat. The boy had no idea what he was in for. Wil grinned faintly and considered wishing the Scot luck. Then again, not all of life's lessons were learned at

Cambridge, and who was he to curtail any young man's libertinism? Fatigue settled on him as the champagne and brandy wore off. He wasn't sleeping well, and he did not need Haydock to determine the reason.

A slurring voice caught his ear. "Romany royalty, I understand?" Lord Somerset bent to kiss Syeira's hand.

Wil watched him use his bulk to hem the girl in, rubbing higher up her arm with fat fingers. Somerset was his friend. He was also, right then, an insufferable boor. Wil didn't know which was worse. The fact that he could not have Syeira or the fact that all the gentlemen of his acquaintance seemed to want to try. The Romany princess whispered something, moving politely away from Somerset to take up a place beside her brother.

Valkin barely noticed the exchange, so engrossed was he with the women at his table, but he smiled when his sister joined his party and led her in to dine. Offering his arm to Lady Huntingdon, Wil followed after Lord Clifton. He barely spoke to his dining companion, nodding in response to whatever she said. He was far too interested in watching Roger leaning toward Syeira.

Taking up a spare glass in lieu of his supper, Wil clenched his fist, gulping savagely at his drink. He had no appetite at all. The meal seemed interminable. A hundred niceties might be required before he gained a chance to speak with his princess.

***

The Earl of Haversham had been invited as a gesture of goodwill. His sister, Syeira noted, had had the grace to decline her invitation, which was a pity. She'd liked to have at least met the sister of the coward who considered her Romany disposable—and tradeable. Syeira knew Haversham by sight. She also knew he'd had the hardihood to request 'other' recompense in exchange for Brishen's debt. She did not require her father's shame to elucidate her as to the earl's meaning. He had asked for a girl. Or, possibly, girls. As if her father, or any *sher-engro*, would agree to such a thing, much less head of the royal Romany House. Watching the earl currently slithering his way around the card room, Syeira shuddered. This was a man with no honour, a coward and a fool to boot. She stiffened at his approach.

"Cross your palm with silver, lady, and you'll do what for me?" Haversham leered. "I had no idea Brishen had you to offer." He loosed a lecherous laugh, grabbing her by the arm.

"You will step back, sir." Syeira's voice carried above the reel music as she leaned away, drawing back her free hand to strike his face. "Now."

Out of the corner of her eye, she saw Valkin rise as quickly as Lord Clifton, but Wil moved faster than anyone. He was suddenly there, taking Haversham by the arm, breaking his grip. Catching Syeira's palm with his own as though he meant to take her hand, he spoke over-loudly, contriving a worldly smile even as his eyes glinted dangerously.

"Did I hear you call for your carriage, James? I believe you'll find it more comfortable to wait in the hall."

Lowering his voice, Wil insisted, "You will apologise to the princess, or *I* will call *you* out. And I believe you have run out of seconds to hide behind." Pinning Haversham's arm to his side so hard Syeira expected to hear bones crack, Wil kept his eyes on the coward's face. Lord Clifton appeared on the earl's other side, pinning his other arm. He raised his dark brows at Wil and waited.

The earl winced, stammering a little. "Terribly sorry to give offense, Princess Brishen." Haversham glared directly at her, his face purpling in a most unbecoming way.

Syeira returned his glare as, without letting go of either arm, the Clifton brothers moved their guest smoothly to the door, consigning him to the care of Hudson and several burly footmen. Valkin resumed his seat, nodding to the two men in silent acknowledgment.

Chapter Twenty-Nine

"*Oh.* You should have let me slap him, Wil." Syeira's anger was still heated as Wil returned to her side. "It's no more than he deserves."

Wil's lips quirked, his eyes warm. "That may be so. Still, I do not want you hurt, Syeira."

"Hurt?" She very nearly choked, looking vainly around for a wine steward. "I am not afraid of such a *dinnelo*. I can look after myself."

"I do not doubt you, Syeira." His smile remained with no hint of jest.

Syeira's brow rose. He believed in her then, the first Englishman to do so. She looked down at her hands, clasping wine instead of Wil, cleared her throat, reaching for calm. "Nevertheless, I thank you. It is not always so when Romany women move among your countrymen."

Wil gazed down at her in a way that made the blood pound dangerously in her veins. "I did not wish the earl's attendance. I beg your pardon, unreservedly."

Syeira's careful attempt to maintain a cool, discreet distance evaporated with the heat of his tone. "I will pardon this, if you tell me what *truly* happened with his sister." She looked up at him.

"Ah, yes, well, that one was rather my fault, I'm afraid, princess," Roger broke in. "I believe the—er—lady in question had her sights set on becoming a duchess. I met her in Spain. I confess, I was unwilling. *Most* unwilling." He shuddered without meaning to and Syeira felt a pang of pity for the scheming Miss Haversham.

"Wil stepped in to pay her some attention and, ah, distract her somewhat and it got, well, a little out of hand," Roger explained.

"When she saw she couldn't marry the first son, she decided I would do, and it was my painful task to tell her no." Wil lifted his brows lightly, shrugging off the clear second-hand treatment. "I didn't set out to hurt her feelings."

"I am certain you did not," Syeira said, her voice warm and soft as she looked at him.

"You could have avoided the duel if you'd simply..." Roger let his sentence finish itself.

Wil groaned. "Don't make me blush for your manners too, Roger," he warned. Roger turned to apologise, but Syeira waved it away.

"This is not needed, my lord. Romany houses discuss these things openly. They are family matters." She turned to Wil. "You did not wish to take the easier way out, Wil?"

Wil's expression did not alter. "I thought then that the duel *was* the easier way out." Roger laughed and, seeing an opening at a card table, excused himself.

As soon as Syeira finished her wine, Wil caught her hands in his again, looking earnestly into her face. "My home is not a fit place for the House of Brishen tonight." His face still held traces of anger and a sort of furious embarrassment.

"Valkin seems well satisfied." Syeira attempted a smile, watching her brother lean in to whisper something to one of the women near him. The wine was having its effect there as well then.

Signalling a wine-server with his eyes, Wil prepared to mix another glass for his guest. Syeira stopped his art, accepting the fuller cup and sipping slowly.

"Unmixed wine is not too strong for you?" Wil asked.

"Not in this moment." Syeira swallowed with pleasure. The richness of the wine calmed her from within. "It is good wine, I thank you. It soothes me."

"It ought to be. Clifton Hall's preserves are some of the best in the country. I don't suppose the Romany have receipts for wine."

"Because we move around so much?" Syeira laughed, taking another appreciative sip. "It is true that we cannot cellar preserves in barrels or anything like, but we do possess receipts for our own fortified beverages. Romany spirits are as powerful as those of the English, Wil. The means by which we create them are merely different." She smiled at him over the rim of her glass.

***

"It is a comfort to know that differing traditions may still offer common ground." Wil watched her watch him, her tongue slipping out to moisten her lower lip.

He cleared his throat, blinking at the noise and crush of folk around them. Across the room, he felt Roger's glare honing in on him. Glancing behind Syeira, he saw a similar expression on Prince Brishen's face. He dared not look for Lady Huntingdon. All three death-stares together might prove effective. In any case, he preferred to look at Syeira.

How he longed to be alone with this woman again like they were in the kirkyard, soaked to his skin and hearing her cracked whisper. *Love.*

He still did not know what he wanted to say in response, so instead he said, "Can you truly read palms?" He extended his arm when she nodded. Opening his palm, she examined him steadily, smoothing slender fingers over his far larger hand. Wil took a long swallow of brandy as her fingers slid over his. He hadn't thought this through. He thought desperately of Miss Haversham. It helped, a little.

"Your lifeline is this one," she began, tracing his skin with a tender fingertip. "Do you see how it runs long and deep? This is a good sign for a long, active life, Wil."

Her touch was exquisite. It was all Wil could do to keep himself from pulling her into his arms. "What about—is there something called a heart line?" His face was close to hers now, her uneven breath warming his skin.

Her fingertip gently traced another curved line across his palm. "Your heart line is strong. You are a man capable of great love, Wil." She released him.

Wil instantly caught up her hands again, stroking them gently with his thumbs. He said nothing, but he wanted to… Oh, how he wanted to hold her, to free the fire within her, to free the one in him. To speak of love as she'd spoken of it. He took a breath, wondering if he'd find the courage to say such a thing. A stab of pain shot through him, like a ragged whisper in a rainstorm. It was love then, this pain. He was certain now. This softly shimmering veil between them had a name, as well as a temperature. It was love. *Love.*

He felt, acutely, the crush of people all around him, around *them,* and he'd never wished for more space at Clifton Hall in his life.

There was one thing he could think of to do, in such a place, among such company, burgeoning as he was with such feeling. Bringing his feet together as correctly as he knew how, he bowed low and properly. His princess drew back, surprised.

"Syeira," he began, quite formally, lifting his eyes to her astonished face. "May I have this dance?"

The music began and he waited, feeling more than usually awkward in a silence that seemed to stretch. He straightened and put out his arm. "Syeira?"

"I do not know this dance, Wil." She glanced at the lines forming down the room. "I do not wish to embarrass you."

Wil smiled. "I assure you that such an outcome is quite impossible. Come, I will count the steps for you," he paused. "If you will allow me to lead?"

She placed her hand by his as they joined the lines of dancers. Wil was somewhat grateful the musicians played an old Scottish reel. Both Romany *and* English societal codes would likely be smashed to smithereens if they played a waltz. Syeira's bare hand beneath his was more than enough to ignite his blood.

The music sped up as the count switched from three beats to two. Syeira stumbled briefly against Lord Somerset. Watching his friend leaning in far too closely, whispering as he attempted to step her towards an obliging alcove, Wil blinked as Syeira stepped suddenly forward. Somerset grimaced in pain as she mouthed an apology. Turning at the head of the reel, she faced Wil once again, giving the finest performance of mild unconcern he'd yet seen, though her cheeks seemed darker. As the music tapered, Wil accompanied her off the floor.

"What on earth?"

Syeira looked him straight in the eye with an arch smile. "I *may* have caught his toe with my shoe."

Wil looked down. "Your shoe?"

Syeira grinned, lifting her skirt the smallest distance. Wil glimpsed black leather before Syeira let the silken fabric fall. "I am a Romany woman, Wil. I *always* wear riding boots."

"Even to a ball?" Wil grinned back.

"*Especially* to a ball." Syeira laughed. "In truth, I do not own anything like the delicate little shoes your English ladies call 'slippers'. They are of little use in a Romany camp." She looked back at the frowning gentleman with the obviously throbbing toe. "He is a friend of yours, this lord?"

Wil shook his head, glancing back at Somerset. "Not anymore. What did he say to you?"

Syeira's eyes darkened with her expression. "*That* I will not repeat, not even to you, Wil. It is not the first time an Englishman has suggested such a thing. I do get so tired of it." Her voice was weary now as she looked around. "I thank you for your dancing lesson. You are extremely patient, especially with so many of my missteps."

"I noticed no missteps." He glanced down at his shoes and back up into her eyes. "And I thank you," he smiled. "For taking mercy on my toes."

Syeira laughed, and Wil with her until he turned back to the room, sighing as Roger bore down on them, far too deliberately in Wil's opinion, with Lady Huntingdon in tow. Wil saw his brother's intent. He only wondered that Roger did not see Her Ladyship gazing up at him with all the dewy-eyed delight she seemed to keep in reserve, and Wil turned, equally as deliberately, drawing Syeira into his arms as the first strains of the next waltz began. Whether this was madness or mercy—or self-preservation—he didn't quite know, but that he wanted Syeira in his arms, and *only* his arms again, was a truth he was rapidly coming to accept.

The heat that seemed to move through him whenever she was near slowed down now, taking long moments to seep into each part of him until he was warmer than he should have been. Warmer than he'd ever been, and far too warm for such visibility.

He felt her shiver, lean in, and hold that closeness as though she were giving herself a gift. His lips were so close to her temple now. His knee brushing the front of her skirts, the shift and sway of silk against his thighs. Against hers. This close, the heat was impossible. His breathing shifted, shallowing and somehow harder.

He swallowed and breathed. He was out of step now, out of time but he didn't dare stop. He couldn't. The rhythmic sway of her hips beneath his hands was too hypnotic, and his palms ought to be on her waist, he realised a moment too late, not sliding down towards her curves, her thighs, her warm, moist—*Oh god, what the hell was he thinking?*

She coloured prettily, offering no objection. Offering nothing but herself, in his arms, which was more than enough. He bit his lip, repositioning his hands. He did not wish others to get the wrong idea about what was appropriate with her.

"Wil," she murmured, lifting her face until her lips hovered inches below his, parting slightly as though she were about to kiss him, but she simply followed his count, gazing at him with darkly misted eyes, and savouring the warm glow of this sweet moment. He stared right back, trying to move automatically now, but he couldn't. He wasn't even sure he remembered the dance, though he'd been waltzing since the age of twelve.

Never in his life had he been more aware of the shift and movement of the woman in his arms, each breath lifting her breasts, the way the light played over her neckline. He twirled her out to the floor and back in again. Too fast, she stumbled. He caught her up, regaining her balance against his shoulder. A light, easily and swiftly corrected mistake that started a fire beneath his skin and from that point on he simply held her tight until the dance ended. Mercifully, crushingly complete.

They stilled, as the other dancers did, Syeira's cheeks flushed and Wil seemingly feverish. He didn't even have the wherewithal to look at the others in the room. To see whom, if anyone, he had scandalised this time. He stared at his princess, watching the rise and fall of her breasts as she panted from his dance. From being led by him.

The sheen of her eyes startled him. She stared wildly around the room. Perhaps she thought to fly out to the woods again, or to a cooler corner where those dark rose cheeks of hers might find some relief. She looked as frightened as the day of the duel. Following her gaze, Wil saw Lord Clifton and Prince Brishen staring at the both of them. He imagined a thousand things he might say to her if they were alone and *not* caught between the twin glare of two glowering brothers.

"I—I wish to retire, Wil." Syeira shook her head and seemed to shudder. "It is not rude to do this?"

"Not at all. Allow me to escort you, princess." He held out his arm and bowed, realising she'd made the best decision for both of them. How mortifying to find that Syeira was braver than he. He noted he was not surprised. Her courage was one of the things he loved about her.

The champagne, brandy and estate wines were in full flow. The behaviour of those gathered was unlikely to improve and pointless politeness was certainly not part of any tradition Syeira valued. This he already knew. He looked down to see something like pain dulling her eyes. She was far better off retiring to bed. Alone. Without him. Or anyone to love and be loved by. Existing traditions suddenly felt like the emptiest cruelty in the world.

Once at her door, he handed her into her room, wished her a goodnight and turned, intending to leave her room quickly. To remove himself from all temptation. He did not expect *her* to kiss *him*. To catch his hand as he reached the door, turn his face to hers and run her palm over his new-shaven jaw, holding him in place for this briefest of moments.

He stopped in surprise as Syeira stood on tiptoe to pull his lips to her own, pressing her soft mouth onto his, before he tenderly drew her lower lip into his mouth, stroking her tongue with his. His mouth took possession of the kiss in a rush, and she opened to him, giving him her breath, sighing into him as he outlined her plum-coloured lips with his tongue before diving back into her heated, wet warmth.

His hands came around her waist. Through cool, water-fine silk he felt her skin, burning for him. He groaned deep in his throat, pulling her tightly to him, fingers moving to lightly stroke one softly swelling breast, straining through the silk under his hand. Wil smiled as her lips parted further, moving his mouth to penetrate more deeply the warm, moist softness inside her lips.

His hands slid over silk-covered curves, pulling pins from her cascading midnight hair. Wrapping her dark, silken tresses around his hands, he kissed her eyes, her cheeks, her smooth golden throat. She gasped and whimpered, struggling with his waistcoat buttons.

Wil reached for her skirts, seeking the heated moisture between her thighs. A blazing heat rose within him as she pushed tightly against his fingers, bucking her hips, pressing into him eagerly, tiny moans falling from her lips, driving him closer to insanity. He took her mouth again, pulling her closer as he stroked her, feeling her hardened nipples burning tightly through his shirt as her hips moulded to his burning groin. Wil felt himself moving rapidly beyond control.

Pulling himself back with a roar of frustration, he stared at her.

The look of her—hell. Intense pain speared him and it went far beyond the one in his groin. It *hurt* to see her like this. Her lips swollen and wet from his kiss, her pupils dilated with desire, her wild hair tousled where he'd grabbed it, her breasts swollen and full with her nipples still tempting him through the passion-mussed silk. Her eyes held a blaze of longing, echoing his fierce, hot passion. His breathing was so loud he feared they'd hear him below stairs.

Swearing under his breath, he closed his eyes. God help him, he'd been about to take her here and now, up against the wall, without sparing even the space of a breath to reach the bed or the floor. He thought briefly of her underclothes. Hardly any, he remembered. *Hardly helping.* He opened his eyes. The heat between them crackled, then cracked.

Wil spoke into the long silence, voice grating in his throat. "I will not do this to you, Syeira. I promised myself. I promised Valkin." Not a single syllable left his mouth without a struggle.

"Another vow made about me, not to me." Syeira did not trouble to hide her bitterness. "You promised for yourself, Wil. You cannot promise for me—and you did not offer me anything. I wanted something for myself. For *me.* Because no one asked *me* at all. Not even you." Her voice caught, but she barely paused. "Besnik is quite capable of leaving me on this shelf for the rest of my days. This is my choice. *You* are my choice." Her voice was low and tempting now. Too tempting.

"I would not have stopped."

Desire-darkened eyes gleamed in the firelight. Her husky whisper almost broke his resolve. *Her choice.* It suddenly occurred to him that she did not have many choices she could make for herself, and she had chosen *him.* His heart shook in his chest again. Tenderness welled within him.

But the girl did not know what she was saying.

"Believe me, Syeira, I could *barely* stop. Another moment and I assure you choice would have been immaterial. For either of us." Raking a shaking hand harshly through his blond locks, Wil spoke gently, as though soft-spoken words dulled this pain. "I will not be responsible for hurting you or your family."

Her eyes misted with tears and he could not bear it. Knowing he hurt her flayed like needles in his skin. His fists curled in frustration.

The fire in his blood demanded release. He'd given his word to Prince Brishen, and her brother was right. To offer Syeira any hope was unfeeling. Wil buttoned his waistcoat, bowed and left.

As he pulled her door closed, he heard her quiet weeping. It took every ounce of self-control to remain on his side of her door. He longed to go to her, comfort her, hold her. He ached to do it. Denying her desire hurt far more than knowing he must deny his own, the pain of walking away from her slicing deeper than any he'd ever known, but he could do her no good. He had never felt more useless.

He paused on the landing to arrange his dress. The denial was not hers alone. Far from it. He dared not look too closely at what he felt for her. If he did… Well, he would not trust himself to take his leave this night. Or any night.

She had chosen him.

He slammed his fist into his thigh. It couldn't matter. She was beyond any man's reach, for a moment or forever. He flinched, but there it was again: that subtle, quiet shift within. Since when had he even *thought* 'forever' when it came to taking a lover? One who wanted him. Who wanted *him*. When had a woman last kissed *him*? Desired *him*? Not merely the pleasure he lavished over her body, or his access to the duchy, but truly wanted Captain Wil Clifton for himself?

This is my choice. You *are my choice.*

He felt…grateful. Honoured. Blessed. Definitely different, and almost pleased to be so. 'Almost' would have to be enough then, for what could he offer her? *Yourself, perhaps?* The small voice inside him spoke louder than it was used to doing. Wil closed his eyes against the pain of refusing this advice.

He stilled his heart into silence and gritted his teeth. To dream of her, of them, of anything beyond this night's kiss was madness. He had no other choice but to walk away. Syeira had said it herself: *There is nothing you can do.*

But what if there was? Did he—*could they*—have any chance? If they did, *would* he—?

In that moment, Wil knew. If it were possible to possess this woman truly, he would run any risk, take any chance, for her. He'd do anything for this bright warmth burning between them. If he were free to allow her choice, he would choose her right back. Choosing their love felt like the only right decision, even if all the attendant circumstances called it 'wrong'. If it were at all possible to turn towards his princess, he would not walk away from this tenderness, this wonder. From the woman who chose *him*. Wil closed his eyes tight against the pain of it. He'd had no idea desire could hurt this much. It took him like a musket wound. No, worse. Like his soul was being ripped in pieces. Swearing under his breath, he descended the stairs.

Chapter Thirty

Syeira was powerless to halt the tumult inside her. Why had she kissed him? Oh, *why* had she kissed him? She'd been here too long, spent too many weeks away from her home and family. She'd all but forgotten, she'd nearly allowed her heart to matter more than her duty—or her pride. Suddenly she wanted to be away from more than the stuffiness of the assembly downstairs. She wished to leave Clifton Hall. Slip quietly out to the stables, find Grygry and be gone. It was too hard to breathe in this place, the walls of her room too close. Running to the drapes, Syeira scrabbled frantically at the rusted iron catch. Swinging the mullioned window out wide, she leaned into the night, drawing in gasps of air, tasting the freedom of deepening dark and not caring when the wind whipped her dark hair to wildness. Why should the air feel any calmer than she did herself?

Slowly her breaths calmed and her body stopped shaking. Placing her palms together, she breathed deeply thrice. She kept her mind on the wind, the chill, the cold welcome of the night air. Anything, anything to cool the fire she had allowed to burn too brightly for one shining, joyful moment of heat and heart. She *would* be calm, she would be collected. She would insist this scorching warmth leave her cheeks this instant.

Her traitor-heart pounded knowingly beneath skin still hot from Wil's touch. The warmth of his hands stroking her still burned like a firebrand. Syeira wrapped her arms around herself, holding tight. The turmoil of unspent desire left her aching for a love she was bound to deny herself—and Wil. Turning away from this love was the deepest pain of all.

She needed to be busy, to work. Taking the flint from the mantel, she struck it and soon had a crackling fire chasing the chill air from her bones. No doubt it was foolish to leave the window pinned open on such a cold night but she could no longer bear this closed-in feeling. The sense of being trapped in this place with an Englishman who did not know what to do with her heart would rob her of her rest. She refused to lose sleep over this love of hers.

No part of what she'd said to Wil was feigned, but when it came to seduction, she did not have the skills. The lovemaking lessons she'd received from her mother and aunts were so long ago. Until now, Syeira had made no effort to recall her education in *camello*. Such thoughts mocked the emptiness of her womanhood.

Placing her gown carefully in a cupboard, she shook out her plain silken shift and readied herself for bed. Still, she couldn't stop her mind from going over what had occurred. Surely it was a *good* thing Wil had left when he did? What else did she expect? That he would not feel as bound as she? That it would not hurt quite so badly to want to be touched by him? He'd refused her, baulking at her choice. Perhaps he wasn't the man she thought him. Perhaps he didn't want her the way she wanted him. How could her own heart mislead her so?

She recalled far too clearly the morning of the duel and the closeness of his body to hers. No, she had not misunderstood. His refusal wasn't due to any absence of desire. He was bound by other restraints. Respect for her brother. Respect for Brishen. Trapped by promises he'd made to honour Brishen's vow—a vow that never should have been made at all, much less kept. Until this moment, Syeira had never dared acknowledge the depth of her frustration and her anger at being held in a state of such suspension. For the first time in her life, she felt torn between her family and someone she loved as much, possibly more. Her fragile peace was breaking apart and she was afraid.

She picked up the poker, stirring the fire listlessly. The gentle warmth reminded her of Wil. Well, right now everything did. That he cared for her family's troubles was one of the reasons she loved him. So why did his unswerving commitment to Brishen's honour now irritate her so? She disdained the *gadjo* who operated without integrity. Was it so galling that the man she loved was better than many of his countrymen?

Listening to the howling wind outside, Syeira felt less enclosed by the ancient stone walls. She tied all the curtains back with silks, watching the sky. She wondered if she was to bear witness to another storm splattering her frustration across the windows of Clifton Hall, feeling again the kindred response within her own soul.

She remembered the ancient superstition that the Romany could 'call in a storm' whenever they wished. Tonight, Syeira wished it were true. Right now, she wished for nothing more than wild skies and some kind of deluge to drive this feeling of abeyance from her mind. She could not erase it from her heart. That was truly a foolish fantasy.

She must give up her impossible dream of love before it destroyed her from the inside out. Syeira shook her head. Sitting before the glass, she brushed out her hair, making a vow of her own.

"I will not grow hard and cold and bitter, like this place," she said aloud. The secrets of her heart were hers to keep, whether her love was permitted or no. Twining her hair in a simple braid, she remembered her mother. Princess Syeira Brishen needed no one's permission to choose to love whom she wished.

Turning down her covers, she settled into bed, wondering what her Mama would say to her now. Would she approve of her eldest daughter choosing an Englishman to give her heart to, even if said daughter could do no more than dream over him? Mama had not tarred all Englishmen with the same brush. Indeed, it was she who had been so well known to Baron Bristol and his daughter, Wil's grandfather and mother. Would Mama have permitted Baroness Eliot's son to court the pride of Brishen? Syeira smiled. She had a feeling her Mama would have liked Wil. *In healing, as in love, timing matters.*

All the Romany had observed proper death rites to honour Stefan Besnik, but Syeira had grieved her wasted love alone. The love that, after his death, had no place to go. No one who received it or returned it. No one who even desired it. For whom among the Romany would dare flout her father's promise? A promise everyone knew had been given in the name of the Romany king, or *krallis*.

That pain was made worse by the helplessness that gripped her, and the entire House of Brishen, as her father's illness progressed to the point where she feared for the safety of her family. While Brishen tracked the deterioration of their once-proud *krallis*, their princess faced the emptiness of a life alone. A life lived without the love she had stored in her heart for far, far too long. A love she was forbidden to give to any other Romany man.

This was the honour she felt called upon to preserve, and she *must* preserve it. This is what her brother—all of Brishen—expected.

Family honour, at all costs. Even at the price of her heart? Syeira closed her eyes against the pain. *Yes. Even if it costs my heart.*

Her throat closed over again, tears pricking behind her eyes. A heavy, jagged breath escaped, threatening to become a sob. She took another breath. Hadn't she cried enough tears over this already? She honestly thought she'd long since stopped grieving the waste of her heart.

Wil, she was certain, was expected to marry as the duke dictated. Syeira grimaced at the idea of Wil with Lady Huntingdon. What sort of wife might she make for him? *And why is this any concern of mine?* But it was, she felt it as powerfully as she felt the attraction between them. It was not in the nature of a Romany to deny their instincts. This was truly why she had kissed him. This, and the weariness of being separated from the liveliness of knowing another. From the warmth and pure, simple joy of courtship, of touch. Of love. She understood it could not be hers, but did she have to give it all up so entirely? So unbearably? Was this truly her family's choice for her? Could she not choose something more for herself?

Syeira shivered in the too-large bed. Clifton Hall was not a warm family home by any means. Everything about the hall felt cold to her. Everything except Wil, and he'd refused her out of the same manacled sense of duty that chafed her soul so badly.

Syeira swore in all the languages she remembered. It didn't help stem the tears. She cried until her throat was raw, her body too limp to move, and her heart empty. As she drifted into an exhausted sleep, one thought remained rooted in her mind: Tomorrow, she would speak with her brothers about returning to *ker*, for she could no longer stay here.

Chapter Thirty-One

Wil made his way to the quieter wing of the hall, further from the clinking glasses and too-loud laughter. He noticed a fire had been laid in the library. Kneeling, he lit the flint before sinking down in the leather-wing chair behind the centuries-old oak desk. Exactly where he'd been sitting when Lydia had rushed in to hug and kiss her gratitude for the most wonderful afternoon she'd had in years. He smiled. Wil was glad she'd not missed the duke at all this Easter, but there remained something indescribably sad about the furtive way such good things at Clifton Hall always came about. A sadness that reminded him painfully of his gentle mama.

Sighing, Wil drew his quill toward him and trimmed it. The room was a trifle dark, but perhaps it was a mercy he could not see the portraits of Cliftons who'd served the crown for centuries frowning down on what must, to them, amount to treason. He felt as clandestine as when he'd hidden behind the bookshelves as a boy to spy on a young Roger kissing his first heiress.

He opened the lower right-hand drawer slowly, as though a viper were concealed within. Someone—Hudson, he supposed—had assiduously preserved General Wallis's paper. The correspondence had been carefully smoothed and dried, though the ink remained badly smudged. Still, the note was short. Wil didn't need to refer to it in composing his response.

Dear General Wallis,
I thank you for your letter and for your confidence.

He stopped, staring at the mostly empty page. All he had to do was compose his acceptance, and dance Lady Huntingdon closer to the duchy in celebration. It seemed simple. It *was* simple. So why was it so impossible to pen his acquiescence?

Pressing his lips together, he remembered the softness of Syeira's mouth moving over his. Her hands holding him to her as though he were important. As though he mattered—him and *only* him. All thoughts of Lady Huntingdon faded to echoes.

He heard a voice and footsteps. Scattering sand over the page, Wil laid aside his quill.

"Wil? You here?" Roger's speech sounded scarcely the proper side of slur. "It's blacker than Hades." His brother stumbled about the room, lighting some tapers before steadying his balance. "That's better."

Was it?

Generations of Cliftons glared down at them, heirs and officers all. Wil glanced up, sighing. "A pressing matter of business."

"So pressing you left Lady Huntingdon unpartnered for the waltz?" Roger turned to face him. Foxed or not, he still managed to skewer Wil with a look.

Roger's tone shifted slightly as he glanced at the paper on the desk. "Are you replying to General Wallis?"

"How did you—?"

"Lady Huntingdon whispered a little something in my ear." Roger looked more severe than usual. "I thought to prevent you from making the gravest of mistakes."

"Courting a lady of the ton who most certainly prefers Lord Clifton to Captain Clifton is not exactly wise, Roger," he replied, surprised to hear something like steel-plated certainty in his words. "*Marrying* her is certainly not a game worth playing."

"I did not mention marriage." Roger looked as though he'd swallowed something sour. "A harmless flirtation is all I was suggesting. She feels admired, her father admires the duchy as well as his daughter, and the ladies of the salon admire you as Major Clifton. Or do you mean to turn down your commission?"

"I came in here to compose my acceptance," Wil replied unsteadily. He didn't miss the look that crossed his brother's face. As if Wil's words had sobered Roger up.

"Have you accepted?" he asked sharply.

Wil was spared from answering.

"Good evening, gentlemen. How goes the revelry?"

Wil looked up to meet the ominous gaze of the Romany prince. He wondered how long he'd been absent from the ballroom. Wil stood, bowed and moved out from behind the desk.

"I want to thank you both for your actions earlier this evening," the prince began.

"Haversham ought never to have had the hide to attend." Wil's jaw clenched at the memory. Roger nodded in agreement, adding his apologies.

"That waltz is another matter." Brishen stared at Wil with a look that reminded him uncomfortably of Syeira's glare.

Wil held himself steady in the face of Valkin's scowl. "What about it?"

"Do you imagine no one noticed?"

Wil swallowed slowly. "I imagine all parties were rather busy with their own affairs, Prince Brishen. Did you find Lady Huntingdon satisfactory?" He paused. "On the dance floor?"

Brishen stepped forward but Lord Clifton inserted himself smoothly between them. "Gentlemen, I beg you will consider the furniture." He glanced repeatedly between his brother and his friend. "You will consider *me*." He spoke loudly, and with the authority of Lord Clifton.

"Of course, Roger. I do not intend *coorava*. That is, to mill. In fact, I wish to speak with you both. About Syeira."

Wil opened his mouth to decline, but Roger said, "How about we do so over a drink?" He stepped away to ready three glasses of scotch. *On top of all that brandy and champagne?* Wil shook his head.

"Take it." His brother's voice seemed unnecessarily hard. "You'll need it, Wil."

Wil stared at him from the opposite end of the sofa, curving his palm around the crested crystal. Both Cliftons looked toward the prince as he placed his drink on the desk and faced Wil, his expression darkened with sorrow.

"I have watched the sadness in my sister's eyes for three long years," Valkin said heavily. His gaze lit on Wil and something hopeful flickered. "Perhaps that can change."

Wil stilled, unable to speak. He waited for Valkin to continue.

"Romany traditions have a—flexibility to them that is sometimes useful. The promise that holds Syeira is only binding for my people.

No Romany but Besnik can wed her." He took a breath, that dark stare heavy with expectation as he looked at Wil. "It does not preclude an offer being made to her by a *gadjo*. That is, a gentleman who is *not* Romany."

Wil's heart stalled in his chest. Did the prince mean…?

"What do you propose?" Roger asked.

"If one of you wishes to make an offer for my sister, it may be possible to parlay a solution with the House of Besnik. I believe I can persuade them to this." His words sounded measured and his tone neutral. "I also believe I can convince my father to permit the match, if it is to a man of honour."

"You can't mean—" Roger began.

"He means me," Wil broke in. "Don't you, Brishen?"

The prince inclined his head in affirmation. "I do. I am also aware you have a certain reputation, captain." He fell silent, dark brows drawn in as he continued his examination of his hosts in silence.

With every appearance of outward composure, Wil withstood the prince's cool appraisal. Heart hammering, he waited.

Lord Clifton spoke first. "Come, man, Wil's manners are arguably less reproachable than both of our own." He squared his shoulders. "Are you questioning the captain's integrity?"

Their guest acknowledged this point with a nod. "Manners are one thing, my lord. Honour is another. A Romany courtship is not the same as walking out with a girl of the ton." Valkin sipped his drink. "Any insult to my sister and you will face not only myself, but all the men of my house."

"All?" The prince had kept his voice studiously level but Wil knew a threat when he heard one. Air tensed as his muscles tightened.

"Syeira has three brothers besides myself, captain. There are at least a dozen others at *ker*. Brishen is not a large house but we are not without allies."

"Neither is Wil," Roger stated.

Valkin appeared to choose his next words carefully. "I am not a fool, Wil, and neither are you. I spoke a warning. Not a call to arms."

Wil looked down at his drink, as though admiring the play of light over amber, but in truth, to avoid the eyes of the others. He'd had no idea it lay in his power to secure Syeira's freedom. *There is nothing you can do*, she had said. But this, this was something he could do. Something he could give her. *Marriage?* The fact that he did not reject the idea outright didn't surprise him, his outlook having altered so dramatically in the past few weeks.

He took a breath, met Valkin's shrewd gaze and held it, laying a quelling hand on Roger's arm. "I never intended to marry, sir. However, neither would I allow my wife to suffer an indignity such as that of which you speak. Our mother—" He broke off, unwilling to air quite so much family linen even in the company of a trusted acquaintance.

"I will not betray a woman I have sworn to protect and lo—" He swallowed and broke off. *Bloody hell.* This was worse than any interview with the duke. The hypocrisy of those exchanges always insulated him from feeling. An absence of feeling was hardly the case here. *Surfeit, more like.* "Your concern is understandable. I will not call it justified."

The prince let go a relieved breath. "I thank you for your candour." His lips relaxed into a smile. "I have vowed to do everything I can to secure my sister's happiness. Until now I have been of little enough use to her. I would not pursue this were I not tolerably convinced of your regard for her. I see you care for her. You honour her. I will permit you to court Syeira if you wish. I myself will chaperone." He fixed Wil with his imposing stare once more. "Do you wish to court her?"

Wil studied the scotch in his glass as though he were to pass a test on its colour. He held it to his lips, then set it down, pushing it entirely away. He needed no further dulling of his wits this night. The idea of Syeira as his betrothed was intoxicating enough. The thought of warm, honeyed skin, that shy smile. Even her proud glare heated his blood. A vision came to him. Slender hands tracing lines on his palm. Curvaceous hips shifting beneath silken cloth. Golden arms encircling his neck, the scent of roses and cinnamon.

He took a longer swallow of Roger's scotch, uncertain he had anything to say as yet. Was he truly discussing courtship and marriage? An alliance that could see him exiled from Clifton Hall? He remembered the shattered look in Syeira's opal eyes when she told him of her circumstances.

There is nothing you can do.

He recalled her broken utterance—*Love*—in the streaming rain and the pressure of her heart-stopping kiss this evening. Her barely whispered avowal as he left her rooms. *This is my choice.* You *are my choice.*

"Wil?" Roger spoke his name as though afraid of his answer.

He might well be. Wil was not *un*afraid of it himself.

And she had chosen *him*.

Slowly, he felt himself nodding, dimly aware of the prince's speech outlining the rules for courting the Romany princess. He barely took in what was permissible, and what was not. How these kinds of agreements were fulfilled or broken off should the couple prove to be unsuited. This last piece of information escaped Wil entirely. He knew, to the depths of his bones, that it was unnecessary.

"You may find marriage to the princess acceptable," the prince continued. "If so, you must make an offer for her to my father. I will deal with Besnik."

"And if he chooses *not* to make an offer? If he finds he does not want her?" Roger asked. It was a perfectly reasonable question under the circumstances and difficult to phrase tactfully, but the implied insult to Syeira had Wil across the room in a flash, one hand on Roger's collar, the other clenched in a furious fist inches from his chin. His brother caught his arm, easily pushing him aside. Looking over Wil's shoulder to Brishen, Lord Clifton appeared to nod in time with their guest.

"As I thought," Roger exhaled. "Not a chance in hell." He sipped his drink, seeming to form his next words with care. His tone was milder than Wil expected. "Wil, I am here in your interests, and I need hardly add, my own." Lord Clifton glanced down at his empty scotch glass. "I remind you that the duke expects you to marry as he directs. Something silly, with money. Until then, you are dependent on his allowance." Roger looked over at his friend. "You have my utmost respect, Brishen, and I greatly admire the honour of your house, but I would be remiss in my filial duty if I failed to point out that should Wil marry your sister, our father will most assuredly cut him off. Your royal status notwithstanding."

The prince did not appear in the least offended. "Brishen can provide the living." He grinned. "It will be a different life, but not a bad one. You would be Consort to the Princess Syeira, and a part of Brishen."

"There is also the matter of your commission, Wil." Roger would not be deterred, and he was quite right.

"I have until the end of the quarter to decide," Wil informed them.

Leaning in, Roger stared hard at Wil. "You do truly mean to do it then?" His dark eyes were wide with amazement. "Defy the duke?"

The space between them overflowed with words unsaid. Wil sighed, allowing his silence to speak for him.

"One more thing, Wil."

"Yes, Roger?" He looked up, wincing at the hurt in Roger's eyes.

"You won't be able to return." Lord Clifton spoke softly, clearly aware of the pain he gave them both now. "Not until I succeed His Grace. You must know this."

Nodding, Wil gripped Roger's shoulder. He couldn't speak. No words came to him. No words, but a greyish sort of sadness settled somewhere behind his ribcage. Not wanting to come home was one thing. Knowing he *could not* was something else entirely.

Could he have imagined wanting to remain at Clifton Hall a month ago? Before the Romany? Before Syeira?

Tonight seemed to be the night for paining all those he loved best. *Loved?* An image of Syeira's eyes flashed before him. *Yes. Loved.*

"I wonder, is there a Romany word for 'irony'?" He tried for a smile, not quite succeeding.

"No, Wil." Brishen's voice was low, as though the prince himself was afraid of tipping some sort of careful balance that could slip either way on a breath. "It is your decision. If you, or Syeira, do not choose to wed, I may have the satisfaction of seeing the princess smile tomorrow, and the next day, and the day after that. Until our time here is over. It is a great deal more than she has had lately or may ever have." When Wil said nothing, the prince rose slowly, wincing as he touched his fingertips to his torso. "I will speak with my sister in the morning. Now, if you gentlemen will excuse me. I promised a charming young lady a palm reading."

"I thought only Romany women could read palms." Roger put his glass down and stood.

"True." Valkin grinned wolfishly. "Quite, quite true, Lord Clifton."

His brother laughed, following his friend out.

Wil sat alone by the fireplace, thoughts whirling as wildly as his arms had spun Syeira across his ballroom. His princess did not deserve to be held captive to her father's vow. By her own admission, she chafed at it. She wanted and deserved her freedom. What better gift could he offer her?

He had never seriously considered taking a wife. He enjoyed having his choice of lovers. Avoiding the alliances the duke pushed at him had likewise pleased him. His status as the duke's backup and his father's money made playing rakehell far too easy. But Wil had not been near an 'eligible' woman in weeks. He'd found it remarkably difficult to feel even mildly displeased that he'd been dismissed by so many past lovers. They'd simply ceased to amuse him. The change lay with him. In the realisation that, whether sanctioned by the duke or not, he truly had a choice when it came to his future. For the first time in his life, Captain Wil Clifton faced the bone-jarring question: What did he *really* want?

Chapter Thirty-Two

Syeira hardly slept that night, rising before dawn. She readied herself quickly and quietly, packing her leather bag and donning her Romany riding habit. She couldn't bear to face Wil over breakfast today. She'd visit the village to see how the children did, before speaking with Valkin. His wound was mostly healed and would bear the strain of travel if he took care. Long days of riding risked pulling at his new-grown skin, but it was time for Brishen to move on.

Preoccupied with her thoughts, she cannoned directly into a firm, hard body directly outside her door. Strong hands caught her up and set on her feet. She looked up, aghast as Wil took her hands in his own.

"Whatever are you doing here?" she blurted out, wishing he'd look anywhere but at her, too aware of how she must look. Eyes gritty and heavy-lidded with weeping, face pale as if she were ill. Despite all the fairy tales told to young children, there were no curing herbs for wasted love.

"You rise early." Wil avoided her question.

"I thought to go out." She sounded breathless—*damn it*—as she tried to pull herself together. "I've been indoors too long."

"Then I'm glad I came to find you. I wished to—to invite you to come riding this morning?" He spoke as though he were afraid of something. "With me, I mean."

Syeira stared at him. "I cannot."

"Prince Brishen has agreed to chaperone," he said, hurriedly. "Your father's vow does not forbid this." Wil watched her the way a cat might watch someone pour out milk.

Syeira simply gazed back at him, realising the cleverness of Valkin—and the arrogance. An Englishman courting a Romany woman flew in the face of both sets of their strictest traditions. So outrageous, it seemed, that there were no specific rules forbidding this. Trust the Romany prince to find a way round their father's vow without breaking it.

"Prince Brishen spoke with me last night, after I returned to the lower rooms."

Syeira dropped his hands as though they burned. "You and my brother? You spoke?"

"Yes."

"About me?" Syeira's rising temperature had nothing to do with desire. "Valkin spoke with you about me?"

Wil squared his shoulders. "I beg your pardon," he replied. "I do not understand."

The effrontery of it. Not for the first time did Syeira curse her brother's arrogance. She breathed out slowly through her nose. Of course, Wil did not understand. This *is* how such matters are managed by the English. Why would Captain Clifton comprehend her feelings in this moment? It was exactly the sort of thing Valkin did. Well-meant, but high-handed in the extreme.

"You will excuse me, captain. I am angry with my brother, not with you. This is a family matter." She took another breath. "I do not like being disposed of as though I were one of Valkin's racehorses. *Again.*" Her tone was sharper than she intended. Wil was not to blame.

Wil nodded slowly. "I see."

Syeira watched him back away from her once again, feeling all of last night's pain anew. Was she truly so proud in this moment? She swallowed, banishing the image of this same man walking away from her last night. That was the past and she would no longer allow it to hold her hostage. Wasn't that a choice she'd made last night too, as the wild wind blew across her room? Some kinds of passion could not be conquered. Some kinds of love were worth the risk, no matter how stormy the odds. Certainly, her heart was worth this little matter of pride.

After all, she had chosen Wil. She had said so. Was it now truly her choice to watch him go, on a point of Romany pride he did not even comprehend? He was an Englishman. An Englishman she loved. Syeira's heart barely caught her up in time.

"Wil."

He turned, silent and dignified, poised at the top of the stairs. For a moment, she simply *looked* at him, admiring the shape of him, from his polished riding boots to his too-English cravat, sunlight picking up the fairness of his head, keeping his eyes in shadow. Her gaze touched him, her fingers warming as she remembered the firm hardness of his torso, her body heating at the memory of his lips on her skin.

She discerned the heart that beat with kindness in that handsome chest. She knew him. Loved him. Chose him. And now, he was choosing her. *Asking* to choose her. Syeira knew what this might mean for her. She understood it might mean the end of Wil's life at Clifton Hall. Last night, she had risked her heart for a kiss and a lover. This morning, Captain Wil Clifton risked himself. There was only one thing she could think of to say in the face of such courage.

"I accept your invitation," she curtsied briefly. "I thank you."

"No, I thank *you*, Syeira."

She couldn't help but grin as a joyous smile lit his face.

***

"I'll see you at breakfast?" He flushed, without troubling to hide it from her.

Syeira nodded. "I must first speak with my brother." Her smile was gone and replaced with a look Wil hoped never to see her direct towards him in his life. Dear God, she had spirit. He continued downstairs, not envying Brishen in the slightest. Syeira was not a woman to be trifled with. *If a man must take a wife...*

He had never seriously considered such a thing before, so why was he smiling?

"Sir?" Hudson passed his master on the stairs and stopped dead. "Is there something amiss?"

Wil laughed out loud at the mystified expression on his valet's face. "Not a thing in the world, Hudson. Why do you ask?"

Hudson gestured at him. "It's barely dawn, and you're up and...smiling."

His man seemed so bemused, Wil couldn't help but smile wider as he fell into step beside his valet. "Have Nero readied for a ride immediately after breakfast. Find something quiet for Brishen to ride. He is still healing. The little bay mare for the princess will suit. Is it clear?"

"Er—yes, sir." Hudson replied.

Wil grinned at him. "Thank you. Ask Eddy to prepare an outdoor meal, if you would."

"Yes, Captain."

"And Hudson?"

His valet waited.

"No saddles."

"Sir?" There was no concealing his man's shock.

Wil swung himself round the balustrade and went into breakfast. "No saddles, Hudson," he called out. "Today we ride Romany fashion."

Chapter Thirty-Three

Syeira entered her brother's sickroom, the door slamming shut behind her. "I wish to speak with you."

Valkin started, dropping his riding jacket on the floor. "It is the custom to knock, my sister, my *pen*." He bent to pick up his jacket, wincing.

"Is it not also your custom to speak with both parties before arranging personal matters between yourselves?" She did her best to keep her anger warm, but when he winced again as he attempted to pull the jacket on, she slapped his hand away. "Here, let me help." Were all men so irritating? "Your muscles will be stiff for some time and the skin is still new." She helped him into the jacket, fastened his buttons and stood back to appraise her handiwork. "You are obviously aware that Captain Clifton has offered to take me riding?"

"Yes," her brother replied cautiously.

"He also said you have agreed to allow him to court me." Syeira tied his sash unnecessarily tight. Relenting a little when she heard him gasp, her glare did not falter as she held her brother's eyes.

Valkin favoured her with one of his appraising stares. "You do not wish to go riding with Captain Clifton?"

Without taking her eyes from his, Syeira made a tutting noise in her throat. "This is not the point, Valkin. The point is I am not an Englishwoman."

"Of course you're not. I doubt Clifton would court you if you were. They seem to bore him." Valkin furrowed his brow. "I fear I am missing something. What is this about?"

Syeira took a long-suffering breath. "It is not how we Romany do this. I should have been part of your interview with the captain." She scowled at her brother, future *sher-engro* of House Brishen and soon to be her *krallis*. "I am a Romany woman, Valkin. Not a filly. You did not think to inquire as to my desires at all? I feel like an

Englishwoman. It is no wonder so many of them are so unhappy—and I do *not* like it."

Dawning realisation in her brother's expression. *Finally.*

"You are right, Syeira," her brother acknowledged. "I should of course have discussed this with you too. Excuse my interference."

Syeira calmed at once. "Not 'too' Valkin. *First.* As for excusing you, I shall try." She nodded towards his boots. "You'd best get those on quickly."

"What for?"

Syeira stared. "For *riding with Captain Clifton.* He said you have agreed to chaperone, is it not so? I do not wish to keep him waiting."

"You *wish* to be courted by him now?"

"I never for a moment intended otherwise," she replied. "This is *my* choice."

"Umm, Syeira?" Her brother held out his boot. "Could you—ah?"

"I have my own toilette to attend to." She spun on her heel and took her leave, pretending not to hear the Romany prince muttering under his breath that he did not understand women at all and it was a good thing he had no wife. Syeira silently agreed, although she personally believed that the right kind of wife would sort this arrogance of his right out.

***

Racing ahead of Wil and Valkin, Syeira sent the little brown mare cantering across the park, her wild hair cascading behind her. She glanced behind. Wil was close, Valkin's mount trotting along a fair distance away.

Syeira felt happier than she had in years, though it might all be in vain. She didn't care and was determined to give herself as much of a life as she was permitted. Pulling her mount to a stop as she reached the copse of trees, she blushed, laughing as Wil pulled up beside her, lightly bumping his thigh up against hers.

"You bested Nero," Wil said.

"You allowed me the win," she replied, still breathing heavily. The movement brought Wil's eyes to her breasts, jade eyes darkening with desire. The charge between them seemed to grow hotter.

Wil grinned. "Let you win? Not exactly. I admit to holding Nero back so I could study your form, Syeira."

"Have you seen enough then?"

Wil laughed and shook his head, which was answer enough.

Lifting her face up to the sun, Syeira smiled in sheer joy at the beauty of the day, then froze in place as she spied a rider galloping towards them. Her mouth dried. An awful presentiment stole through her.

"I think it is Janfri," she said, as Valkin rode up. Their grouping halted, watching as the boy came towards them at speed.

Her belly tightened as she glanced at Valkin, the happiness fading from his face as it fled from hers. Could she not be spared even one day of joy? Sadness pooled somewhere behind her eyes. She could not feign any other feeling in this moment. Wil's knuckles whitened with tension as they curled tightly into Nero's dark mane, his lips curling into a smile of comfort, a smile of support. She breathed again, her heart lifting a fraction.

"Valkin," Janfri called, racing towards them. "Valkin." The boy paused, catching his breath. "Papa is dying. We are summoned."

Valkin swore. "How long?" he asked in Romany.

"A day. Two. No more."

Manoeuvring the mare until the animal stood beside Grygry, Syeira reached one arm awkwardly towards her little brother and squeezed him in a hug as best she could.

"Do not be afraid, Janfri." She repeated herself in English for Wil's benefit, including him even though this was family business. Shaking off the heaviness behind her eyelids, she looked at their host. "I beg your pardon, Wil. Our father—"

She could not form the words 'Our father is dying.' She could not make such a hopeless statement become real. Her tears fell slowly and she shook her head to clear them, struggling to keep herself from shaking. Valkin and Janfri closed in, mounted on either side of her, each Romany looping their arms around the shoulders of the other, until they formed a little knot of mourners. Janfri's shoulders shook against hers. Valkin held them all steady.

"Syeira."

That soothing voice again. Low and rich, like sandalwood and honey. Wil's voice. Syeira looked up into eyes of gold-green and the strangest feeling came over her, as though she knew precisely how far above a heavy storm cloud the sun truly shone. A smile curved across her face as she drank him in, absorbing the warmth of his presence and the kindness he showed to them now. She'd never felt more grateful.

Wil closed his eyes, clasping his hands under his chin. "Are you ready, Syeira?"

Valkin nodded encouragement as both he and Janfri readied their breath. Syeira closed her eyes, placing her hands together. "We are ready, Wil."

The four of them breathed deeply. Then twice more, each inhalation steadying them in the present. Each exhalation preparing them for the loss to come.

Syeira turned her mount in readiness. "I am sorry, Wil."

"As am I," Valkin held out his hand.

Wil shook it, nodding solemnly. "If there is anything you need from the house, we will assist you." His concern was soothing, like the rich timbre of his speech.

"I thank you." Valkin spoke a few urgent words to Syeira, before he turned together with Janfri, kicking their mounts into a gallop.

"What did Valkin say?"

Syeira's eyes dropped to her mare's neck. "He—he said I may say my farewells privately." Syeira stared after her brothers, now two small markers in the distance. "My brother is not as careless as he appears," she mused. "Like most men, he feels more than he reveals." Eyeing Wil from beneath half-closed lashes, she continued. "I behaved improperly after your assembly yesterday, but I cannot honestly offer to beg your pardon."

"Why not?"

"I am always honest." Her heart thundered at her as she marshalled her courage and met his gaze full on. "I am not sorry."

"Neither am I." Wil's gaze locked on hers.

The now-familiar heat flared between them. Syeira blushed, watching Wil shift atop his horse, her heart drumming in time with this feeling, this moment, this powerfully tender sensation within her breast. *For what, after all, is the point of courage in half-measures?* Her Mama had taught her that.

"Well?" Wil's deep voice roused her. "Do we attend on your father?"

Syeira stared. "You can't mean to attend me to his bedside?"

"That is exactly what I do mean, Syeira. Are you going to lead, or shall I?"

Syeira did not move. "You wish to meet my father?"

"Of course. We are courting, or had you forgotten?"

Forgotten? Impossible.

"I am—I am surprised. And, also, Papa is…" She looked down, away from Wil's too-perceptive gaze. Her fingers threaded through the little brown mare's mane. "Papa is not terribly complimentary as regards Englishmen. He is not often aware of his speech." She raised her head, met his gaze, and saw only tenderness and concern.

Wil simply shrugged. "Is that all? I am the son of the Duke of Carston, Syeira. The man offends half the realm before elevenses. Your father's illness is not of his choosing." He softened his tone. "Besides, I attend on him to be useful to you."

"To me?

"To you, Syeira." The way he spoke her name was a balm. She wondered if she'd ever become accustomed to his gentle consideration. To the beautiful way he simply cared.

"Thank you, Wil." Her heart was too full to say much more. She gazed at him a moment before nudging the mare into a canter. "Follow me?"

Chapter Thirty-Four

They arrived at the Romany campsite directly behind Valkin and Janfri. Syeira's brothers didn't question Wil's presence. They simply shook his hand after they'd all dismounted and thanked him for attending them.

Wil gazed about him as they led their mounts through the camp. Dozens of coloured tents established a sort of semi-circle at a fairly uniform distance from the large central fire, which seemed the focal point of about every activity, and of these there were many. Several young Romany men were working young horses in a penned-off enclosure. Some dozens of older Romany women bent over their kettles, coaxing the great fire while younger girls assisted, running to and fro with sticks for the fire or various ingredients to add to the cooking. A few Romany women nodded over distaffs or seemed to be drying herbs in another open space, suitably distanced from the busy comings and goings of men, women and children near the fire. Everyone seemed to have their tasks to perform and set about them accordingly.

A silent sentinel of men stood in a wide circle around them all, armed with sticks, rifles and what looked like a kind of club. Their hostility towards Wil was palpable, until Valkin and Syeira eyed each one in turn. After this, the men took no notice of him at all.

"Our perimeter guard," Syeira explained.

"Even on a bounded estate?" Wil asked, then he understood. Their *sher-engro* was dying. His heir was out riding with the English. The Romany could not risk their families in this moment. They *would* not. A powerful feeling moved through him and he felt again their warmth, their closeness of filial affection that had impressed him ever since he'd first encountered Brishen. His response persisted as a kind of wistful envy. Their sense of family was visible everywhere he looked.

From mothers nursing their infants while they stirred meals over kettles and pots, to sisters carrying food across to the horsemen who were ready to rest. Nothing underlined the care and protectiveness quite so much as those silent, watchful men standing at even intervals. One faced inward, the next outward, and so on. Each one was accompanied by a dog who remained alert at the feet of the guard to whom he belonged. There was as much tradition here, as much history, as Wil felt at the Little Chapel. He felt far more comfortable than he'd expected. Perhaps all that mattered was that there *were* traditions to which a man might anchor himself.

Syeira stopped to kiss the small knot of men and women who came up to them as they walked through the camp. Then she gestured toward him. "This is Captain Clifton. Wil, my brothers and sisters. Narilla is the youngest. Then Chal, Daiena and Tornapo." She looked around. "Reyna must be attending Papa."

Syeira's sisters seemed uncertain as to whether or not they ought to curtsey. Wil shook his head. "This is no time for that. I am here to assist in any way Brishen may require. Please, ask for what you need." He stepped back, deferring to the prince and princess. This wasn't about him. They were the leaders here.

He looked down in surprise when Syeira slipped her bare hand in his. Smiling, he allowed himself to be drawn into the throng as the prince and princess were pulled towards the only walled dwelling he could see. It was a large wooden caravan set some way off from the tents of the rest of Brishen. Smoke curled from the chimney into the cobalt sky. Wil wondered if all of Brishen took shelter there when the weather proved inclement. He thought of the storms that ravaged this part of the country and shook his head. Nothing brought a family closer than weathering all storms, including death.

"I must attend Papa." Syeira turned to Wil, leaned up and kissed his cheek. Right there before her entire house. "I will be back as soon as I can." She knocked lightly at the carved wooden door. It opened wide as a Romany girl only slightly younger than Syeira herself flew at her with tears in her eyes.

"Syeira." The girl's choked sob spoke to her distress, and her relief.

"Reyna." Syeira held her sister for a long moment.

Despite the tears streaming from her eyes, Reyna stared at Wil over Syeira's shoulder with the same speculative look the Romany prince had speared him with during their interview. After a silent moment, she stepped back from Syeira, cleared her throat and curtsied, her gaze turning from him to her older sister. Syeira introduced them to each other.

Reyna looked from Syeira back to Wil. "It will ease his mind to meet you in time, Captain."

Wil bowed. "What can I do?"

"There is nothing more to be done."

Wil nodded then turned to Syeira. "I will remain in your camp until you call for me."

Valkin spoke a few words to some of the younger Romany men as the family entered the caravan in order. The look on Syeira's face as she passed in tightened Wil's chest. He would go nowhere until he had somehow seen to her comfort. However, he could not wait idly to be summoned. Everywhere he looked, the Romany were active, busy and purposeful. The need to act, to participate, to do *something* gripped him.

He turned to the men around him. "May I assist you gentlemen at all?"

They smiled and nodded, drawing him across to the fire where he was offered a pillowed seat before one of the tents. Two men sat beside him, handing around river water and wild apples for all three of them. One was older, and the other might be his son.

"Eat, captain," said the older man. "The *sher-engro* will call for you soon enough."

It sounded like a warning, especially when both men laughed.

Wil cleared his throat. "Exactly how ill is your *sher-eng*?" He'd pronounced the word incorrectly. The men grinned.

"*Sher-engro*." The older of the men pronounced it slowly, waiting for him to repeat it back.

"*Sher-engro*?" Wil asked, relishing the clap on his back the other man offered.

"Very good, sir. Like your woods." He smiled, his teeth bright against his dark mouth.

"You've had some success with your hunt then?" Wil asked and was gratified when both men nodded. "And your *sher-engro*?" He asked again, slowing his speech this time.

The man shook his head. "He does not hunt with us, captain. He is sick. A very bad sickness. He will not see two more suns, so his daughter says. The prince and princess are everything to us now. They take good care of Brishen."

Wil nodded, not knowing what to say.

The men rose, sighing. They both looked tired. Wil rose too.

A screeching wail from behind interrupted them and the older man glanced toward a tent where a woman was emerging, a swaddled babe in her arms. The look on the young father's face was like being struck in the heart. His joy was infectious as he presented his young wife and infant child to Wil, smiling and insisting Wil hold the child for the briefest of instances. Wil saw the uncertainty in the mother's face. Clearly, she was not quite sure an Englishman's arms were the safest place for her new babe. He held the child in close and gazed down into a pair of the darkest eyes he'd ever yet seen. The babe gurgled up at him. He rocked the child gently with an instinct he had not known he possessed. The strangest sensation moved through him. Calm and a sense of rightness as he noted the young family's devotion to one another, as an almost physical thing he could touch and attach himself to. He traced the chubby little cheek, smiling when the child grasped his finger and gripped it oh-so tight.

"A fine child, sir. Ma'am," he commented when he handed the child back. Wil shook the father's hand. "I thank you for sharing your meal with me. Allow me to offer this trade. You are one of the perimeter guard?" The man nodded. "I will stand guard in your place until I am called. You may then take some rest with your family— yes?"

The young mother favoured Wil with the brightest smile he'd yet seen in the camp. She nodded, thanking him before retreating in to her family's tent with a whirl of ruffled skirts.

Wil moved to take up his station. He didn't know what had possessed him to offer such a trade, but he liked it. Facing out towards the trout lake, he watched the landscape for any sign of approach. He stood at attention, feeling important, useful and valued, feeling *wanted*. The sensation was so powerful he was grateful he faced the lake.

He glanced around the perimeter, taking in all of the guardsmen. All of them were taking care of the people of Brishen, from the tiny baby he'd held to the ailing *sher-engro* in his caravan saying a last goodbye to his children. They could take this time because the rest of their house allowed it, as the young father could spend time with his family because Wil stood guard. Suddenly, Wil felt it. This was family. This sense of connectedness enabled Brishen to do their duty without resentment. Each one of them was valued, and that value was continually being shared.

A boy ran up as he stood there, watching the horizon for any threat to Brishen.

"Captain Clifton?"

"I am."

"*Sher-engro* asked for you."

"Thank you—er, Chal?" The boy bore a striking resemblance to Janfri.

Chal nodded. "Knock, captain, and you may enter. I must find another guard in your place." The young father took his position in the circle, eyes scanning the grounds for the unlikely arrival of any threat.

Wil followed Chal to the caravan, knocked softly on the wooden door and stepped back.

Chal passed inside as Syeira opened the door, her eyes overflowing. "Papa is failing." Her voice broke. Wil pulled his princess close, pressing a gentle kiss to her temple. "It is slow and his mind... He is not making sense."

He held her tight. It felt so *good* to feel her leaning into him, to have her need him. Want him. Choose him. It was time for him to voice the choice he'd already made.

Before he could speak, Syeira pulled away and gestured for him to enter. The caravan was dimmed to semi-darkness by shawls covering the windows. There was a fire in the little wooden stove and that, plus the abundance of people in the space, made for a warm interview. Wil tugged at his cravat as he approached the foot of a carved wooden bed.

A wizened old Romany man lay swathed in the down and silk coverlet, propped up with dozens of cushions. His eyes were closed. Beside him, at the head of the bed, and with his hand holding his father's, the Romany prince acknowledged Wil with a nod of his head.

Syeira took up her place on her father's left, holding his other gnarled hand between hers. Her eyes were bright with grief and more unshed tears.

Wil looked at each member of the Brishen family in turn. All of them had tears in their eyes or running down their faces. Not one of them even tried to master their grief, sharing it instead here in the circle of their family, witnessing the loss of their dear Papa. The power of it took his breath away. That they allowed him to stand in this place with them spoke of an esteem for him, a regard, a love. Wil was grateful, honoured, connected. A surge of emotion took him, so raw, so powerful, he shook with it, bowing his head in awe.

The old man seemed made of paper as he opened his eyes to stare at Wil. "*Sarishan*," he whispered, closing his eyes again.

Wil bowed. "Good morning, *sher-engro*."

The Romany king's eyes did not open again.

"He cannot hear you, Wil." Syeira's voice was sad and small and full of grief. "He is no longer awake."

"Is he—?" Wil could not say the words aloud. Every person in that room was already in mourning.

Syeira shook her head. "Not yet. Soon, I think." She raised her hand and held it out to him. He moved to her side, folding his palm over hers. She hunched into him, slow tears spilling over her lovely cheeks. Wil thought the blanched look on her face might haunt him forever.

Valkin passed his hand across his eyes. Even from across the caravan, Wil could see his shoulders shaking. Wil realised he was shaking too. His breaths came too heavily. A roaring sound filled his ears and he closed his eyes, trying to steady his breath. Syeira's other three sisters were already weeping quietly, their brothers' arms around them, holding them firmly together. Other than the soft sobs and the rattling breaths from the bedclothes, the caravan was so quiet Wil could hear each pop from the wood stove.

A knock at the door made them all jump. Chal opened the door to one of the guards, whispered and closed it again. He spoke a few short words in Valkin's direction. The prince stared and Syeira stood up with a little cry, her hand clenching inside Wil's own.

"What?" Wil glanced from Chal to Valkin to Syeira. "What is it?" He rose beside his princess, an awful foreboding invading his chest. He felt as he did before a battle, teetering on the edge of loss.

Valkin stood up. "Besnik have sent for the princess. The *sher-engro*'s wife is dead and he wishes to marry Syeira."

"No." Wil's stomach clenched. He swore viciously.

Valkin cleared his throat. "Do you wish to marry the princess, Wil?"

In that moment, Wil knew what to do. He could not—he *would not*—let this happen. He looked at Syeira, nodding. He heard a sound from his princess. Something between a gasp and a sob as she withdrew her hand from his. He glanced at her, but he couldn't make out her expression in the darkness. "What happens now?" he asked Valkin, glancing at the old man in the bed.

"This is now about timing." Valkin informed them all. "Besnik cannot ask that Syeira leave House Brishen at the moment. I shall speak with the messenger and parlay us a little grace. We cannot delay unduly. Papa's word still stands while he lives." He glanced meaningfully at his father before surveying his siblings. "I'll need all my brothers."

The royal men of Brishen filed out.

Chapter Thirty-Five

Syeira said a few words to her sisters and looked at Wil.

"May we speak outside?" She spoke in tones that sounded wooden and forced.

"Of course, princess." Wil bowed, following her from the caravan.

Once outside, Syeira faced him, dark eyes flashing a storm warning. "Wil, what is this? Why did you tell the prince you wish to marry me?"

Wil stared as though she were speaking Romany instead of English. "We are courting for a reason, or did you forget?"

Syeira made a dismissive sound in her throat. "Do you think I do not know that that was a game?"

"A game?" Wil heard his voice harden. Carefully, he forced himself to reply. "I'm afraid I am the one who does not understand."

"A way to placate my brother and—and have a day or two of joy. A—a *kindness*." Her eyes welled as she stared back at him, the pain so clearly evident that his own heart hurt to see it.

"I appreciate it, Wil. I do. It is only that—"

She blinked hard, her last few words so garbled he could barely make them out.

"I beg your pardon?"

She breathed in deeply. "I appreciate your kindness. I do not want to marry *kindness*."

Wil stared at her. "You appreciate my *kindness*?"

Syeira stepped back, away from him, well out of reach. "What is the difference if I marry Besnik or if I marry you? He wishes to wed me out of duty. And you?" Her cheeks flushed with mortification. "You would marry me only out of pity. I do not understand this."

"You think this is about *pity*?" Of course she did. How could she not? She had spoken to him of love and he had turned away. She had chosen him, and he had left her weeping alone in her room. But that was before he knew himself. Words would not be enough this time.

A kind of buzzing began in his ears as he reached for her, the drumming of his heart beating out a rhythm: *Please say yes, please say yes, please say yes.*

Syeira didn't move away when Wil closed his hands on her shoulders, pulling her to him. As his mouth met hers, he caught her gasp between his lips, sighing when her tongue met his. *Oh God, the heat of this one kiss.* Wil forgot her position, and his own. All he felt, all he knew, was the rightness of his mouth on hers. A union that could no longer be denied.

"Pity be damned," he whispered fiercely, feeling her shiver as he pulled her closer, her response to his kiss already more than he could stand.

The buzzing in his ears grew louder, resolving into a murmuring. A low sound that he recognised as a kind of humming. Wil looked up, breathing hard. The guard he'd stood in for was leading a rapidly growing crowd of onlookers in a soft chorus. He grinned at Wil as though all the riches of England were suddenly before him.

The man's wife stood at his side. Bringing her hands together, she began a slow clapping. The action was taken up by her family. Then, one by one, all the Romany gathered, joining in until the rhythmic clapping surrounded them. Everywhere Wil looked, he saw joyful faces smiling back at him. He heard the soft humming in his ears and felt lighter and strangely calm. So *this* was family. This was community. This was the way of Romany love. He put his hand to his chin, shook his head and smiled. *What now?*

The young Romany wife looked at Syeira with a profoundly serious expression, speaking quietly under cover of the steady clapping.

Wil looked down at the reluctant smile on Syeira's face. "What did she say?"

Syeira was already blushing. "She asked me why I would speak such nonsense to my betrothed."

Wil grinned, inclining his head to the lady who had assisted his suit. He turned back to his princess. He would have preferred to declare his heart privately rather than before her whole camp, but perhaps this was better. It was certainly different.

Stroking her golden cheek with his hand, Wil locked his gaze on hers, holding her so close it was as if they shared one breath. "You once told me I was a man capable of great love," he said. "Do you remember, Syeira?"

She nodded, her dark eyes fixed on his as the clapping echoed across the lake.

"I chose you without realising. I did not know myself then. I did not understand. I never said I love you Syeira, but I do." His eyes prickled with emotion. "I choose *you*." He looked down to find his love mirrored in her shimmering tears.

She leaned against him, sobbing in earnest. At the look on her face, an awful feeling undercut his joy. The clapping began to slow. An omen, a warning, the balance within him tip, tip, tipping. Tipping the wrong way.

"Wil, I cannot accept." His princess shook her head, moving away from him again. "I cannot remain at Clifton Hall."

Wil shuddered. "What? I would not ask it of you, Syeira. I would not ask it of myself and before you ask if I need my father's permission to marry, I do not." He grimaced.

"You will lose your living."

"I shall find another. I am not entirely useless you know. Second sons rarely are." He smiled. "Is—is this your only objection?"

"No."

Pain lanced through him so deeply he felt felled, like a tree whose heart was cut out, axe-stroke by axe-stroke. The clapping picked up tempo a little, echoing the frantic pounding within his breast. *Don't give up, don't give up, don't give up.*

"Wil, you cannot give up your family. I will not allow it."

He hesitated. This was the hardest sacrifice for him. "*You* will not allow it? Syeira, you and your Romany taught me that home is the people you love, not the place in which they reside. The people I *love*, Syeira. And chief among them is you."

All of Brishen were assembled now, clapping faster. Wil felt them all watching, *willing* him to see this through.

She was backing away, but he walked slowly towards her, taking his pace from the rhythmic clapping on all sides. "Brishen will be my family. Besides, I'll not lose Roger and Lydie. The duke cannot live forever, and he is so rarely at the hall I daresay we shall visit more than he." His voice slowed to silence as she stopped moving and he came to stand before her, facing his princess with all of Brishen beating out the rhythm of his love. If she didn't accept him now…

***

Syeira gazed at him, dark eyes wide, hardly daring to believe. *Could this be true?* Could the man she chose, be choosing her? Surely she was slipping into some sort of feverish dream, as though she'd mistaken mint for pennyroyal. The heat of his gaze, the warmth where his fingers met hers, and oh, the rhythm of her heart was enough to lead the rest of her in a wild dance.

"Can it be true?" Carefully, hardly daring to breathe now, Syeira lifted her palm to Wil's torso, measuring his heartbeat against her hand. Wanting to be sure, she leaned in, her ear flat against his chest to hear it. His heart hammered in rhythm with her own. Tilting her head, she stared up at the man she loved. Reaching up, she pulled his face down, kissing him once, full on the mouth. The clapping broke out of its rhythm, becoming thunderous applause so loud it frightened the horses. Wil laughed, pressing her to his side. Syeira smiled at her Romany and her smile became a laugh. They applauded that too.

Then, with her lips beside his ear, she whispered, "I love you, Wil."

"Marry me, then."

At her nod of acceptance, her lover's face warmed into a smile so widely open, so entirely directed at her, that she never wanted to see it leave his eyes.

The caravan door opened and her three sisters stood there.

"I beg your pardon my sister, my *pen*. Could you please assist?" Reyna's eyes were starry with mixed tears as Syeira stepped up to the caravan door and held her close.

"Of course. Did we wake Papa?"

Her sister shook her head, speaking in English for the benefit of their guest. "No. He is still not conscious. But none of us are deaf, Syeira." Her smile at Wil tempered the sadness in her eyes. "The prince will send for you when his parlay is complete, captain."

Syeira arched a brow at Wil. "As you will learn, there are no secrets in a Romany camp." She sighed, disappearing inside the little doorway.

Chapter Thirty-Six

Wil rode back to Clifton Hall by the road. He needed to make his farewells to his brother and sister. The heaviness in his chest reminded him how difficult his departure would be. Still, it wasn't forever, and his military service had taught him the value of reliable correspondence.

Slowing his canter as he approached the steward's cottage, Wil thought to have a word with Yates while he was here. Thank him for his work. Yates's boy stood by the gatepost.

"Good afternoon, captain." He bowed.

Wil smiled. "An excellent bow, Master William. Good afternoon to you. Is Mr Yates at home?"

The boy shook his head. "Papa was summoned to the hall by His Grace."

"What?" Swinging Nero abruptly towards the hall without a word of goodbye, Wil set off at a gallop. He was forced to pull up nearer the stables when he found the duke's carriage blocking his path.

Handing Nero off to the grooms, he covered the remaining distance on foot, pausing to listen before entering by a side door. Hearing little in the way of expletives or exploding porcelain, Wil found the eerie silence less reassuring than overt outbursts.

Passing the second breakfast room, he heard sobbing. *Lydia.* Wil stopped, knocking gently.

"Wil." His little sister flew at him, a ball of white fur tumbling to the floor with an indignant yip.

"Lydie, what is it?" She was sobbing so hard her whole body shook as he held her.

She managed to utter the words, "Papa's home," before another storm of sobs overtook her.

"Reason enough."

"And Miss—Miss Lee is with him. They are at l-luncheon and she—she sent me away. Told me to eat in th-the nursery."

Wil closed his eyes, hugging his sister tight, rubbing her back as he'd seen Syeira do to calm her. Was there no end to the duke's cruelty? And how dare he bring that whore here? Wil swallowed hard past the ball of fury in his throat. "Never mind, Lydie. I daresay you're in better company here."

"She does not look like my governess at all." Her voice hitched, but she was no longer sobbing.

"No. I imagine not." He sighed, wishing he could take Lydie with him. "I imagine too that you will not have to endure her for much longer."

"What is it you mean, Wil?"

He could not explain without hurting his sister further. He stood, straightening her dress as well as his own, reflecting on the very great talent His Grace possessed for reducing females to tears everywhere he went. He shook his head, tugging on the bell pull.

A footman arrived a moment later. "You will serve luncheon for Miss Clifton and myself in here." He smiled as Lydia's mouth turned up at the edges—finally. "I must write a letter while we await our luncheon," he told her when the footman departed. "Can you keep yourself and your puppy occupied while I do so?"

Lydie nodded, moving with her puppy to the chairs by the fireplace.

Taking his seat behind the old oak desk, Wil watched his sister settle down with a book. Sighing, he took up his quill. Slowly, as though it hurt to do it, he drew out the letter he'd begun days earlier.

Dear General Wallis,

I thank you for your letter and for your confidence. I regret I am unable to close with this commission before the end of the quarter.

I understand the Earl of Horsham to be seeking a similar purchase. May I suggest an introduction from Lord Clifton?

I am unable to present you myself. My absence from London will be of some duration.

It has been my honour to serve His Majesty.

Capt. Warwick Clifton, Esq.

His note resigning his captain's commission was even shorter. He sanded both papers, locking them away from His Grace's sight. Wil stiffened at the door opening behind him.

"Breathe, Wil. It's only me." Roger's voice was a welcome relief. "I am come to see after Lydie." He held out his hand and his sister hurried over to him, slipping her fingers through his. "And to get out of there, in truth."

"Is it true he brought a—" Wil stopped, biting his tongue.

Roger nodded. "His Grace is furious, by the way. He does not like to leave London mid-Season. Someone has been indiscreet. He came up when he heard 'Clifton Hall is infested with gypsies'. That's a quote." He sank into one of the chairs and rubbed his face.

Wil winced. "I beg your pardon, Roger. Permitting Brishen to camp on the estate is my doing. You ought not to bear his ill favour because of my decision."

"The duel was as much my doing as it was yours, Wil." He smiled humourlessly and then broke out in a proper grin as he offered Wil his outstretched hand. Wil took it.

"Well? Do I have the honour of addressing the princess's consort-elect?"

"You do indeed, though I must brook a slight delay." Wil filled his siblings in on his proposal. "It is decided and I will not be stopped."

Roger sat and stared at Wil, seemingly speechless. Leaning back, he studied his brother with a speculation of which Wil had not believed him capable.

"I've never seen you like this before, Wil. You aren't nearly the rake you like everyone to believe, are you? Although, I should not be surprised. Unlike His Grace and myself, you have always possessed the *capacity* to love someone better than yourself." He clapped a hand on his brother's shoulder.

Their sister's gaze flicked between brothers as though she umpired a game of lawn tennis. Wil knew she'd caught up when Lydia flew at him again, shrieking with joy this time.

"Syeira will be my sister? Oh Wil, Wil, *Wil*." It seemed she could not contain her delight. "She will live here with me?"

Wil's heart nearly broke then, as he realised she still did not understand. The door opened and two covers were brought in by silent staff. Gone were the smiles and general candour he'd seen at

Clifton Hall in recent weeks. All warmth was replaced with the cold hauteur for which his father, and Clifton Hall, were renowned. Wil barely prevented his lip from curling in distaste.

When the servants were gone, he knelt, facing his sister. "Lydie, Syeira will not be able to stay here at the hall."

"Then where will you live when you are married?" His sister's delighted countenance froze in place.

Roger uttered a sort of sighing moan. Wil closed his eyes, opening them again to meet his sister's gaze.

Her eyes filled slowly with tears to spill down her cheeks. "You're leaving, aren't you?"

"I'm sorry, Lydie." He pulled her into the tightest hug he could, holding her until she leaned back.

"It's all right, Wil." She faced him, blotchy face, snotty nose and all. "I'm all right. Of course you must go. Syeira deserves the best and my brothers *are* the best." Wil's heart ached as she took a huge, shaky breath and straightened her stance. He shrank inwardly at the idea of leaving her at Clifton Hall.

"Look after her," he said needlessly to Roger.

"Of course." Roger was hardly one for tears, but Wil saw the sadness in his face. He imagined it echoed the look on his own. "The princess will make you happy, Wil. She loves you, you know."

"I know," Wil replied, his voice thick and soft with pain. "And I will miss you both."

Lydia sniffed a little, taking her place at the table. She looked at Wil but he shook his head. "I must face the duke." He grimaced at Roger. "You are certain he will forbid me?"

Roger laughed, not unkindly, as he commandeered Wil's cover. "Oh my, yes. He'll cut you off without a penny. But I'd give a good part of my inheritance to see the duke's face when you break the news. A *good* part."

Wil smiled faintly. He wasn't even sure why he'd asked. Hope, perhaps. The vain hope that a son's happiness mattered a little more to his father than increasing the consequence of a duchy that was already more bountiful than any one generation could possibly require.

He stood watching his brother and sister for a long moment. Roger teased Lydie as they began to eat, until she smiled a little. Breathing too deeply past the dull ache in his breast, he left.

Hearing hoofbeats as he passed the main door, Wil was out the front before Oates or any of the duke's men could attend. The Romany bay horse stood snorting on the gravel as Chal Brishen jumped to the ground, handed him a note, and bowed.

Tearing open the Brishen seal, Wil's mind ran through frantic scenarios. *If Besnik have claimed her already, if she is lost to me…* He did not doubt he'd go after her. This feeling in his heart was too strong, too powerful. He could not give her up. He simply *would not* let her marry another man. He looked down, hardly able to read the words before him, written in Valkin's hurried scrawl.

Sir,

   Tonight we bury our father. I am responsible for Syeira now. My consent you have. Besnik arrive in three days to attend Papa's death rites. It will be best for Syeira to be married before this time.
   VB.

PS: Your steward has given us notice. Brishen must depart the duchy by dawn.

Three days? Even a duke's son could not marry so quickly. *Damn.*

Wil looked wildly around for some sort of guidance. His eyes met the eager dark gaze of Chal. "You have my condolences, Chal."

Chal nodded his thanks, tutting impatiently. "I believe our new *sher-engro* is hoping to hear your plan." Chal gazed at him, seeming to convey some sort of secret by his looks. "There is no one who parlays better than Valkin." He bowed again. "Papa's death rites do not take three days, captain."

Wil stared at him, realisation dawning far too slowly. "Do I take it Syeira can be ready to travel before Besnik arrive?"

Chal clapped his hands. "I am also to tell you that all of Brishen must be beyond the borders of your duchy by dawn." The boy paused. "*All* of us."

Wil understood. Brishen would not risk the law. Not even for their princess.

He turned at the sound of Roger's voice behind him. "Have the Princess Brishen brought here as soon as your father is laid." His brother stood at the top of the stone steps, looking at Chal. "Tell her to bring a bridal gown and enough swag for a week."

Chal looked from one Clifton brother to the other. "*Which* one of you is she marrying?"

"Him." Pointing his finger delightedly at his brother, Roger snorted. "Most assuredly *him*." When he stopped laughing long enough, he tried out his most ducal glare on the child. "Well? What are you waiting for? Get to it, man."

Before the thunder of hooves had faded from his ears, Wil turned to his brother. "You have a plan?"

Roger tapped the side of his nose gently. "Brishen has a plan. He simply needs you to follow it. There is no wilier a gentleman in the country than the Romany prince. Or king he is now, I suppose. You see how he found you 'extra' time? He expects you to use it. The princess needs to be out of here before Besnik arrive."

"I have no objection to Gretna, but do you have a plan for the duke?"

Roger shook his head. "Being in love seems to have addled your brains, Wil. His Grace has this day completed a *very* exhausting overnight journey with a *very* young lady. I doubt either he or Miss Lee will remain in the lower rooms after dinner."

"I hope not. He's had Yates order all of Brishen off the estate."

"Did you expect anything else?"

Wil sighed, shaking his head. "No. Still, they have a funeral to arrange. Yates might have—"

"Yates can only do as His Grace directs. You know this as well as I. Now, are we going in?" He jerked his head toward the window of the salon where their father sat at luncheon with his latest trollop.

Wil stared at his brother. "We?"

Roger grimaced. "No one should have to endure His Grace's rage alone. Besides, I want to see how such a thing is done. I may have to gainsay him myself someday. Shall we say a quarter hour before I join you?"

Wil shook his head and smiled. "You are unfailingly generous, Roger."

"I am," Roger agreed.

***

Knocking loudly on the door of the salon, Wil did not await any command to enter. His Grace did not bother to rise at the sight of his second son, barely even lowering his fork before waving Wil to a seat. He waved his companion away with the same gesture, then used said fork to shovel more meat into his mouth. Wil stood until Miss Lee left, bowing as slightly as he could. An under butler poured ale then arranged bread and meats before him. Wil waited until the lackey left them entirely alone.

He looked up at the duke. "I am leaving Clifton Hall to marry the princess Brishen."

His Grace dropped his cutlery with a clang as he thundered, "Are you out of your senses?" A dribble of gravy on His Grace's chin glistened and dripped lower, the brown of it even browner and shinier against the livid purple of the duke's jowls. "Why would you do this thing? Is the girl—have you—"

His father seemed to gather himself like tamping down powder before releasing a volley. His next words were not so much spoken as spat at his son. Indeed, a fleck of snowy spittle appeared at one corner of His Grace's lips.

"Am I expecting a grandchild, sir?" It seemed the only reason the duke could comprehend for Wil's decision. "The girl has trapped you, then?"

"Of course not."

"Then you haven't touched her? Harmed her in any way?" his father demanded, sharp grey eyes narrowing to tips of steel.

"It may indeed be unique for a Clifton to marry a woman *before* taking her, but I assure you that it is quite my intention, Your Grace. I would never harm the princess, and I will be the first man to call out anyone who tried. That goes for those who stain the honour of her house as well, sir."

"Yates has orders to clear these gypsies from my lands," the duke sniffed as if he hadn't heard a word Wil said. "They are to leave the duchy immediately. Your gypsy whore will be gone by— *What the devil?*"

"Say that again," Wil demanded, fighting to free his arms as Roger held him back. It was as well for the duke that Lord Clifton entered the room at that moment, or His Grace the Duke of Carston would have found himself flat on his back on the floor.

"Wil. Wil." Roger locked him in the sort of death-grip of which their wrestling tutor would be proud. "*Wil.* Calm down man."

"If you speak of her that way again, you will meet me in Paddington, and all of London shall *know*, sir." Wil shook his brother off, addressing the duke in deadly tones. Fisting his hands, he clenched his jaw so hard he felt in danger of cracking teeth—and not his own.

The duke's jowls wobbled as he seethed, finally managing to speak through tightened lips: "These people have been known to ask savage recompense." His Grace sniffed again, as though his son were a bad smell instead of a man. "However, I am sure they can be bought."

"You'll find no one from the royal house is for sale." *Including the consort-elect to the princess.* "There is no need in any case."

"What do you mean, boy?" The duke looked thoroughly wrong-footed.

"I am quite determined." Wil bit back a smile, enjoying himself now. "Sir."

The Duke stood taller than his sons, his fury evident. "You are quite aware you will be cut off?"

"I am." Wil felt the steadiness in his spine as he stood his ground. This was not about besting the duke. This was about his, Wil Clifton's, *life*. The Little Chapel bell sounded loudly in the silence. Brishen were burying their *sher-engro*. The duke turned slowly towards the melodic tolling.

"What the devil is that?"

Wil's answer came with a smile that reached to his heart. "The sound of a new tradition, Your Grace."

His future happiness lay with Syeira, not this man. Wil would do whatever needed to be done and face whom he must, be it Besnik or the furious peer glaring at him across the Clifton Hall salon. Wil watched his father curiously, surveying His Grace with the most complete sense of calm. He'd never seen the duke so angry. The man's face was a truly alarming shade of puce.

"We shall speak more of this at dinner," His Grace concluded.

"I think not. I came to inform you of my choice, sir. Not to be dissuaded. Besides, I have orders to be beyond your borders by dawn." Wil stood firm in the horrified silence that followed. Tiny sounds he'd never noticed before crept in to fill it. Dogs rustling in sleep beneath the table. The clock on the mantel ticking too slowly. Buzzing from some sunshine-warmed insect beyond the window.

"Then you are no son of mine." The duke turned away, his tone final.

Roger stood between them, calmly miserable.

Wil, on the other hand, felt better than he had in years. There was freedom in choosing a future for himself. A future that led away from the unhappiness at Clifton Hall.

***

An hour before sunset, Wil met Roger out front with a carriage and four of the duke's best horses. His brother had had the sense to cover the livery. Hudson presented Wil with a set of fresh Romany linen. Wil stripped off immediately, changing his costume in the open air. Hudson hurriedly sent the serving maid back inside. His master laughed. "Is this your way of telling me I need to smarten up, Hudson?"

The valet made a sound that might have been a cough. "I have made inquiry, sir. Consort to the princess Brishen requires specific attire." He proceeded to tie a royal blue sash about his master's hips. Wil was now clad for ceremony in the Romany fashion, with his throat bare and no coat at all.

As he completed the quick change, the Romany horse came pounding up, bearing Syeira mounted behind her brother. She was clad in a black gown and shawl and carried a small swag. She passed her swag to Wil before swinging down. Wil placed his arm firmly around her shoulders, drawing her in close.

"Papa is laid," she murmured. Wil took her hands in his, squeezing them tight. Glancing briefly up at her brother, Syeira smiled softly. "Thank you, Chal."

The young boy nodded. "Sarishan." He smiled at both of them, staring at Syeira for a long moment before turning his mount to ride rapidly away. Syeira watched her youngest brother until he was out of sight, releasing a breath. She looked up, her loving smile tinged with sadness.

Wil looked down at his princess. "Is it too strange for you, a wedding on the heels of a funeral?"

Syeira shrugged heavily. "Perhaps, but I stood by Papa's grave thinking that life is always mixed this way." She smiled softly. "A little joy, a little sadness. A little grief, a little hope. Is it too fanciful, Wil?"

He shook his head with a smile. "Not if it also comes with love, Syeira."

Her eyes brightened as she looked up at him, the love he felt echoed in her gaze.

"Shall we be on our way?"

She nodded, then gripped both his hands in hers, a frown furrowing her brow. "Have you seen your father?"

Wil nodded, the scorch of shame in his cheeks. "I am glad you were not there, Syeira," he said quietly. He didn't want to tell her the full details of his interview with the duke. It was enough to say, "I'm to be cut off."

At Syeira's horrified gasp, Wil squeezed her hands tight. "It's no more than I expected."

"But Wil—"

"But nothing," he finished. "My life is about you now, Syeira. About *us*. It's not about the duchy at all. Do you understand my love?"

Syeira nodded, fresh tears spilling down over her smile. Wil kissed her brow, holding her tight.

Roger stepped forward then, his expression serious. "I want you to know not all the Cliftons think like His Grace. I intend to stand up for you."

Syeira uttered a small, sharp sound of delight, placing her hands over her mouth as her tears dried.

"Roger, you can't—" Wil began.

"I most certainly can," Roger replied. "And I'll knock you down myself if you raise any further objection. You are not yet wed. Syeira still needs a chaperon and all of Brishen are in mourning. Do I understand these traditions right, princess?"

"You are correct, my lord."

"There, you see? I'm coming to Gretna with you and we'll see if that doesn't dent the duke's false dignity a little."

"I won't have you damage your prospects on my account, Roger. You're his heir," Wil began.

"Precisely. And if he intends to make good his threat, he might find I intend to enter the regular army and serve on the front lines."

"You could be killed."

"We'll see how he likes the threat of having no Clifton heirs at all then. It will be years before Lydie can oblige him. I stand with you and there's an end to it. You are not the only Clifton who holds honour and family dear."

Wil clasped his brother's hand and forearm. "Thank you."

"Yes." Syeira echoed Wil. "Truly, my lord. Thank you." She leaned up, kissing her new brother lightly on his cheek.

"It's Roger, if you don't mind," he said, his cheeks faintly flushed. "As we're very nearly relations by marriage." Roger squeezed her hand then stepped back, allowing Wil to hand his princess into the carriage. Wil climbed in behind her. Roger took his seat on the coachman's box and they were off.

As the carriage lurched, Wil turned to Syeira. "The road to Scotland is long and dull, my sweet. I've been considering what we might speak of while we travel."

Syeira quirked her brow. "I believe we were speaking of love."

"I believe we were. I want you to know how much I admire the way you ride." His voice was light, with a husky undertone.

Dark eyes grew wider with curiosity.

"What has riding to do with love?"

"Did you know," he continued conversationally, "that you may ride without a horse?" His voice deepened with every word.

Syeira stared at him, doubting.

Wil leaned across the coach and kissed her, taking great care not to touch her. There would be time for that soon enough. "Allow me to explain," he began.

Chapter Thirty-Seven

Syeira looked down at her anvil ring and smiled to herself as they arrived at the little farmhouse Roger had leased for them. She stepped down from the carriage and looked around. "This is a sweet place for a honeymoon."

"Yes. Roger tells me it also has a herb garden and an orchard."

"Oh, may we see them?"

"Of course," Wil replied, smiling as he led her through the garden. "I know you'll not be satisfied until you see *all* the plants here."

"Thank you, Wil."

"My motivations are purely selfish, Syeira," he said with a wolfish grin. "Tonight is our wedding night and I want your undivided attention."

Heat spread out from her centre at his words and it stayed with her as they toured the gardens. Not that this surprised her. Whenever she was around Wil she felt barely contained. A look from him, a touch, a caress set her trembling with desire. Merely the thought of his kiss was enough.

She shivered in the chill evening air, pulling her furred cloak more tightly about her. Scotland was colder than she remembered. Wil had insisted on her cloak as his wedding gift. There was nothing she could give him that matched its value, so she hadn't. This was love, and love was not a trade.

They went inside where a fine dinner awaited them. They chatted and flirted but didn't touch, the tension mounting until she'd never been more aware of herself or him. Finally, they were finished eating and she retired to their room while Wil banked the fire downstairs.

A merry blaze had been set in the huge fireplace in their room, lending heat and a sensual light to the scene. A light tapping drew Syeira's attention to the door. "Come in." She untied her cape, turning to greet her husband.

Wil slipped into the room and stood gazing at her with those jade eyes she loved so much. "I could look at you forever, my love," he murmured, his voice low and deep. Heat rose to her cheeks and her knees quivered.

He held her gaze as he removed his boots, his sash, and threw his shirt across the room. Her eyes roved over his lean, muscled curves, taking in the light dusting of golden hairs on his chest she hovered there, her breath hot and tight in her throat.

Wil understood. He gave her a dazzling smile. Only his breeches remained. Her tongue slipped out to touch her lower lip as she gazed back at him.

"Sweet, sweet Syeira. You are breathtaking."

She trembled at his words. "Mmm, I thank you. But perhaps you can do more than love me with your eyes."

Wil was beside her in an instant. "Not only my eyes, princess." He took her mouth in a fierce kiss, running his wicked tongue over her lips. She pressed into him as her fire rose to match his.

She moved her palm over his chest to the pale golden hairs of his stomach. She hesitated only a moment before sliding her hand down over cloth. His breath hitched as she grazed the tip of his heat.

He caught her hand, breaking the kiss only to whisper, "Not yet," before diving between her lips again.

As they kissed, he worked the buttons of her silk gown, loosening its ties. She wore a simple silken shift he parted easily, and then he was touching her bare skin, caressing her wonderingly. Syeira barely breathed as he touched her, pooled heat rising to flickers of wicked flame.

"You're so soft, so golden, Syeira. So beautiful." He ran his fingertips across her skin, causing warm wetness to bloom between her thighs.

"I'm yours, Wil," she whispered. *So very, very his.*

Syeira moaned as his fingers grazed her nipples, stroking softly, holding her to him with a searing kiss that had her shuddering with longing.

He sank down on the plush rug before the fire, pulling her with him, his breath hot on her skin now as he drew her tender flesh into his mouth, tasting her, laving her, creating a rising heat within. He stripped off her skirts, running his hands lingeringly over her thighs.

She lay before him, naked, her body burning with undeniable fire, with shimmering, desperate need.

There was nothing to stop them now. His touch trailed heat over each part of her, exploring her body with slow, aching tenderness. As he brushed her centre, she pressed urgently against his fingers.

"Please, Wil," she whispered.

"Not yet."

He kissed her again, his mouth tracing a path across her jaw to her ear. He whispered all the ways he wanted to touch her, and how much he loved her, and how sweet and beautiful she was. He kissed down her throat, tangling his hands in her hair. He kissed her breasts, shifting above her with gentle, deliberate momentum.

He drew each tight, hardened peak into his mouth, sucking hard. Syeira cried out, bucking against him. He smiled, turning his attention to her abdomen, fiery kisses tracing a path to her navel now. He tongued her there. Syeira cried out again, not knowing what words she used or even which language, only aware that she had surrendered completely, utterly, to the deepest, sweetest sensation she'd ever known.

His breath heated her skin as he bit lightly at her stomach. Moaning, she threaded her fingers through his hair, holding his mouth to her body in a mute plea for more. As Wil stroked her centre with one slow, wicked finger, Syeira moved against him wild, hot, desperate.

He kissed lower as she twisted against him. He looked up at her, smiling as he held her hips in place then made her gasp when he placed his mouth on her centre, kissing her there. Pleasure rippled through her in wave after searing wave as he lavished her with this most intimate kiss. She writhed, screaming in his arms, his tongue a flame sending wildfire through her being. She could not feel the rug beneath her, or his hands at her hips. In all her dreams she had never imagined anything like this.

"*Burroder.* More. Oh, Wil, more. More. *Please*," she cried out as he took her closer to the edge of pleasure than she'd ever thought possible. She cried and whimpered and moaned. Wil continued his attentions until her breathing changed. She grabbed at his hair, screaming in ecstasy as her body peaked and pulsed and shook, warm, molten fire flowing through her.

It wasn't until he touched her face that she realised there were tears on her cheeks. He kissed them away then took her mouth again, holding her. As tremors of release tumbled through her, he whispered his love, kissing her neck until she shivered with desire, burning for him now, beyond reason. He pulled off his breeches with a savage motion, turning back to her, gripping her hard against him.

He eased back, watching her.

Her lips parted slightly in awe at what she saw on his face. She lifted her hand, curving her palm over his firm, smooth heat.

Wil shuddered as she stroked him. He groaned, taking her hand, kissing it, easing her body beneath his. Her eyes drifted closed as he stroked sensuously at her thighs, her hips, her soft, wet centre. His urgent heat pressing hotly against her, she tensed, gasping.

He stilled. "Syeira, look at me," he whispered, his voice deeper than ever.

She opened to him. Wil inhaled a ragged, jarring breath. "I don't want to hurt you, my sweet. Do you understand? There may be some little pain, but only this once and then never again. I swear it. If you ask me to, I will stop now. Sweet, sweet Syeira, I will not hurt you. Tonight must be *your* choice."

Syeira reached up, touching his face, feeling her consort smile as he turned into her palm, kissing it. His eyes glinted in the firelight. She felt his desire for her, her own body hotly ready for his.

"Oh Wil, I do love you." She pulled his mouth back to hers, her sighs becoming ragged as his fingers moved over her again. He traced the curve of her shoulder, her breasts, her abdomen, her navel, caressing the fire at the heart of her.

She shifted her thighs apart. He pressed into her gently, his tip teasing her. "Tell me, my love. What can I do?"

"Don't stop," she whispered. "Love me now and never stop."

Wil kissed her, pressing deeper as she moaned in pleasure, arcing against him. He slid deeper still and lifted his head to stare down into her eyes, then sheathed himself within her hot, wet core.

The sensation of his flesh buried in her molten fire undid her. For a moment, she couldn't breathe as he moved deep within her, possessing her, filling her, loving her so absolutely. She caressed him, writhing against him, crying out, begging for more. His warm breath against her breasts was ecstasy as he plunged still further into her. She could only gasp and close her eyes as he slid in and out of her fiery centre.

She thought she could take no more but then he tilted her hips, rocking against her. She cried out, her breaths coming shallow and broken now, nearly sobbing as the pleasure of him moving inside her increased. Her hands came around his back, pressing him further inside, gripping his shoulders until her nails shred his skin. He groaned, taking her mouth in a savage, deep kiss.

He rolled until she found herself staring down in surprise. He gripped her hair, which spilled over them both and lengthened inside her, touching every part of the fire within her.

Looking up, Wil smiled his dazzling smile. "This is where you ride, my sweet." Syeira caught a glimpse of something there leashed tight, begging to break free.

Linking her hands with his, she moved against his rigid flesh. Small movements at first, so slowly, and oh, the sensations within her. Each inch of him thrusting deeply, the tension in her mounting as she quickened their pace, watching him holding on, barely aware of anything other than Wil moving powerfully inside her, shifting the parameters of her world with each upward thrust.

The fire within her building, building, threatening to consume her utterly until she tipped over some indefinable edge, falling into the joyous, shuddering heat, screaming and crying and begging it to take her as she rode him into a blazing fire of ecstasy, shuddering together in devastating release.

***

Wil smiled as she lay against him, her dark hair sliding over his chest. "I always love watching you ride."

Syeira laughed, the sound husky and sensual. "It is allowed for the consort to watch the princess all he pleases. There is nothing now that is not permitted."

He kissed the top of her head lazily. "*Nothing?*" He felt himself harden again, winding her midnight hair through his hands. Tugging lightly, he lifted his lips to hers, leaning in to the dark warmth of her mouth. He wanted to spend the rest of his life showing his princess all the ways he loved her.

According to his palm, his life spent loving Syeira promised to be a truly long one.

AUTHOR'S NOTE

It is not feasible to summarise an ancient and noble culture in a short a note. Instead, I offer some of the research and insights from which I have been fortunate enough to benefit.

The arrival of the Romany people in continental Europe dates from much earlier than the Regency period, and the traditions of various tribes or houses vary with the geographic region in which they travel. I concerned myself with the UK Romany only.

Romany people have been present in England since the 1500s. The first record of arrivals began in Scotland in 1505, and in England from 1513. In 1530 the Government passed "The Egyptians Act," establishing a foundation for a prejudice that still exists today. Some readers may recall the manner in which the Romany people are portrayed in Austen's *Emma*, where they are termed "gypsies."

The term "Romani" is more popularly used today than "Romany," though in the Regency period "gypsy" would have been correct among the English. However, in today's world, the term "gypsy" is often considered a slight, which is why I altered it in my story.

Always a Princess includes some few anachronisms, which I have detailed below:

1. Romany caravans: The covered wagons now so popularly identified with the Romany people were not commonly used in England until the 1850s. They were found on the continent a little earlier. The word *vardo* is used more often than *covo*, but both are accurate.

2. Romany royalty: The title "King of the Gypsies" has existed in England since at least the 1600s. It may be inherited, or bestowed, and sometimes simply claimed. One of the most famous *royal* Romany families of England were the Boswells. They were large in

number and often negotiated between the English and the Romany, which is how their reputation grew.

3. Romany Language: Much of my information for this comes from a Romany-English manuscript I discovered, dated from about 1865. I have detailed a few of the words below.

Bostaris translates, literally, as bastard.

Brishen means born during a rainstorm and seemed to fit both the passionate nature of the family and the Lancashire weather to which I made my characters subject.

Coorava "to chin" means to fight, similar to the Regency era slang "to mill with me."

Covo as per the note above, is one of the words for caravan.

Dinnelipénes means follies or nonsense.

Dinnelo means a fool (from the similar root word to that above).

Dosta means enough.

Grygry is a child's name for Valkin's horse, the word "gry" means horse.

Sarishan is a fairly common Romany greeting, meaning "how are you?" and possibly "peace to you."

Sher-engro means head-man, and every Romany house (or tribe) has one.

Syeira is the Romany word for princess as well as a fairly common girl's name. It was not unusual for Romany girls to have names like this, or to be named after flowers.

Further Reading:
These are a few of the available resources, for those readers who are interested:

Smart, B. C.; Croften, H T (1875) *The Dialect of the English Gypsies*
MacRitchie, David (1894) *Scottish Gypsies under the Stewarts*
Acton, Thomas Alan; Mundy, Gary (1997) *Romani culture and Gypsy identity*

With thanks to the University of Hertfordshire Romani Studies Unit, my own family history, and the inspiring Roma who have shared their stories with me.

ABOUT THE AUTHOR

Clyve Rose is an award-winning author of historical fiction in Australia and the US. She has been writing historical romance for the best part of two decades. The first piece she published was a fictional biography of an erotica writer who made a living crafting extremely explicit dating profiles for online chat sites.

Clyve lives fairly simply these days, sharing her home with a small white demon dog and a budding Amazonian warrior. She believes that love is the highest and strongest force known in the world, and that it only manifests when we are our best and truest selves. She'll continue writing about love in all its various, glorious forms, and that one day her epitaph will read *Just one more read-through*.

When she isn't writing fiction, she can be found pounding the sand at any of the beautiful beaches near her Australian home. She's addicted to short-haul ocean swims and researching quirky historical fashion trends.

CONNECT WITH CLYVE:

Website & blog: clyverose.com
Twitter: @clyverose
IG: @clyverose
FB: Clyve Rose

www.BOROUGHSPUBLISHINGGROUP.com

If you enjoyed this book, please write a review. Our authors appreciate the feedback, and it helps future readers find books they love. We welcome your comments and invite you to send them to info@boroughspublishinggroup.com. Follow us on Facebook, Twitter and Instagram, and be sure to sign up for our newsletter for surprises and new releases from your favorite authors.

Are you an aspiring writer? Check out www.boroughspublishinggroup.com/submit and see if we can help you make your dreams come true.